The Baby Bequest

Center Point
Large Print

Also by Lyn Cote and available from
Center Point Large Print:

Their Frontier Family

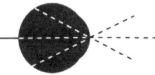

The Baby Bequest

Lyn Cote

CENTER POINT LARGE PRINT
THORNDIKE, MAINE

This Center Point Large Print edition is published
in the year 2013 by arrangement with
Harlequin Books S.A.

The text of this Large Print edition is unabridged.
In other aspects, this book may vary
from the original edition.
Printed in the United States of America
on permanent paper.
Set in 16-point Times New Roman type.

ISBN: 978-1-61173-926-8

Library of Congress Cataloging-in-Publication Data

Cote, Lyn.
 The Baby Bequest / Lyn Cote. — Center Point Large Print edition.
  pages cm
  ISBN 978-1-61173-926-8 (Library binding : alk. paper)
  1. Large type books. I. Title.
 PS3553.O76378B33 2013
 813′.54—dc23
                                                        2013028195

I am come that they might have life,
and that they might have it more abundantly.
—*John* 10:10

And be ye kind one to another, tenderhearted,
forgiving one another, even as God for
Christ's sake hath forgiven you.
—*Ephesians* 4:32

To Carol, Nan and Chris, my knitting pals!
And in fond memory of Ellen Hornshuh,
a special lady

Chapter One

Pepin, Wisconsin
August, 1870

Clutching the railing of the riverboat, Miss Ellen Thurston ached as if she'd been beaten. Now she truly understood the word *heartbroken*. Images of her sister in her pale blue wedding dress insistently flashed through her mind. As if she could wipe them away, she passed a hand over her eyes. The trip north had been both brief and endless.

She forced herself back to the present. She was here to start her new life.

The sunlight glittering on the Mississippi River nearly blinded her. The brim of her stylish hat fell short and she shaded her eyes, scanning the jumble of dusty, rustic buildings, seeking her cousin, Ophelia, and Ophelia's husband. But only a few strangers had gathered to watch the boat dock. Loneliness nearly choked her. *Ophelia, please be here. I need you.*

The riverboat men called to each other as the captain guided the boat to the wharf. With a bump, the boat docked and the men began to wrestle thick ropes to harness the boat to the pier.

As she watched the rough ropes being rasped back and forth, she felt the same sensation as she relived her recent struggle. Leaving home had been more difficult than she could have anticipated. But staying had been impossible. Why had she gone against her better judgment and let her heart take a chance?

The black porter who had assisted her during her trip appeared beside her. "Miss, I will see to your trunk and boxes, never fear."

She smiled at him and offered her hand. "You've been so kind. Thank you."

Looking surprised, he shook her hand. "It's been my pleasure to serve you, miss. Yes, indeed it has."

His courtesy helped her take a deep breath. She merely had to hold herself together till she was safely at Ophelia's. There, with her cousin—who was closer than her sister—she could mourn her loss privately, inwardly.

Soon she was standing on dry land with her luggage piled around her. She handed the porter a generous tip and he bowed his thanks and left her. Ellen glanced around, looking for her cousin in vain. Could something have happened to her? Even as this fear struck, she pushed it from her mind. Ophelia was probably just a bit late. Still, standing here alone made her painfully con-spicuous.

A furtive movement across the way caught her

attention. A thin, blond lad who looked to be in his midteens was sneaking—yes, definitely sneaking—around the back of a store. She wondered what he was up to. But she didn't know much about this town, and she shouldn't poke her nose into someone else's business. Besides, what wrong could a lad that age be doing?

She turned her mind back to her own dilemma. Who could she go to for assistance? Who would know the possible reason why Ophelia wasn't here to meet her? Searching her mind, she recalled someone she'd met on her one visit here a year ago. She picked up her skirts and walked to Ashford's General Store.

The bell jingled as she entered, and two men turned to see who had come in. One she recognized as the proprietor, Mr. Ashford, and one was a stranger—a very handsome stranger—with wavy blond hair.

Holton had the same kind of hair. The likeness stabbed her.

Then she noticed a young girl about fourteen slipping down the stairs at the rear of the store. She eased the back door open and through the gap, Ellen glimpsed the young lad. Ah, calf love.

Ellen held her polite mask in place, turning her attention to the older of the two men. "Good day, Mr. Ashford. I don't know if you remember me—"

"Miss Thurston!" the storekeeper exclaimed and

hurried around the counter. "We didn't expect you for another few days."

This brought her up sharply. "I wrote my cousin almost two weeks ago that I'd be arriving today."

The storekeeper frowned. "I thought Mrs. Steward said you'd be arriving later this week."

"Oh, dear." Ellen voiced her sinking dismay as she turned toward the windows facing the street. Her mound of boxes and valises sat forlornly on her trunk at the head of the dock. How was she going to get to Ophelia? Her grip on her polite facade was slipping. "I could walk to the Steward's but my things . . ."

"We'll get some boys to bring them here—"

The stranger in the store interrupted, clearing his throat, and bowed. "Mr. Ashford, please to introduce me. I may help, perhaps?" The man spoke with a thick German accent.

The man also unfortunately had blue eyes. Again, his likeness to Holton, who had misled her, churned within. She wanted to turn her back to him.

Mr. Ashford hesitated, then nodded. "A good idea." He turned to Ellen. "Miss Ellen Thurston, may I introduce you to another newcomer in our little town, Mr. Kurt Lang, a Dutchman?"

Ellen recognized that Mr. Ashford was using the ethnic slur, "Dutch," a corruption of *Deutsche*, the correct term for German immigrants. Hiding her acute discomfort with the insult, Ellen extended her gloved hand and curtsied as politeness demanded.

Mr. Lang approached swiftly and bowed over her hand, murmuring something that sounded more like French than German.

Ellen withdrew her hand and tried not to look the man full in the face, but she failed. She found that not only did he have blond hair with a natural wave and blue eyes that reminded her of Holton, but his face was altogether too handsome. And the worst was that his smile was too kind. Her facade began slipping even more as tears hovered just behind her eyes.

"I live near the Stewards, Miss Thurston," the stranger said, sounding polite but stiff. "I drive you."

Ellen looked to Mr. Ashford a bit desperately. Young ladies of quality observed a strict code of conduct, especially those who became school-teachers. Should she ride alone with this man?

Mr. Ashford also seemed a bit uncomfortable. "Mr. Lang has been living here for over six months and is a respectable person. Very respect-able." The man lowered his voice and added, "Even if he is a foreigner."

Ellen stiffened at this second slur from Mr. Ashford.

Mr. Lang himself looked mortified but said nothing in return.

With effort, Ellen swallowed her discomfort.

The man couldn't help reminding her of someone she didn't want to be reminded of. More important, she would not let him think that she embraced the popular prejudice against anyone not born in America.

"We are a nation of immigrants, Mr. Ashford," she said with a smile to lighten the scold. She turned to Mr. Lang. "Thank you, Mr. Lang, I am ready whenever you are."

Mr. Lang's gaze met hers in sudden connection. He bowed again. "I finish and take you."

She heard in these words a hidden thank-you for her comment.

A few moments later, she stood on the shady porch of the store, watching the man load her trunk, two boxes of books and her valises onto the back of his wagon along with his goods. She noticed it was easy for him—he was quite strong. She also noticed he made no effort to gain her attention or show off. He just did what he'd said he'd do. That definitely differed from Holton, the consummate actor.

This man's neat appearance reminded her that she must look somewhat disheveled from her trip, increasing her feelings of awkwardness at being alone with the stranger. She'd often felt that same way with Holton, too. His Eastern polish should have warned her away—if her own instincts hadn't.

At his curt nod, she met Mr. Lang at the wagon

side and he helped her up the steps. His touch warmed her skin, catching her off guard. Rattled, she sat rigidly straight on the high bench, warning him away.

Just then, the storekeeper's wife hurried out the door. "Miss Thurston! Ned just called upstairs that you'd arrived." The flustered woman hurried over and reached up to shake hands with Ellen. "We didn't expect you so soon."

"Yes, Mr. Ashford said as much. I'd told my cousin when I was arriving, but perhaps she didn't receive my letter."

"The school isn't quite ready, you know." Mrs. Ashford looked down and obviously realized that she'd rushed outside without taking off her smeared kitchen apron. She snatched it off.

"That's fine. My cousin wanted me to come for a visit, anyway." Ophelia's invitation to visit before the teaching job began had come months before. Ellen suffered a twinge, hoping this was all just a minor misunderstanding. Then she thought of Ophelia's little boy. Little ones were so at risk for illness. Perhaps something had happened?

She scolded herself for jumping to conclusions. After a few more parting remarks were exchanged, Mr. Lang slapped the reins, and the team started down the dusty road toward the track that Ellen recognized from her earlier visit to Pepin.

The two of them sat in a polite silence. As they

left the town behind them, Ellen tried to accustom herself to the forest that crowded in on them like a brooding presence. The atmosphere did not raise her spirits. And it was taking every ounce of composure she had left to sit beside this stranger.

Then, when the silence had become unbearable, Mr. Lang asked gruffly, "You come far?"

"Just from Galena." Then she realized a newcomer might not know where Galena was. "It's south of here in Illinois, about a five-day trip. You may have heard of it. President Grant's home is there."

"Your president, he comes from your town?"

She nodded and didn't add that her hometown had a bad case of self-importance over this. They'd all forgotten how many of them had previously scorned Ulysses S. Grant. "Before the war, he and his father owned a leather shop." She hadn't meant to say this, but speaking her mind to someone at last on the topic presented an opportunity too attractive to be missed. She found President Grant's story extraordinary, though not everyone did.

"A leather shop?" The man sounded disbelieving.

"Yes." She stopped herself from saying more in case Mr. Lang thought that she was disparaging their president. The wagon rocked over a ridge in the road. Why couldn't it move more quickly?

"This land is different. In Germany, no trades-man would be general or president."

Ellen couldn't miss the deep emotion with which Mr. Lang spoke these few words. She tilted her face so she could see him around the brim of her hat, then regretted it. The man had expressive eyebrows and thick brown lashes, another resemblance to Holton. Unhappy thoughts of home bombarded her.

As another conversational lull blossomed, crows filled the silence, squawking as if irritated by the human intrusion. She felt the same discontent. She wanted only to be with dear Ophelia, and she wasn't sure she could stand much more time alone with this disturbing stranger.

She sought another way to put distance between them. "I am going to be the schoolteacher here. Do you have children?" Ellen hoped he'd say that he and his wife had none, and hence she would not come in contact with this man much in the future.

"I am not married. But I have two . . . students."

"I'm sorry, I don't understand," Ellen said, clutching the side of the wagon as they drove over another rough patch, her stomach lurching.

"My brother, Gunther, and my nephew, Johann. They will come to school."

This man had responsibilities she hadn't guessed. Yet his tone had been grim, as if his charges were a sore subject.

"How old are they?" *Do they speak English?* she wanted to ask. She sincerely hoped so.

"Gunther is sixteen and Johann is seven." Then

he answered her unspoken question. "We speak English some at home. But is hard for them."

She nodded out of politeness but she couldn't help voicing an immediate concern. "Isn't your brother a bit old to attend school? Most students only go to the eighth grade—I mean, until about thirteen years old."

"Gunther needs to learn much about this country. He will go to school."

The man's tone brooked no dispute. So she offered none, straightening her back and wishing the horse would go faster.

Yes, your brother will attend, but will he try to learn? And in consequence, will he make my job harder?

The oppressive silence surged back again and Ellen began to imagine all sorts of dreadful reasons for her cousin not meeting her on the appointed day. Ellen searched her mind for some topic of conversation. She did not want to dwell on her own worry and misery. "Are you homesteading?"

"*Ja.* Yes. I claim land." His voice changed then, his harsh tone disappearing. "Only in America is land free. Land just . . . free."

In spite of herself, the wonder in his voice made her proud to be an American. "Well, we have a lot of land and not many people," she said after a pause. If she felt more comfortable at being alone with him, she would have asked him to tell her about Europe, a place she wished to see but probably never would.

"Still, government could make money from selling land, yes?"

She took a deep, steadying breath. "It's better not to look a gift horse in the mouth."

More unwelcome silence. She stole another glance at him. The man appeared in deep thought.

"Oh," he said, his face lifting. "Not look gift horse . . . to see if healthy."

"Exactly," she said. She hadn't thought about the phrase as being an idiom. How difficult it must be to live away from home, where you don't even know the everyday expressions. Homesickness stabbed her suddenly. Her heart clenched. Perhaps they did have something in common. "It must have been hard to leave home and travel so far."

He seemed to close in on himself. Then he shrugged slightly. "War will come soon to Germany. I need to keep safe, to raise Johann."

"You might have been drafted?" she asked more sharply than she'd planned. During the Civil War, many men had bought their way out of the draft. Not something she approved of.

"*Ja*—yes—but war in Germany is to win land for princes, not for people. No democracy in Germany."

"That's unfortunate." No doubt not having any say in what the government did would make being drafted feel different. Ellen fell silent, exhausted from the effort of making conversation with this man who reminded her so much of Holton. She knotted her hands together in her lap, as if that would contain her composure. Would this ride never end?

"We—the men—we build the school . . . more on Saturday," he said haltingly.

This pleased her. She wanted to get her life here started, get busy so she could put the past in the past. "How much longer do you think it will take?"

"Depends. Some men harvest corn. If rain comes . . ." He shrugged again, seeming unable to express the uncertainty.

"I see. Well, I'll just have faith that it will all come together in the next few weeks. Besides, the delay gives me more time to prepare lessons."

At that moment, Mr. Lang turned the wagon down a track and ahead lay the Steward cabin. Ellen's heart leaped when she saw her cousin, carrying her baby, hurry out to greet her.

"Ophelia!" she called.

Mr. Lang drew up his team. "Wait," he insisted. "Please, I help." He secured the brake.

But Ellen couldn't wait. She jumped down and ran to Ophelia, the emotions she'd been working so hard to keep at bay finally overtaking her. She buried her face in Ophelia's shoulder and burst into tears. Her feelings strangled her voice.

Chapter Two

"Why weren't you at the river to meet me?"

Ellen grasped her cousin's hand desperately as Mr. Lang drove down the track away from them. She had managed to pull herself together enough to bid Mr. Lang goodbye and thank him for the ride, but she was glad to see him leave—his presence had pushed her over the edge emotionally. The man had only been kind to her, but being alone with him had nearly been more than she could bear.

"Why weren't you at the river to meet me?" Ellen repeated.

Ophelia pulled a well-worn letter from her pocket. "You said your boat would dock tomorrow. 'I will arrive on the sixteenth of August,' " she read.

"But that's today."

"No, dear, that's tomorrow. It's easy to lose track of days when traveling. I know I did."

Ellen thought her own mental state must be the explanation. As Ophelia guided her to a chair just outside the log cabin and disappeared inside, Ellen tried to appear merely homesick and travel-weary, not heartsick. She must master herself or this thing would defeat her. She stiffened her spine.

Soon Ophelia bustled into the daylight again and offered her a cup of tea. "This will help. I know when I arrived I . . ." Her cousin paused, frowning. "I cried a lot. It's a shock leaving family, leaving home." She sat down beside Ellen and began nursing her little boy.

Ophelia had thoughtfully offered her an excuse for her tears and she would not contradict her. Yet the invisible band around her heart squeezed tighter. Ellen took a sip of the tea, which tasted like peppermint. "I'll adjust."

"Of course you will. You've done right coming here. Pepin has the nicest people, and those with children are so happy to have a teacher. They can't wait to meet you."

A weight like a stone pressed down on Ellen's lungs. She'd never taught before. Would she be good at it? "I'm glad to hear that."

"The schoolhouse with your quarters isn't finished yet, but Martin and I will love having you spend a few weeks with us."

That long? How could she keep her misery hidden that long, and from Ophelia, who knew her so well? "I'm sorry for arriving early and putting you out—"

"You're not putting me out," Ophelia said emphatically. "Having family here—" the young mother paused as if fighting tears "—means a great deal to me."

Touched, Ellen reached out and pressed her

hand to Ophelia's shoulder. "I'm glad to have family here, too." *Family that loves me,* she thought.

Her cousin rested her cheek on Ellen's hand for a moment. "I'm sorry I missed Cissy's wedding."

The image of Holton kissing her sister, Cissy, in their parlor, sealing their life vows, was a knife piercing Ellen's heart. What had happened had not been her naive younger sister's fault, she reminded herself. "Cissy was a beautiful bride," she said bravely.

"Oh, I wish I could have been there, but we couldn't justify the expense of the riverboat fare and the time away from our crops. It seems every varmint in Wisconsin wants to eat our garden and corn." Ophelia sounded indignant. "You'd think our farm was surrounded by a desolate desert without a green shoot, the way everything tries to gobble up our food."

Ellen couldn't help herself; a chuckle escaped her. Oh, it felt good to laugh again.

"It's not funny."

"I know, but *you* are. Oh, Ophelia, I've missed you."

And it was the truth. Ophelia had been a friend from childhood, slipping through the back fence to Ellen's house, escaping her own overbearing, scene-making mother.

"I miss your parents. They were always so

good to me," Ophelia said in a voice rich with emotion, rich with love and sympathy.

The cousins linked hands in a silent moment of remembrance.

"They were good to me, too," Ellen murmured. Strengthened, she released Ophelia's hand. "But they are with God and I am here with you. To start a new life, just like you have."

"Ellen, about Holton." Her cousin paused, biting her lower lip.

Ellen froze, her cup in midair. What about Holton? What could Ophelia possibly know? And *how?*

"I wondered . . . My mother wrote me that when he first came to town, he was making up to you . . ."

Ellen suffered the words as a blow. She should have foreseen this. Ophelia's mother, Prudence, completely misnamed, was also one of the worst gossips in Galena. Of course Aunt Prudence would have told Ophelia how, when he first came to town, Holton had buzzed around Ellen, only to switch his attentions when her prettier, younger and easier-to-manage sister came home from boarding school in Chicago.

Ellen tried to keep breathing through the pain of remembering.

At that moment, Ophelia's husband, Martin, walked out of the woods, a hoe over his shoulder and a dog at his side, saving her from having to speak about Holton and his deception of her. She had gotten through mention of the awful day of Cissy's wedding without revealing anything. No doubt it would come up again, but perhaps every day that passed would distance the pain.

This move would work out. It had to.

As she thought of her future in Pepin, the handsome but troubled face of Kurt Lang popped into her mind. What was wrong with her? Did she have no defense at all against a handsome face? A handsome face belonging to a man that might mislead and lie just as Holton did?

She vowed she would never again make the mistake she'd made with Holton. Never.

Kurt found Gunther sitting beside the creek, fishing. The lanky boy was too thin and his blond hair needed cutting. A pang of sympathy swept through Kurt. His brother was so young to carry their family shame.

Gunther looked up, already spoiling for an argument. "I did my chores and Johann did his."

And just like that, Kurt's sympathy turned to frustration. He knew why Gunther simmered all the time, ready to boil over. But the lad was old enough to learn to carry what had happened to them like a man.

Upstream, Johann, who had been wading in the cooling water, looked up at the sound of Gunther's voice. He waved. "Hello, *Onkel* Kurt!"

The barefoot boy splashed over the rocks and ran up the grassy bank to Kurt.

Kurt pulled down the brim of the boy's hat, teasing. Johann favored his late father's coloring with black hair and brown eyes. "You keep cool in the water?" Kurt asked in careful English.

Johann pushed up the brim, grinning. "Yes, I did." Then the boy looked uncomfortable and glanced toward Gunther.

In return, Gunther sent their nephew a pointed, forbidding look.

Kurt's instincts went on alert. What were these two hiding?

His guess was that Gunther had done something he knew Kurt wouldn't like and had sworn Johann to secrecy. Kurt let out a breath. Another argument wouldn't help. He'd just wait. Everything came out in the wash, his grandmother used to say and was said here, too.

"You bring me candy? Please?" Johann asked, eyeing Kurt's pockets.

"Candy? Why should I bring you candy?" If he wasn't careful, he'd spoil this one.

"I did my chores this week."

After feigning deep thought for a few moments, Kurt drew out a small brown bag. "You did do your chores well, Johann." Kurt lapsed into German as he tossed the boy a chunk of peppermint. Then he offered another chunk to his brother.

Gunther glared at him. "I'm almost a man."

Irritation sparked in Kurt's stomach. "Then act like one."

Gunther turned his back to Kurt, hunching up one shoulder.

Kurt regretted his brusque tone, but he couldn't baby Gunther. Everyone said that had been the root cause of their father's downfall. Their father had been a very spoiled only child who had never grown up. Kurt would not let Gunther follow in their father's disastrous footsteps.

"Your schoolteacher arrived today."

Kurt stopped there, realizing that the unexpected meeting had upset him. Miss Ellen Thurston was a striking woman with a great deal of countenance, but so emotional. He'd heard all the gossip in town about her. She was a well-educated woman and a wealthy man's daughter, and her family was even in government in Illinois. Far above his touch. His brow furrowed; he recalled the scene at the Stewards', her brown eyes overflowing with tears. Why had she burst into tears like that? He shook his head again. Women were so emotional, not like men.

But wondering about the new schoolteacher was just wasting time. His life now was raising Johann and guiding Gunther. Brigitte's betrayal tried to intrude on his thoughts, but he shook it off—he did not want to spare one more thought for his former fiancée.

"I'm not going to school," Gunther insisted.

Kurt stiffened.

"*Nicht wahr?*" Johann asked and went on in German. "I think it will be fun. At least we will get to meet some others here. I want to make friends. Don't you want to make friends, Gunther?"

A fish took Gunther's bait, saving them from another angry retort.

The deep pool of Kurt's own sorrow and shame bubbled up. He inhaled deeply, forcing it down. Would the weight he carried never lift? Kurt watched his brother deftly play and then pull in a nice bass. Kurt tried encouragement. "A fine fish for supper. Well done."

Gunther refused the compliment with a toss of his head.

Kurt's patience began slipping. Better to leave before he traded more barbed words with the lad. He relaxed and spoke in German, "Catch a few more if you can. Johann, help me put away what I bought at the store. Then we will look over the garden to see what needs picking."

Johann fell into step with him. Kurt rested a hand on the boy's shoulder. Again he thought of the schoolteacher, so stylish and with soft brown curls around her aristocratic face. He'd anticipated a plain woman, much older, with hair sprouting from her chin. What was Miss Ellen Thurston doing here, teaching school? It was a mystery.

Then, in spite of the sorrow that never quite eased, Kurt began teasing Johann about how much peppermint he thought he could eat at one time.

Things would get better. They had to.

Riding on the wagon bench, Ellen dreaded being put on display for all of Pepin today, nearly a week after arriving. But the men had decided to hold a community-wide workday on the school and attached living quarters, and she must attend and show a cheerful face to all. In light of the wound she carried and concealed day by day, it would be one long, precarious ordeal. She had to portray confidence above all.

When the Stewards' wagon broke free of the forest into the open river flat, she welcomed the broad view of the blue, rippling Mississippi ahead. She took a deep breath. The normally empty town now appeared crowded and her heart sank another notch—until an impertinent question popped up: Would Mr. Lang come today? Ellen willed this thought away.

Ophelia touched her hand. "Don't worry. You'll get to know everyone in no time and then this will feel more like home."

Ellen fashioned a smile for Ophelia. If only shyness were her worry. "I'm sure you're right."

"You met my friends Sunny and Nan last year. They are eager to make you welcome."

Ellen tried to take comfort from her cousin's words.

Ellen and Ophelia joined the ladies who were storing the cold lunch in the spring house behind the store. Then they gathered in the shade of the trees with a good view of the unfinished log schoolhouse and claimed places on a rectangle of benches. Small children rolled or crawled in the grass in the midst of the benches, while older children played tag nearby.

Though scolding herself silently, Ellen scanned the men, seeking Kurt Lang. He had made an impression on her and she couldn't deny it. She also couldn't deny that she resented it.

"Miss Thurston," Mrs. Ashford called. "This is my daughter Amanda." Mrs. Ashford motioned for a girl in a navy blue plaid dress, who appeared to be around fourteen, to come to her. "Make your curtsy to the schoolteacher, Amanda."

The thin, dark-haired girl obeyed, blushing. With a start, Ellen recognized her as the girl she'd seen slipping downstairs to meet a boy on the day Ellen had arrived.

Ellen took pity on the girl, obviously enduring that awkward stage between girlhood and womanhood, and offered her hand. "I'm pleased to meet you, Amanda. Your dress is very pretty."

Mrs. Ashford preened. "Amanda cut and sewed it all by herself. She is the age where she should be finishing up her learning of the household arts. But Ned and I decided that we'd let her go to school one more year, though she's had enough schooling for a girl."

Ellen swallowed her response to this common sentiment, quelling the irritation it sparked. *Enough schooling for a girl.* Her older brother's wife, Alice, had the gall to tell her once that the reason Ellen had never "snared" a man was she had had too much schooling for a woman. *I couldn't stand my sister-in-law's sly rudeness and innuendo a day longer.* What would this storekeeper's wife say if she announced that she intended to earn a bachelor's degree and perhaps teach at a preparatory school someday?

Ellen limited herself to saying, "I will be happy to have Amanda in my class."

The men began shouting words of instruction and encouragement, drawing the women's attention to the schoolhouse. They were coordinating the positioning of four ladders against the log walls, two on each side. With a start, Ellen spotted Kurt Lang as he nimbly mounted a ladder and climbed toward the peak of the joists.

Ellen felt a little dizzy as she watched Mr. Lang so high up in the air, leaning perilously away from the ladder. An imposing figure, he appeared intent on what he was doing, evidently not the kind to shy away from hard work.

As she watched, a barefoot boy with black hair and a tanned face ran up, startling her. "You are teacher?" he asked with an accent. "The girls say you are teacher."

"Yes, I am going to be the teacher. Will you be one of my students?" Was this Mr. Lang's nephew?

He nodded vigorously. "I want school. I like to read."

"Good. What's your name?"

"Johann Mueller." He pointed toward the school. "My *onkel* Kurt." Then he pointed to a teenager standing by the ladders. "My *onkel* Gunther." The boy said the name so it sounded like "Goon-ter."

Ellen noted that Gunther, working with the men on the ground, wasn't paying attention to the work going on around him. He was staring across at Amanda. She then recognized him as the young man Amanda had slipped out to see that first day she'd come to town.

Over the hammering, she heard Mr. Lang's voice rise, speaking in German, sounding as if he were scolding someone. She caught the name, "Gunther."

She saw Gunther glare up at Mr. Lang, then grudgingly begin to work again.

Ellen felt sympathy for the younger brother. Why was Mr. Lang so hard on him? He was just a boy, really.

Johann bowed. "I go. Goodbye!" He pulled on his cap, gave her a grin and ran toward the children.

Mrs. Ashford pursed her lips, looking peevish. "I hope you don't have trouble with those Dutch boys." She nodded toward the unhappy Gunther. "That one's too old for school and Mr. Ashford told Mr. Lang so."

Ellen agreed. A sixteen-year-old could stir up all kinds of trouble at school, not only for the other students, but for her. Mr. Lang, of course, probably hadn't thought of this. She drew in a breath. "I'm sure he thinks it best for his brother."

"Well." Mrs. Ashford sniffed. "I think the homesteading law should have specified that land was only for Americans, not for foreigners."

Ellen bit her tongue. The homesteading law had been designed specifically to attract people from other countries to populate the vast open area east of the Rocky Mountains. There simply weren't enough American-born families to fill up those vacant acres.

Ellen recalled Mr. Ashford's whisper that Kurt was respectable even if a foreigner. It must be difficult for Mr. Lang to face this prejudice against immigrants day after day. Even though she didn't agree with Mr. Lang's treatment of his brother, she felt a keen sympathy for him—he and his charges had a difficult path ahead of them in so many ways.

This very feeling of sympathy led Ellen to resolve to keep her distance from Mr. Lang as best she could.

• • •

Hours later, the lunch bell rang. The men washed their hands at the school pump and gathered around the tables. While the women served the meal, the older children were permitted to sit by their fathers and listen to the men discuss the progress of the school building.

Despite her decision to keep her distance, Ellen tracked Mr. Lang's whereabouts and listened to catch his words.

For distraction, she insisted on donning an apron and whisking away empty bowls to replenish them. As she approached Mr. Lang's table, she heard him laugh—his laughter was deep and rich. Just as she reached him with a heaping bowl of green salad, he turned and nearly swept the bowl from her arms.

"*Tut mir leid*! I'm sorry!" he exclaimed, reaching out and steadying her hold on the bowl with his hands over hers.

The unexpected contact made her smother a gasp.

"No harm done." She set the bowl on the table and stepped back, slightly breathless. Perspiration dotted his hairline and his thick, tawny hair had curled in the humidity. She nearly brushed back a curl that had strayed onto his forehead. The very thought of it made her turn away as quickly as possible to get back to work.

As she made her way to the next table, she

noticed Mrs. Ashford's daughter pause before slipping into the trees. The girl looked over her shoulder in a furtive move that announced she was up to no good.

Ellen recalled how Gunther had earlier been staring at this girl. A kind of inevitable presentiment draped over Ellen's mind. She glanced around. Gunther was nowhere to be seen.

What to do? After listening to Mrs. Ashford's opinion of foreigners, Ellen didn't want to think of the repercussions in this small town if someone found the two young people together. And she didn't want people gossiping about Amanda— she knew how that stung.

She excused herself and followed Amanda into the cover of the trees, threading her way through the thick pines and oaks. She hoped the young couple hadn't gone too far.

She also hoped she wouldn't find them kissing.

When she glimpsed Amanda's navy blue plaid dress through the trees, the young girl was testing the flexed muscle of Gunther's upper arm. A timeless scene—a young man showing off his strength to a young, admiring girl. Innocent and somewhat sweet. However, that wouldn't be how the Ashfords would view it.

At that moment, she heard footsteps behind her. She swung around to find Kurt Lang facing her. She jerked backward in surprise.

Before she could say anything, Mr. Lang

glimpsed the couple over her shoulder. His face darkened. He opened his mouth.

Impetuously, without thinking about her actions, Ellen shocked herself by reaching up and gently pressing a hand to Mr. Kurt Lang's lips.

The lady's featherlike touch threw Kurt off balance. He grappled with the cascade of sensations sparked by her fingers against his lips.

"Please, you'll embarrass them," she whispered, quickly removing her hand as her face flushed.

She was so close, her light fragrance filled his head, making him think of spring. He fought free of it. "They need to be embarrassed," he replied emphatically. "I see you follow the girl Gunther likes. Then I see Gunther is not at table. He is not to flirt with this girl. He is too young."

"But do you want everyone to hear, to know?" she cautioned.

Kurt thought about the wagging tongues, and realized she was right. "No. But I must discipline him. He must do what he is supposed to."

The lady bit her lower lip as if she wanted to say more but then she fell back.

"Gunther." He snapped his brother's name as a reprimand.

In an instant, Amanda dropped her hand, blushing. Gunther jerked back and glared.

"We're not doing anything wrong," Amanda said in a rush.

The schoolteacher preceded him toward the couple. "No, you aren't," she said evenly, "but slipping away like this would not please your parents, Amanda. Why don't you go back before you're missed?"

Kurt admired her aplomb. She was definitely a lady of unusual quality.

"Yes, ma'am." Amanda snuck a last look at Gunther and then hurried away.

The lady schoolteacher sent him an apologetic look filled with an appeal for the young couple. Why did women want to coddle children?

When the two females had moved out of earshot, Kurt told his brother what he thought of such a meeting. The boy flushed bright red and began to answer back.

Kurt cut him off. "You embarrass me in front of your teacher."

Instead of apologizing, his brother made a rude sound and stalked away. Kurt proceeded back to the tables.

The other men were finished eating. With the hot sun blazing down, they lingered at the shaded tables, talking and teasing one another about minor mishaps during the morning's work. Kurt envied their easygoing good humor, wishing he could participate, but inside, he churned like the Atlantic he'd crossed only months before.

He could not afford to lose his brother as he'd lost his father.

An older man sitting in the shade away from the tables in a rough-hewn wheelchair with his feet propped up motioned for Kurt to come to him.

Kurt obeyed the summons. "Sir?"

The older man reached out his hand. "You are Mr. Kurt Lang from Germany. I've seen you come to worship and I've been wanting to meet you, but my days of calling on folk are over. I'm Old Saul."

"I hear you were pastor before Noah Whitmore." Kurt shook the man's hand and sat on a stool beside his chair. "I'm pleased to meet you, sir."

"Just call me Old Saul."

Kurt digested this. People here thought differently about social status. Few wanted titles of respect beyond Mr. and Mrs. or Miss. It puzzled him. But he was never left in doubt of their low opinion of him, an immigrant.

Old Saul nodded toward the lady school-teacher. "I didn't think I'd still be here to greet Miss Thurston, but God hasn't decided to call me home just yet." Then he looked directly into Kurt's eyes. "You carry a heavy load. I see it. You're strong but some burdens need God's strength."

The old man looked frail but his voice sounded surprisingly strong. Kurt didn't know what to make of what he'd said, yet for the first time in many days, Kurt relaxed, feeling the man's acceptance deep within his spirit.

"It's hard starting out in a new place," Old Saul continued, "but you'll do fine. Just ask God to help you when you need it. God's strength is stronger than any human's and God is a very present help in times of trouble, Mr. Kurt Lang. Yes, He is." Then the older man's gaze followed the lady teacher.

Kurt could think of nothing to say so he watched the schoolteacher, too. Even though she was dressed simply, she had that flair that lent her a more fashionable look. He thought of her following the Ashford girl and his brother, trying to protect them from gossip. She must have a caring heart.

Miss Ellen Thurston, the lady schoolteacher.

Kurt drew in a breath and before anyone caught him staring at her, he turned his attention back to Old Saul. *She is far above me, a poor farmer who speaks bad English.*

Chapter Three

Ellen's heart beat fast as she prepared to ring the handbell on the first day of school. Children, obviously scrubbed and combed and wearing freshly ironed clean clothing, had begun gathering over the past half hour and milled around the school entrance.

Then she glimpsed trouble. Mr. Lang marched into the clearing, his face a thundercloud. He grasped his brother Gunther's arm and headed straight for her. Little Johann ran behind the two, trying to keep up.

Oh, no, she moaned silently. Didn't the man have enough sense not to make a public scene?

As she rang the bell, the children ran toward her, looking excited. But when they reached her, they turned to see what she was looking at with such consternation, and watched the threesome heading straight for her.

Ellen racked her brain, trying to come up with some way to avert Gunther's public humiliation. In the moment, she only managed to draw up a welcoming smile.

"Good morning, Mr. Lang!" she called out in a friendly tone, hoping to turn him up sweet.

She watched him master the thundercloud and nod toward her curtly but politely. She turned to the children, hoping to move them inside. "Children, please line up by age, the youngest students in the front."

Some jostling and pushing happened as the line shifted.

Mr. Lang halted at the rear. Gunther tried to pull away from him, but couldn't break free. Looking worried, Johann hurried past them to the front of the line as instructed.

"Eyes forward," she ordered when children turned to look back at Gunther. She set the school bell down on the bench inside the door and then asked the children their ages and did some re-sorting in the line. She sent the children in row by row, keeping Gunther and Mr. Lang at the rear.

Finally, the older children went inside. Mr. Lang released Gunther to go with them with a sharp command in German.

Ellen stepped forward, intercepting Mr. Lang before he could turn away. She lowered her voice. "I wish you hadn't called so much attention to Gunther. He already stands out as it is."

"Gunther disobeyed. He is my brother, Miss Thurston. I must do what I think is best."

Helpless to better the situation, Ellen struggled in silence. Obviously Gunther had balked at coming to school. Mr. Lang had excellent intentions, but this public humiliation would only bring more adverse attention from the other children. Was there ever a schoolyard without hurtful taunting?

"Perhaps you should take a moment to remember your school days, recall how children treat newcomers," she said in an undertone.

He looked up, showing surprise.

Hoping she'd given him something to think

about, Ellen turned to go inside to take charge of her classroom.

Gunther slouched on the bench by the back door as if separating himself from the rest. She didn't say a word, hoping to let the whole situation simmer down. How was she going to gain Gunther's cooperation and reach him?

From her place with the other older children, Amanda Ashford peered at him until Ellen gently reminded her to face forward.

At the front of the class, Ellen led the students in a prayer, asking God to bless them as they began the first year together in this new school, smiling as brightly as she could. With a heavy heart, Ellen sighed. This promised to be a challenging year of teaching. However, uppermost in her mind was the image of Mr. Lang. His square jaw had been clamped tight and his eyes had been angry, but underneath she'd seen the worry.

What drove the man to push his brother so? And how could she help Gunther—and Mr. Lang?

By the end of the day, Ellen had the beginnings of a headache. The children for the most part were well behaved but most of them had little or no experience in a classroom with other students. Concentrating on their own lesson while she taught a different lesson to another age group taxed their powers of self-control.

Ellen had kept order by stopping often to sing a

song with the children. This had occurred to her out of the blue and worked well, bringing a release of tension for her as well as the students. Grateful that the school year started in warm weather, she also had granted them a morning and afternoon recess in addition to the lunch recess.

Now their first day together was nearly done. From the head of the classroom, she gazed at her students, fatigue rolling over her. "Students, I am very pleased with your performance on this, our first day together. I think that I have been fortunate in starting my teaching career with a very bright class. However, we must work on concentrating on our studies. I haven't punished anyone today for not listening and not sticking to their own work, but I may have to tomorrow. Do you take my point?"

"Yes, Miss Thurston," they chorused.

"I will do better," Johann announced in the front row.

Some of the students tittered.

Ellen frowned at them, letting them know this mocking would not be tolerated. And she didn't reprimand Johann for speaking out of turn, since she liked his eager reply and most other students nodded in agreement. "I am sure each of you will. You are fortunate to have parents who care about you enough to build a school. Now pick up your things and line up as we did to go out for recess. I will meet you at the door."

Ellen hadn't planned to do this, but she recalled that her favorite teacher had always waited at the back of the schoolroom and had spoken to each of them on their way out. She had looked forward every schoolday to those few precious words meant just for her.

She took each student's hand in turn and thought of something pleasant to say, showing that she had noticed them specifically. Each student beamed at the praise, and she promised herself to end each schoolday this way.

Finally, she faced Gunther and offered her hand. "Gunther, I hope you'll find school more pleasant tomorrow."

He accepted her hand as if her gesture in itself insulted him and he wouldn't meet her gaze. Then he stalked off with Johann running to keep up with him, talking in a stream of rapid German.

She slipped inside and immediately sank onto the bench at the back of the room as if she could finally lay down the load she'd carried all day. If Mr. Lang had been there, she would have gladly given him a good shake.

During afternoon recess two days later, Ellen watched the younger children playing tag. Then she noticed that the older children had disappeared. Where? And why?

Then she heard the shouting from the other side of the schoolhouse, "Fight! Fight!"

She ran toward the voices and unfortunately the younger children followed her.

There they were—Gunther and Clayton sparring, surrounded by the older boys and girls. As she watched, horrified, Clayton socked Gunther's eye. Gunther landed a blow on Clayton's jaw, making his head jerk backward.

She shouted, "Stop!"

At the sound of her voice, the older children surrounding the two combatants fled from her.

She halted near the two fighting. The fists were flying and she didn't want to get in the way of one. "Clayton Riggs, stop this instant! Gunther Lang, stop!"

Neither boy paid the slightest attention to her. She couldn't physically make them obey. Or could she? She ran to the pump. Soon she ran back. The two were now rolling around on the ground, punching and kicking each other.

She doused them with the bucket of cold water.

The two rolled apart, yelping with surprise and sputtering.

"Stand up!" she ordered. "Now!"

Gunther rose first, keeping his distance from the other boy. Clayton, though younger than Gunther, matched him nearly in height and weight, rolled to his feet, too.

"Both of you, go to the pump and wash your face and hands. Now." She gestured toward the pump and marched them there, hiding her own trembling. She was unaccustomed to physical fighting and it had shaken her.

She stood over them as if they were two-year-olds while they washed away the dirt and blood from the fight. The cold water had evidently washed away their forgetfulness of where they were. Both looked embarrassed, chastened. Possibly wondering what their elders would say?

She then waved them into the schoolhouse and told them to face the opposite walls near the front. She called the rest of the children inside then.

No child spoke but as they filed in, all of them looked at the backs of the two miscreants. A question hung over them all. What would the teacher do to Gunther and Clayton?

She was asking herself the same question. She knew that Clayton had been taunting Gunther for two days—subtly in class and blatantly on the school ground. She had tried to keep them busy and apart, hoping to prevent fisticuffs. She'd failed.

Now she went to the front of the classroom and faced her students. "I didn't think I needed to tell any of you that fighting on school grounds will not be tolerated."

"Are you going to paddle them?" a first grader asked in breathless alarm.

"The idea that I would have to *paddle* any one of my students is repugnant. I expect my students to show self-control in every situation. No matter what the provocation, fighting is no way to settle an argument. Gunther and Clayton will stand the rest of the day, facing the wall in shame."

The same first grader gasped. Some of the children gaped at her.

"If any more fights take place, I will have to inform the school board and they will mete out corporal punishment. I am a lady."

She added the last as her justification and she saw that her instincts had proven true. The other children nodded in total agreement. Miss Thurston was a lady, and ladies didn't paddle students.

Dear Lord, please don't make it necessary for me to talk to anybody about this.

Later, Ellen rose from the table at the end of another evening meal at the Ashfords, who had finally agreed to let her pay them for providing her meals. Ellen could cook over a woodstove but could only make tea or coffee on the hearth in her quarters.

Though the meal had been delicious, the pleasure had done little to raise her spirits. The lady of the house gazed at her questioningly and then glanced toward Amanda, who was clearing the table. Mrs. Ashford had apparently picked up on Ellen's preoccupation and Amanda's forlorn mood during the meal.

"I hope everything is all right at school," the lady of house said with a question in her voice.

Ellen decided that everyone would soon know what had happened so she might as well be frank. "I'm afraid that two boys came to blows during recess this afternoon." The fight had ended in a nosebleed for Clayton and a black eye for Gunther.

"It wasn't Gunther's fault," Amanda declared from the doorway to the kitchen. "That Clayton boy was making fun of how he talks and calling him names all day. Gunther ignored it till the Clayton boy started saying nasty things about Gunther's uncle and little Johann."

Both Mrs. Ashford and Ellen turned to the girl, stunned. Amanda had never shown such spirit before. Yet Ellen wished Amanda had kept her peace.

"I'm afraid I can't allow fighting between students," Ellen said patiently. "Even if there is provocation. I must maintain order."

"Quite right," Mrs. Ashford agreed. Unfortunately, she added, "I knew that Dutch boy would make trouble."

"It wasn't Gunther's fault!" Amanda stomped her foot.

"That will be enough sauce from you, miss." Mrs. Ashford's face reddened. "Now get busy washing the dishes before I wash your impertinent mouth out with soap."

On this unhappy note, Ellen said her thanks and descended the steps into the deep honey of twilight. Since she'd moved into her quarters, a large room behind the schoolroom, she'd dreaded the lonely evenings, which gave her too much time to fret, which she began as soon as she touched ground.

What should she do about Gunther Lang? Why didn't his older brother realize the situation he'd put Gunther in? Her mind drifted back to home and brought up her sister exchanging vows with Holton. How long did heartbreak linger?

When she walked through the trees into the schoolyard, she was surprised to glimpse Kurt Lang, sitting dejectedly on the school step, clearly waiting for her as his horse grazed nearby. Of all people, he was the one she felt least ready to face—she had no doubt he'd come to discuss the fight.

"Mr. Lang," she said.

He jumped up and swept off his hat. "Miss Thurston, I am sorry I am come so late. But I know Gunther had a fight. Please, I ask—do not put him out of school."

Ellen walked toward him, trying to gather her scattered thoughts. This disturbing man put her at a disadvantage. He was handsome like Holton, but he never tried to charm her like Holton. Mr. Lang reminded her more of a determined bull.

Nothing she'd said so far concerning Gunther had made the least impression on him. She knew in her heart that there was nothing she could do to help Gunther fit in—too much separated him from the other students. But how could she make this man believe her? See he was doing harm to his brother?

Glum about her prospects at persuading him, she sat down on the school step, facing the river. He sat down a polite distance from her. For a few minutes neither of them talked. Finally, she cleared her throat. She would try once more.

"I realize that you want Gunther to learn more English so he is better prepared for life here."

His powerful shoulders strained against his cotton shirt. "Yes, that is so."

Her heart went out to him, a man trying to raise a teenage brother and a little boy by himself. Nonetheless, why did he have to be so stubborn? "But Gunther is too much older and too sensitive about being different from the others. Making him sit with little children won't work."

"Gunther must learn to obey." Mr. Lang's words rang with deep feeling.

She tried to imagine what was driving this man to continue to put his younger brother in such a difficult situation. Maybe if she talked about her family, he might reveal something about himself.

"I have a younger sister." She didn't mention that her elder brother was full of himself or that she'd had a baby brother, too. It cost her enough to speak of her sister Cissy and what her sister had unwittingly put her through. She paused a moment, grappling with her own rampant emotions. "My parents made the mistake of always saying to her, 'Why can't you be more like your sister?' "

Where am I going with this? How is this being helpful?

She shook herself and then drew in a breath. "Nothing you do or say is going to change Gunther's mind or behavior. The struggle is not between you and him. It's really between Gunther and this new set of people, this new place." She sighed.

Several moments passed before he spoke. "You speak truth. But Gunther is too young to know what is good for him."

"Human nature will not be denied." Each word increased her confidence that making the lad attend school would not end well. "Gunther is a young man and we've put him in a situation that wouldn't be normal for any lad his age. You see that."

"Yes." Mr. Lang didn't sound happy or convinced. He rose. "I will keep Gunther home tomorrow. I must go, and think." He bowed his head politely, his unfailing courtesy impressing her once again.

"I think that's best." Ellen watched him don his hat and ride away. She stood motionless long after he'd vanished through the trees. Even after he had disappeared from view, his image stayed with her. A handsome, brave but troubled man. She wondered if his broad shoulders ever tired of the responsibilities he carried. The deep sadness she sensed in him drew her sympathy.

She shook herself and went inside, her own heart heavy. Never far from her mind were the charming words Holton had spoken to her. She reminded herself that she must stop noticing Kurt Lang so keenly. After everything she'd been through with Holton, the last thing she needed was to be the focus of whispers about the foolish old-maid schoolmarm.

Of course it was one thing to stop noticing him. It was another thing to stop thinking of him completely.

Chapter Four

Standing outside the Stewards' cabin after Saturday supper, Kurt tried to figure out exactly what he was doing there. He'd been surprised when the Stewards had invited him and his family to eat with them and Miss Thurston. The meal had been tasty, and he'd enjoyed talking about farming and the fall hunting with Martin, who was about his age. Unfortunately, Gunther had eaten in sullen silence, in contrast to Johann's lively chatter.

As the sun had disappeared behind the trees, a sudden awkwardness Kurt couldn't understand sprang up.

"Mr. Lang," Mrs. Steward said in a voice that didn't sound quite genuine, "I wonder if you would save Martin a trip and drive my cousin back to the schoolhouse?"

The question startled him. And it also startled Miss Thurston. He saw her glance at her cousin.

In Germany, this request would have caused Kurt to suspect matchmaking. Here, however, he could not think that he'd been invited for this reason. So why?

Miss Thurston's face turned pink, revealing her embarrassment.

"Yes," Martin spoke up, sounding as if he'd been rehearsed about what to say, "I have my wife's pony hooked up to my cart. It only carries two adults, so perhaps your brother and nephew can just walk home?"

Now Miss Thurston's face burned bright rose-red.

"I am happy to," Mr. Lang replied, mystified. What else could he say?

Gunther favored both of them with an odd look but gestured to Johann to come with him, and the two headed down the track in the fading light of day.

Kurt took the reins of the two-wheeled cart as Martin helped Miss Thurston up onto the seat beside him. She clung to the side of the bench as Mr. Lang flicked the reins and they started down the track to town. He noticed that she sat as far from him as she could. He hoped she didn't think he'd engineered this so that he could be alone with her.

Kurt couldn't think of anything to say to her. When they were out of sight of the Steward cabin, she finally broke the silence.

"Since we've been given this opportunity to talk, just the two of us, there is something that I have wanted to discuss with you, Mr. Lang." Her voice quavered a bit on the last few words, as if she were nervous.

"Oh?" he said, hoping for enlightenment.

"After the fight at school, you kept Gunther home only one day, right? Have you been sending Gunther to school the rest of this week?"

He stiffened. "Yes, I send him. What do you mean?"

"I thought as much. He has been playing hooky."

"Hooky?" Mr. Lang turned his gaze to her.

"Sorry. *Playing hooky* means not coming to school."

Kurt wanted to explode; instead he chewed the inside of his mouth. But he tried to stay calm for Miss Thurston's sake. "Why does he not obey me?"

"Sometimes it's not a matter of obedience," she replied, sounding hesitant.

"Then what is it about?" he asked, his cheeks burning.

"Isn't this really about whether Gunther learns more English and more about this country?" she replied in a gentle voice. "Our history and our laws? Isn't that what you want, more than his obedience?"

Her question caught him off guard. He stared at her, noticing the wind playing with the light brown curls around her face. Startled by both her question and his sudden awareness of her, his mouth opened, and then closed tightly.

Night was overtaking them. Fortunately the half-moon had risen so he could see to drive. He glanced at its silver half circle above the tree-tops. Then, after many quiet moments, he asked, "What am I to do with him?" He didn't try to hide his anxiety.

"Making him sit with little children won't work," she stated.

"But he must learn. And I cannot teach him." His words rung with deep feeling he couldn't conceal.

"I think private lessons would be best," she said. "I asked my cousin to invite you tonight so we could discuss this without calling attention to Gunther. If I came alone to your place . . ." Her voice faded.

"Private lessons?" he echoed.

"Yes. Why don't you bring him two evenings a

week? I will help him improve his English, and learn American history and government. You can make sure he studies at home on the other evenings."

"That will make more work for you. I cannot pay."

She touched his forearm. "I'm the teacher here in Pepin. Whether I teach in the daytime or evening, I'm being paid." Then, seeming embarrassed, she removed her hand from his sleeve and looked away.

He wished she hadn't taken her hand away so quickly. Her long, elegant hands, covered in fine kid gloves, were beautiful. "You are good. But still, I think Gunther must not be given good for bad behavior."

"Very few sons of farmers attend school beyond eighth grade. Don't you see? It isn't normal for Gunther or good for him."

The school came into view through the opening in the forest. Kurt tried to come to grips with what Miss Thurston had suggested.

Then an unusual sound cut through the constant peeping of tree frogs. Kurt jerked the reins back, halting the pony. He peered ahead through the dark shadows.

Miss Thurston did the same. The sound came again.

A baby crying.

They looked at each other in amazement.

"It's coming from the rear of the school, near my quarters," she said, stark disbelief in her voice.

Mr. Lang slapped the reins and jolted them over the uneven schoolyard to her door. A shaft of moonlight illuminated a wooden box. The crying was coming from inside.

Without waiting for his help, Miss Thurston leaped over the side of the cart and ran to her door. She stooped down and leaned over the box.

The wailing increased in volume and urgency.

Kurt scanned the shadows around the schoolhouse as Miss Thurston called out, "Hello? Please don't leave your child! I'll help you find a home for the baby! Hello?"

No answer came. Only the crickets chirped and toads croaked in the darkness. Then he thought he glimpsed motion in the shadows. He jumped down and hurried forward a few steps but the cloaking night crowded around him. The woods were dark and thick. Perhaps he'd imagined movement.

The baby wailed as he walked toward the teacher's quarters. He joined Miss Thurston on the step, waves of cool disbelief washing through him. *"Eines kind*? A baby?"

"It seems so."

She looked as if she were drowning in confusion, staring down at the baby, a strange, faraway expression on her face. She made no move toward the child. Why didn't she pick up the child? In fact, Miss Thurston appeared unable to make any move at all.

Ellen read his expression. How to explain her reluctance? She hadn't held a child for nearly a decade, not since little William. Her baby brother.

"How does the child come to be here?" he asked, searching the surrounding darkness once more.

"I don't know." The insistent wailing finally became impossible for her to avoid. She stooped and lifted the baby, and waves of sadness and regret rolled over her.

"What is wrong?" he asked.

She fought clear of her memories and entered her quarters, Mr. Lang at her heels. She laid the baby gently on her bed and tried to think.

"Does this happen in America?"

She looked at him. "What?"

"Do women leave babies at schoolhouses?"

"No. I've never heard of this happening before."

The child burst into another round of wailing—frantic, heartfelt, urgent.

Mr. Lang surprised her by picking up the infant. "He is hungry." He grimaced. "And the child needs a clean . . . *windel.*"

"*Windel*?" she asked.

"The child is wet," he replied.

She lit her bedside candle. In the light, she

noticed the child had a dark reddish discoloration showing through his baby-fine golden hair. Was it called a port-wine stain? Memories of her brother so long ago made it hard to concentrate. She could feel Kurt looking at her, most likely wondering why she was unable to take action.

"Do you have an old cloth to dry dishes?" he asked when she offered no solution. "We could use to . . ."

"Yes!" She hurried to the other side of the room, threw open a box of household items and grabbed a large dish towel.

Mr. Lang completely surprised her by snatching the dishcloth, laying the baby on her bed and efficiently changing him.

"You know how to change a diaper?" she asked, sounding as shocked as she felt. She couldn't help but admire his quick, deft action.

"I raised Johann from a baby. We must get milk for this one." He lifted the child. "We will go to Ashford's Store, yes?"

Glad to have direction, she blew out the candle and followed him outside. They rushed past the pony and cart and headed straight for the store. The motion of hurrying seemed to soothe the infant.

Within a few minutes, Ellen and Mr. Lang arrived at the back of the store, at the stairs to climb to the second-floor landing. Moonlight cast the stairwell in shadow so she held the railing tightly as she hurried upward. She rapped on the door, and rapped again and again. The child started wailing once more. Mr. Lang stood behind her, trying to soothe the child. She wrung her hands. What seemed like forever passed.

Then Mr. Ashford in trousers and an unbuttoned shirt opened the door. "What do you . . ." he began forcefully, then trailed into silence, gawking at Ellen.

"I'm so sorry, Mr. Ashford, but we need help," she said.

He stared at them yet didn't move.

"We come in, please?" Mr. Lang asked even as he pushed through the door and held it open for her. She hurried inside, again thankful for Mr. Lang's support.

Mr. Ashford fell back, keeping them by the door, still looking stunned. "Where did that baby come from?"

"We don't know," she nearly shouted with her own frustration.

"We find him on the doorstep," Mr. Lang said. "We need milk and a bottle. You have these things?" His voice became demanding on the final words.

Mrs. Ashford, tying the sash of a long, flowered robe, hurried down the hall, followed by Amanda in her long, white, flannel nightdress. The two asked in unison, "A baby? Where did it come from?"

"It is boy," Kurt said.

"We don't know," Ellen repeated, nearly hysterical herself from the baby's crying. She struggled to stay calm as memories of her little brother bombarded her. "He was left on my doorstep."

"He needs milk. And a bottle to feed. Please," Mr. Lang repeated.

Stunned silence lasted another instant and then Mrs. Ashford moved into action. "Ned, go downstairs and find that box of baby bottles. Mr. Lang, bring that baby into the kitchen. Amanda, light the kitchen lamp."

Grateful to follow the brisk orders, Ellen followed Mrs. Ashford and Mr. Lang. The lady of the house lit a fire in the woodstove while her daughter lit the oil lamp that hung from the center of the ceiling. As if he sensed that help had come, the baby stilled in Mr. Lang's arms, his breath catching in his throat.

Mrs. Ashford began rifling through her cupboard and then triumphantly brought out a tin and opened the lid. "Horlick's Malted Milk," Mrs. Ashford read the label aloud. "Artificial Infant Food. It's something new, made east of here in Racine, Wisconsin."

Standing beside Mr. Lang, Ellen's nerves were as taut as telegraph wire. In contrast, Mr. Lang looked serious and determined. Having him with her had made this so much easier.

The storekeeper entered the kitchen with a wooden box of glass bottles. With their goal in sight, Ellen slumped onto a chair at the small kitchen table. Surprising her, Mr. Lang lay the child in her arms and stepped back.

Again, holding the baby brought Ellen the waves of remembrance. Struggling against the current, she watched Amanda scrub a bottle clean while the older woman mixed the powdered milk with water and set it in a pan of water on the stove to warm. Within a few minutes, she handed Ellen the warm, wet bottle. Ellen wanted to offer the child to Mrs. Ashford, but the little boy flailed his hands toward the bottle and she quickly slipped it into his mouth. He began sucking. Bubbles frothed into the bottle.

Relief swamped Ellen.

Mrs. Ashford sat down at the table near her, watching the child eat. "He's evidently hungry."

"He has good appetite," Mr. Lang agreed, gazing down with a grin.

Ellen released a pent-up breath. She felt as if she'd run a ten-mile race.

"Where did he come from?" Amanda asked again.

"I drive Miss Thurston home from her cousin's," Mr. Lang replied. "We find the baby in a wooden box on the doorstep."

"Did you see anyone?" Mrs. Ashford asked sharply.

Ellen frowned. "I thought I saw movement in the woods. I called out but no one was there."

"I've heard of this happening," Mrs. Ashford admitted, "but I never thought I'd live to see it here. Someone has abandoned this child."

"And on Miss Thurston's doorstep," Amanda murmured.

All of them stared at the baby in her arms.

No other reason could explain the child's appearance. People didn't go around misplacing infants.

Ellen gazed down at the small face that had changed from frenzied to calm. The evidence of tears still wet on his cheeks drew her sympathy, and tenderness filled her.

Who could part with you, little one?

"How old do you think he is?" Ellen asked.

"Hard to say," Mrs. Ashford said, reaching over to stroke the white-blond, baby-fine hair. "But not more than a month old, if that."

"Nearly newborn, then." Ellen cuddled the child closer. The tension suddenly went out of the little body. The baby released a sound of contentment, making her tuck him closer, gentler. More unbidden caring for this child blossomed within her.

"Some people are superstitious about babies born with marks like that," Mr. Ashford said, pointing at the baby's port-wine birthmark. "Maybe that's why they didn't want him."

"Yes, it's sad the poor thing's been born disfigured," Mrs. Ashford agreed.

Ellen stiffened. "On the contrary, I've heard people say birthmarks are where babies were kissed by an angel." Nonsense of course, but she had to say something in the child's defense.

Mr. Lang bent, stroked the child's fine hair and murmured some endearment in German. His tenderness with the child touched Ellen deeply.

"I can't think of anybody hereabouts who was expecting a child. Can you, Katharine?" Mr. Ashford asked.

His wife shook her head.

"But babies don't really come from cabbage patches," Amanda said reasonably, "so where did he come from?"

"That's enough about where babies come from," Mrs. Ashford snapped.

"You better go off to bed," the girl's father ordered and motioned for her to leave.

Ellen sent the girl a sympathetic glance. Some topics were never discussed in polite society. "Good night, Amanda. Thank you for your help."

The girl stifled a yawn as she left. "See you tomorrow at church, Miss Thurston."

The mention of church snapped Ellen back to reality. "I better be getting home then. Dawn will come soon enough."

The baby finished the bottle and Mrs. Ashford placed a dish towel on Ellen's shoulder.

Laying the baby on it, Ellen rose, patting his back. She prepared to leave.

The older couple looked flummoxed. "You can't mean you're going to take this baby home with you to the school?" Mrs. Ashford popped to her feet.

"I don't see that I have any other choice," Ellen said, and waited to see if she'd be contradicted.

Despite her initial misgivings, the truth had already settled deep inside her. Someone had entrusted her with this child and she would not shirk that responsibility.

Mrs. Ashford said something halfhearted about Ellen not knowing how to care for an infant in an uncertain tone that didn't fit the usually over-confident woman. Ellen hadn't appreciated the woman's comment about the child's disfigure-ment, and she also knew without a doubt that the Ashfords shared the common prejudice against the illegitimate, the baseborn. "I'll keep the child. I'm sure someone will realize they've made a mistake and come back for him."

"I hope so," Mr. Lang spoke up. "This is serious thing, to give up one's own blood."

His statement struck a nerve in Ellen. What had driven someone to give up their own child, their own kin?

Mrs. Ashford handed Ellen a bag of rags, three more bottles and the tin of powdered infant food. "Just mix it with water right before you need it."

Ellen thanked them sincerely and apologized for bothering them after dark. The two had been more helpful than she would have predicted. Maybe she had judged them too harshly.

Ellen and Mr. Lang walked down the back staircase with the baby in her arms and the cloth sack of supplies over his shoulder. The toads still croaked at the nearby creek. Ellen brushed away a mosquito, protecting the baby from being bitten.

The baby had slipped into sleep. Still, his lips moved as if he were sucking the bottle. With a round face and a nice nose, he had white-gold hair that looked like duck down. His skin was so soft. She'd not felt anything so soft for a very long time.

Ellen had always told herself that she didn't care for babies much, holding herself back from contact with them. But she knew—when she allowed herself to think about it—that all stemmed from losing her infant brother. His loss had altered her life, and led her to not fulfill her accepted womanly role. This had grieved her mother.

But now everything had changed. This child—who had been given to her—needed her. She bent down and kissed his birthmark.

"William." She whispered the name that still caused such hurt.

"What?" Mr. Lang asked.

"I lost a brother by that name." She couldn't say more.

After a moment, Mr. Lang said quietly, "This baby will cause trouble."

She paused.

"People will talk."

She tilted her head as she gazed up at him tartly. "Everyone will know that this couldn't possibly be my child."

"I . . . Sorry," he stammered. "I do not mean that. I mean, people will not want this child here. If someone gives away a child, no one wants him."

She wanted to argue, but recalling the Ashfords' comments and attitude, she couldn't. "I will keep him, then."

Mr. Lang looked quite startled. "They will not let you."

"Why not?"

He lifted both his hands in a gesture of helplessness. "You are schoolteacher and unmarried. They will say—"

"What do *you* say, Mr. Lang?" she demanded suddenly, prodded by something she didn't yet understand.

He gazed down at her. "I say that troubled times come here. Soon."

She couldn't argue with him. But she wouldn't relinquish the child except to someone who would love him as he deserved. "Good night, Mr. Lang. Thank you."

"Good night, Miss Thurston." He paused as if

he wanted to say more, but then merely waved and headed toward the cart.

She gazed down at the child as she entered her home and shut the door. She moved inside, rocking the child in her arms, humming to him. His resemblance to William, who had died before he turned one, brought back the pain and guilt over his loss, and for a moment, it snatched away her breath. Her little brother had been born when she was nearly fourteen, and he had left them so soon. And even though she didn't want to remember, to be reminded, she couldn't help herself.

She thought of Mr. Lang and how he'd helped her, how he'd also cared for a baby not his own.

"I will call you William," she whispered and kissed him again. "Sweet William."

Chapter Five

The next morning, Kurt waited, hunched forward on the last bench at the rear of the schoolroom where Sunday services were also held. When would Miss Thurston appear with the baby? He sat between a surly Gunther and an eager Johann, hoping neither his inner turmoil nor his eagerness to see her were evident.

A warm morning meant that the doors and windows had been opened wide, letting in a few lazy flies. Men, women and children, seated with their families, filled the benches. Ostensibly Kurt had come to worship with the rest of the good people of Pepin. But he knew he and his brother and his nephew did not look or feel like a family in the way that the rest of those gathered today did. Their family had been fractured by his father's awful choices. Gloom settled on Kurt; he pushed it down, shied from it.

Wearing a black suit, Noah Whitmore, the preacher, stood by the teacher's desk at the front. But Kurt knew that more than worship would take place here today. The foundling child would not be taken lightly. His stomach quivered, nearly making him nauseated, and he couldn't stop turning his hat brim in his hands. He was nervous—for her.

He'd had no luck making the schoolteacher see sense last night. He didn't want to see the fine woman defeated, but to his way of thinking, she didn't have a hope. What would everyone say when they saw the baby? When they heard Miss Thurston declare she intended to keep him?

As if she'd heard his questions, the school-teacher stepped from her quarters through the inner door, entering the crowded, buzzing school-room. With a polite smile, she called, "Good morning!" And then she paused near Noah, facing everyone with the baby in her arms, back straight, almost defiant.

As if hooked by the same fishing line, every face swung to gaze at her and then downward to the small baby, wrapped in the tattered blanket in her arms. Gasps, followed by stunned silence, met her greeting. Kurt had to give the lady her due. She had courage. Her eyes flashed with challenge, and Kurt could not help but notice that she looked beautiful in her very fine dress of deep brown.

She cleared her throat. "Something quite unusual happened last night. This baby was left on my doorstep."

In spite of his unsettled stomach, Kurt hid a spontaneous smile. Her tone was dignified, and when a wildfire of chatter whipped through the room, she did not flinch. Kurt could not turn his gaze from her elegant face. She blushed now, no doubt because of the attention she drew.

Recovering first from surprise, Noah cleared his throat. "Was a note left with the child?"

Everyone quieted and fixed their stares on Ellen again.

"No, the child came without any identification."

"Is it a boy or a girl?" a man Kurt didn't know asked.

"How old is he?" Martin Steward asked. His wife, Ophelia, started to rise, but Martin gently urged her to remain seated. Would Miss Thurston's family support her in her desire to keep the child?

"The infant is around a month old, Mrs. Ashford thought," the schoolteacher said. "He is a boy, and I've named him William." At that moment, William yawned very loudly. A few chuckled at the sound.

Mr. and Mrs. Ashford, in their Sunday best, hurried inside with Amanda between them. "We're sorry to be late," Mr. Ashford said, taking off his hat.

"But we lost so much sleep helping Miss Thurston with the foundling last night," Mrs. Ashford announced, proclaiming herself as an important player in this mystery. "We over-slept."

Kurt watched them squeeze onto the bench in front of him, though plenty of space remained open beside Johann. The simple act scraped his tattered pride. When he noted their daughter steal a quick glance at Gunther, his tension tightened another turn. The Ashfords would never let Gunther court their daughter. That was as ridiculous as if he decided to pursue Miss Thurston himself.

This realization choked him and he tried to dismiss it.

Ellen nodded toward the rear of the room. "Yes, thank you, Mrs. Ashford. I'll need more of that Horlick's infant powder today. So far he seems to be tolerating it well."

Mrs. Ashford perched on the bench, her chin lifted knowingly.

"Well, what are we going to do about this, Noah?" a tall, young deacon named Gordy Osbourne asked, rising. Many nodded their agreement with the inquiry.

Kurt braced himself. Now unrelenting reality regarding her station in life would beat against Miss Thurston.

Noah looked troubled. "Is the child healthy, Miss Thurston?"

Before Ellen could respond, Mrs. Ashford piped up, "He appears healthy, but is disfigured by a birthmark on his head."

"He has what's called a port-wine stain on his forehead," Miss Thurston corrected, "but his hair will cover it as he grows." The lady sent a stern glance at the storekeeper's wife and held the child closer.

Why didn't she see that he'd been right? No one was going to let her keep this child. He realized he'd been mangling his hat brim and eased his grip.

"Unless the mark grows, too, and spreads," Mrs. Ashford said, sounding dour.

"I don't think that has anything to do with the baby's health," Noah commented. "A birthmark will not hurt the child."

"Maybe that's why somebody abandoned him at the teacher's door," Osbourne's wife, Nan, spoke up. "Some people don't want a child with that kind of mark."

"Unfortunately you may be right," Noah said. "But the real question is, does anyone here know of any woman in this area who was expecting a child in the past month?"

Kurt admired Noah's ability to lead the gathering. Was it because he was the preacher, or had he done something in the past to gain this position? In Europe, leadership would have to do with family standing and connections, but here, that didn't seem to matter. No town mayor or lord would make this decision. Noah Whitmore had thrown the question open for discussion—even women had spoken. This way of doing things felt odd but good to Kurt.

Noah's wife, Sunny, rose. "I think I can say that no woman *I know* in this whole area was expecting a baby last month."

"Perhaps someone from a boat left him at the schoolhouse," Miss Thurston said, "because it is the only public building in Pepin, and a little away from town. They would have been less likely to be observed leaving the child."

The congregation appeared to chew on this. Kurt stared at Miss Thurston, remembering her initial hesitation to pick up the child and her mention of a baby brother who'd died. She had known loss, too. Wealth and position could not prevent mortality and mourning. He forced his tight lungs to draw in air.

"Well, we will need a temporary home for the child—" Noah began.

"I will keep the child," Miss Thurston said, and then walked toward the benches as if the matter were settled.

Her announcement met with an instant explosion of disapproval, just as Kurt had predicted.

One woman rose. "You can't keep a baby. You're not married." Her tone was horrified.

Ellen halted. "I don't know what that has to do with my ability to care for a child. I've cared for children in the past."

"But you're the schoolmarm!" one man exclaimed. General and loud agreement followed.

Kurt didn't listen much to the crowd, but watched for the reactions of the young pastor. And Miss Thurston, who'd paused near the front row, half-turned toward the preacher, too.

The pastor's wife silenced the uproar merely by rising. "There is an orphanage in Illinois run by a daughter of our friends, the Gabriels. We might send the child there."

Murmurs of agreement began.

Miss Thurston swung to face everyone again. "I think that is a precipitate suggestion. What if the child's mother changes her mind? I don't think it's uncommon for a woman to become low in spirits soon after a birth."

A few women nodded in agreement.

"What if this woman suffered this low mood and was in unfortunate circumstances? After realizing what she's done, she might return to reclaim the child. I think it's best we wait upon events."

A man in the rear snorted and muttered loud enough for all to hear, "It's probably somebody's unwanted, baseborn child."

Noah stiffened. "I think we need to remember why we are gathered here."

That shut everyone up, suiting Kurt's idea of propriety. A child's life was not a subject for derision.

Noah gazed out at the unhappy congregation. "Miss Thurston is right, I think. A child's future depends on our making the right decision. This is something we need to pray about so we do what God wants. One thing is certain—no woman gives up her child lightly. Someone has trusted us with their own blood and we must not act rashly."

His words eased some of the tension from the room, another sign of Noah's leadership. Again, Kurt wondered about the preacher's past and how he'd come to be so respected here. Kurt's family had been respected in their village, but had lost that over his father's many sins.

"But who's going to take care of the foundling in the meantime?" Mrs. Ashford asked.

"I will," Ellen declared. "He was left on *my* doorstep."

The storekeeper's wife started, "But you'll be teaching—"

"I'm sure we can find someone who will care for the child while Miss Thurston carries out her teaching duties," Noah said, taking charge of the room. "That's something else we will pray about."

Noah raised his hands and bowed his head and began praying, effectively ending the discussion. Kurt lowered his head, too, praying that Miss Thurston wouldn't be hurt too badly when the child was taken from her. Because he was certain that that was exactly what was going to happen, one way or the other.

Ellen's face ached with the smile she'd kept in place all morning during the church service. She wished everyone would just go home and leave her alone. But the congregation lingered around the schoolhouse, around her.

Everyone wanted a good look at William and an opportunity to express their opinion of wicked people who abandoned babies. They also lauded her desire to care for the child—even if she were a schoolmarm, a woman was a woman, after all. Most voiced sympathetic-sounding, nonetheless irritating comments about William's birthmark. Noah and Sunny had helped her but underneath all the general sentiment still held that she shouldn't, wouldn't, be allowed to keep William. Ellen was nearing the end of her frayed rope.

Then Martin came to her rescue. "Cousin Ellen, you're coming home with us for Sunday dinner as planned." He smiled at everyone as he piloted her toward their wagon. When Martin helped her up onto the bench, she noted Mr. Lang and his family, who had ridden to church with the Stewards, sat in the wagon bed at the rear. This man had predicted how the community would react all too accurately. But he didn't look triumphant in the slightest, and for that, she was grateful. He nodded to her and gave her a slight smile that seemed to have some message she couldn't quite read.

As the wagon rocked along the track into the shelter of the forest, Ellen breathed out a long, pent-up sigh. She glanced at her cousin sitting beside her. "Ophelia . . ." She fell silent; she simply didn't have the words to go on.

Ophelia leaned against Ellen's shoulder as if in comfort. "I can't believe this happened."

Ellen rested her head against the top of Ophelia's white bonnet, murmuring, "I'm so glad you're here."

"The Whitmores are coming over after dinner so we can discuss this," Martin said. "We need to decide what to do with this child."

Ellen snapped up straight. "It has already been decided. William will stay with me."

"You can't mean you really want to keep this baby?" Ophelia said, sounding shocked. "I don't know how I'd take care of our little one alone."

Her cousin's stunned tone wounded Ellen, stopping her from responding.

"*Ja*—yes, she does," Mr. Lang said as the wagon navigated a deep rut. "I told her last night that they will not let her."

Mr. Lang's words wounded more than all the rest. He'd been there last night, he'd experienced discovering this child with her. Why wouldn't he take her side in this matter?

She brushed the opposition aside. It didn't matter why he wouldn't support her—it didn't matter why any of them wouldn't support her. She wasn't like other women. She had goals, and now she'd added one more. If she were a weak woman, she wouldn't be here to begin with—she would be living at home under her sister-in-law's snide thumb. But she had struck out to make a life of her own, and that was exactly what she planned to do.

Those who opposed her would not win. All she had to do was come up with a convincing argument to keep this child—and her job. And frankly, she reminded herself, Mr. Kurt Lang's opinion in this matter—in all matters—was irrelevant to her.

Later, in the early dusk, Kurt walked into the Steward's clearing for the second time that day.

Ever since the Stewards had dropped them off after church, he'd been worrying—about William, about Gunther, about Miss Thurston.

"Kurt, what brings you here?" called Martin, who was hitching the pony to his two-wheeled cart.

"Is Miss Thurston here still?" The fact he couldn't easily pronounce the "Th" at the beginning of her name caused him to flush with embarrassment. He tried to cast his feelings aside. He had come to talk with Miss Thurston face-to-face over Gunther's schooling. Altogether, the issue had left a sour taste in his mouth. But a decision must be made—Gunther's playing hooky had forced his hand.

"She's about done feeding the baby and then I'm taking her home," Martin said as he finished the hitching.

"I have come to offer to escort the lady home."

Martin turned to Kurt. "Oh?"

The embarrassment he'd just pushed away returned. Kurt tried to ignore his burning face. Did Martin think he was interested in Miss Thurston? "I wish to speak to her about my brother, Gunther, before school starts again tomorrow."

At that moment, the lady herself stepped out of the cabin with William in her arms. She noticed him and stopped. "Mr. Lang."

Sweeping off his hat, Kurt felt that by now his flaming face must be as red as a beetroot. "I come to take you home, Miss Thurston. And perhaps we talk about Gunther?"

She smiled then and walked toward the cart. "Yes, I want to discuss that matter with you."

They said their farewells to the Stewards, and soon Ellen sat beside him on the seat of the small cart, holding the baby whose eyelids kept drooping only to pop open again, evidently fighting sleep. Kurt turned the pony and they began the trip to town, heading toward the golden and pink sunset. Crickets sang, filling his ears. Beside him, Miss Ellen Thurston held herself up as a lady should. Only last night had he seen her usual refined composure slip. Finding the infant had shaken her. Did it have something to do with the little brother she'd mentioned?

Kurt chewed his lower lip, trying to figure out how to begin the conversation about his brother. "I still don't agree with what you have said about Gunther," he grumbled at last.

"But yet you are here, talking to me" was all she replied.

A sound of frustration escaped his lips. "Gunther . . ." He didn't know what he wanted to say, or could say. He would never speak about the real cause of Gunther's rebelliousness. He would never want Miss Thurston to know the extent of his family's shame. His father's gambling had been enough to wound them all. What had driven him even further to such a disgraceful end?

Kurt struggled with himself, with what to do about his brother. Gunther needed to face life and go on, despite what had happened. Would his giving in weaken his brother more?

"Your brother is at a difficult age—not a boy, not fully a man," she said.

If that were the only problem, Kurt would count himself fortunate. So much more had wounded his brother, and at a tender age. A woodpecker pounded a hollow tree nearby, an empty, lonely sound.

"Gunther and Johann are all I have left." He hadn't planned to say that, and shame shuddered deep inside his chest.

"I know how you feel."

No, she didn't, but he wouldn't correct her. "Do you still think to teach Gunther in the evenings?"

"Yes. As you know, you can send him to school, but you cannot make him learn if he's shut his mind to it. Private lessons would be best."

Kurt chewed on this bitter pill and then swallowed it. "He will have the lessons, then."

"Will you be able to help him with his studies on the evenings when I am not working with him?"

"I will."

"Then bring him after supper on Tuesday." Miss Thurston looked down at the child in her arms and smiled so sweetly—Kurt could tell just from her expression that she had a tender heart. Something about her smile affected him deeply and he had to look away.

She glanced up at him and asked, "Have you told Gunther about this?"

"I tell him soon," he said.

"Good." She sounded relieved.

He, however, was anything but relieved. His fears for Gunther clamored within. They had come to this new country for a new start. He wanted Gunther to make the most of this, not end up like their father had.

They reached the downward stretch onto the flat of the riverside. He directed the pony cart onto the trail to the school. Again, he was bringing her home in Martin's cart and again someone was waiting on her doorstep. This time a woman rose to greet them. What now?

Kurt helped Miss Thurston down. She moved so gracefully as a shaft of sunset shone through the trees, gilding her hair. He forced himself not to stop and enjoy the sight. Instead, he accompanied her to greet the woman.

"Good evening," Miss Thurston said, cradling the sleeping baby in her arms.

The other woman replied, "I am Mrs. Brawley. My husband and I are homesteading just north of town."

"Yes?" Miss Thurston encouraged the woman.

"I have one child and I heard the preacher say this morning that you needed someone to care for the baby." The woman gazed at the child, sleeping in the lady's arms.

"I take it that you may be interested in doing that?" the schoolteacher asked.

"Yes, miss. I could take care of two as well as one."

"May I visit your home tomorrow after supper and discuss it then?"

"Yes, yes, please come." The woman gave directions to her homestead, which lay about a mile and a half north of town. They bid her good-night and she hurried away in the lowering light of day.

"Well, I hope this will solve the problem of William's care during the schooldays."

Her single-mindedness scraped Kurt's calm veneer. "You think still they will let you keep the child?"

She had mounted the step and now turned toward him. "Perhaps you are one of those who think a woman who does not wish to marry cannot love a child, and is unnatural. That is the common *wisdom*."

Her cold words, especially the final ones, startled him. "No. That is foolish."

Her face softened. "Thank you, Mr. Lang."

He tried to figure out why anybody would think that. Then her words played again in his head. "You do not wish to marry?"

"No, I don't wish to marry."

Her attitude left him dumbfounded. "I thought every woman wished to marry."

She shook her head, one corner of her mouth lifting. "No, not every woman. Good night, Mr. Lang. I'll see you Tuesday evening."

"*Guten nacht,*" he said, lapsing into German without meaning to. He turned the pony cart around and headed toward the Stewards' to return it. Thoughts about Miss Thurston and William chased each other around in his mind. Very simply, he hated the thought of seeing her disappointed. What if she became more deeply attached to William and the town forced her to give the child away in the end?

Why wouldn't she face the fact that the town would not let her keep William? He wouldn't press her about this, but in fact, the town *shouldn't* let her keep him. The question wasn't whether Miss Thurston was capable of rearing the child. But didn't he know that raising a child alone was difficult, lonely, worrying? Didn't he know it better than anyone here?

Chapter Six

On Monday morning, Ellen inhaled deeply, preparing to face teaching school with William in the room. With any luck, tomorrow he would be with Mrs. Brawley. But until then, she'd have to make do.

She entered the still-empty schoolroom and set William in his basket on her desk. She gazed down at him as he slept, his little fists clutching the blanket. Every time she looked at him or held him, the feelings she had for him deepened, coiling tighter around her heart.

She walked outside into the air that still held no fall crispness, and rang the bell. The children stopped playing and ran toward her, jostling for their spots in the line. They filed in, taking their seats row by row. When all were seated, she shut the door with satisfaction at their orderliness and returned to stand by her desk.

"You still have the baby," Amanda said and then colored. "I'm sorry, Miss Thurston. I didn't mean to talk out of turn."

Ellen nodded her forgiveness. "It is an unusual situation but until his mother returns—" Ellen's heart clamped tight "—or I find someone to care for William, he will have to come to school.

Now, I will begin with our youngest grade. Slates out, please. The rest of you, please take out your readers and begin reading silently where we left off on Friday."

All went well till in the midst of listening to the fifth graders recite their times tables, William woke with a whimper and then a full-scale cry. The sound raced up her spine. But she reminded herself that she already had a plan for this situation.

Every child stopped and turned their attention to the basket on her desk.

Johann popped up. "Miss Thurston, the baby is crying."

The other students laughed, and Johann looked abashed and sat down with a plunk.

Ellen smiled at him. "I think you may be right, Johann." She lifted the child and checked his diaper. "Amanda, would you be kind enough to take William to my room and change his diaper? I left everything on the table for you. And mix him another bottle of Horlick's. That's all laid out, too."

Amanda beamed and hurried forward to carry William's basket through the door behind Ellen. Ellen motioned for the fifth grader, who had been interrupted, to begin his times tables again. She listened to the boy with one ear and to the sounds of Amanda crooning to William in the next room with the other.

Ellen could make this work—she knew she could. All she had to do now was prove it to everyone else.

After supper, Ellen left the Ashfords and began walking to the Brawley's claim with William in her arms. As she walked, an unread letter from home clamored to be taken out of her pocket. Mr. Ashford, the postmaster, had given it to her before supper.

But she didn't have the strength to face it yet. She would never admit it to anyone, but rising to feed William at least twice each night had exhausted her, flattened her somehow. And she was not sure she could handle what the letter might hold. She would have to prepare herself for the ordeal of reading it.

Walking steadily, she had no trouble finding the newly built log cabin and she called out the familiar frontier greeting, "Hello, the house!"

Mrs. Brawley came outside to welcome her. "You came!" The petite dark-haired woman, who looked barely twenty, sounded relieved.

Ellen noted that she wore a fresh apron and held her own child, who looked to be a few months older than William. Behind her loomed the young man of the house. He did not seem very happy to see Ellen. Nevertheless, she stepped inside and greeted him, offering her hand.

He shook it, all the while grimacing as if he had

a toothache. "I want to make it clear—my wife does not need to work for anybody. I'm able to provide for my family."

Mrs. Brawley blushed and lowered her eyes.

Ellen realized she should have anticipated this. "I understand that, Mr. Brawley. I thought it kind of your wife to help me out in this unusual situation."

He looked somewhat mollified. "I just don't want anybody getting the wrong idea."

"If your good wife and I come to an agreement, I'll make certain everyone knows she is doing it out of the goodness of her heart, and that I'm beholden to her kindness." Ellen scanned the room and found what she'd hoped for—a clean, orderly house.

"Okay, then," he said gruffly, offering what passed for a placatory grin. "I got animals to see to. I'll leave you womenfolk to thrash this out." Pulling on his hat from a peg by the door, he left them.

"Won't you sit down, miss?" The woman motioned toward one of the chairs at the table.

Drawing in a deep breath, Ellen agreed. "Where are you and your husband from?" Ellen asked, thinking how touchy the man's pride had been.

"We grew up west of Chicago, but my husband wanted his own farm so we headed north." The woman sounded as if she'd rather not have come to the frontier.

Ellen had chosen to come to Pepin for her own reasons, not a husband's. "I'm from Galena myself," Ellen said, keeping the conversation going, and soon they were chatting about leaving one's family. The letter in Ellen's pocket reminded her of her own.

"Now, you don't mind taking care of an orphan?" Ellen asked.

"Oh, no, it's not the child's fault," Mrs. Brawley replied quickly. "And I'll treat him just like my own." As they talked more, Ellen noted the woman's ease with William and the excellent attention she gave her own child. When Ellen was satisfied Mrs. Brawley had no prejudice against a foundling, they agreed upon both wage and plan. Mrs. Brawley would pick the child up each morning before school and Ellen would come fetch William each day after school. They shook hands and Ellen left, feeling as if everything were neatly taken care of.

Except for the unread letter from her sister sitting like a hot potato in her pocket.

The letter presented another fiery trial Ellen must endure. Could she bear to read about Cissy and her new husband? After she'd put William down later that night, Ellen finally faced her trepidation. With sure fingers, she opened the letter and began reading.

August 23, 1870

Dear Ellen, dearest sister,

Why did you leave before we returned from our honeymoon? Randolph said something about your wanting to spend a long visit with Ophelia before the school year started. I didn't realize that you'd made the decision to take the teaching position in Pepin definite. Was I so involved in my own affairs that I ignored this?

I know that we've been through a difficult time, losing Mother and Father. But then Holton came into my life and I thought it would make a happy new beginning for all of us . . .

Ellen could read no further, her heart squeezing so tight she felt strangled. She folded the letter and slid it into her music box's secret door. Her fingers trembled and she forced back tears. She gazed around at her one room with its few familiar possessions—the music box, the quilt her grandmother had sewn for her, a sampler her great-grandmother had stitched as a girl in Massachusetts. She clung to these as Holton's betrayal wounded her afresh with every memory of home.

I'll read more tomorrow when I can handle it. She could no longer hold back the tears, and they ran down her cheeks. *I'm glad you're happy, Cissy.*

• • •

On Monday evening, Kurt waited till Johann had gone to bed early as usual. Then he found his brother sitting outside on the bench by the door, gazing at the surrounding forest, the last of the sun's bronzed rays sifting through the trees and branches. Kurt sat down beside him and Gunther made room for him.

Kurt understood Gunther's fascination with the forest. At home in Germany very few forests had been preserved. Had Germany looked like this once—a vast forest with little villages, over-shadowed by the brooding evergreen trees and tall maples? But the beautiful surroundings didn't distract him from his purpose. He'd argued with himself over whether the schoolteacher was right till he was ragged inside. Now he must speak. Tomorrow Miss Thurston would be expecting Gunther for his first private lesson.

"I know you have not been going to school," Kurt said flatly and without preamble.

Gunther started and swung to face him, instantly fired up. "I am too old—"

"*Ja*, you are too old."

This halted Gunther's words. He stared at Kurt.

Kurt inhaled deeply. "But there is still much you need to learn."

Gunther looked unhappy but didn't reply.

"How will you learn about this country without school?"

Kurt asked to force Gunther to deal with the problem as an adult. If he wished to be treated as an adult, he'd have to start acting like one.

There was a pause; cricket song filled their silence and then Gunther suggested, "I could read books."

"Is your English good enough to understand those books?"

"My English is better all the time," Gunther said, some of the edge seeping back into his tone.

Kurt stared at his boots. This still felt like giving in, like letting Gunther get his own way, making him weak.

"Miss Thurston has offered private lessons two evenings a week, starting tomorrow. Do you want them?"

Gunther sent him a look laden with suspicion and folded his arms. "Private lessons? Can we afford that?"

"She says she is the teacher for Pepin and will teach anybody who wants to learn whenever they can come. Do you want to learn, Gunther?"

Gunther eyed him as if he didn't trust him.

"You did not set Johann a very good example," Kurt scolded, frowning, and felt the frown lowering his own mood.

"I couldn't get you to listen to me," Gunther objected.

Kurt bent forward and folded his hands. Their relationship was not the usual between brothers.

It never had been. Their father had never "fathered" Gunther.

Gunther rose. "So I go to school tomorrow after supper?"

"We'll go with you," Kurt said. "Maybe I can learn, too."

This thought obviously startled Gunther. Then the lad grinned. "We go to school together—you and me?"

Kurt shook his head, standing. "Go to bed."

Gunther chuckled and went inside.

Kurt stared at the last of the sunset and thought of Miss Thurston, so pretty and so caring. But she was going to be hurt over this baby and there was nothing he could do to help her.

On Tuesday evening, Ellen stood in the doorway of the school, waiting for Gunther to arrive. Would he? Or would he skip evening school, too?

As she waited, she tried not to think of the contents of her sister's letter, which she'd finished reading before she went to retrieve William from the Brawley's. The letter's contents still upset her stomach and played through her mind. She'd thought she'd left matters in the best way she could, but evidently that had changed for the worse.

She sighed. The autumn days still lingered in a long twilight. Then she saw a trio of shadows approaching. Apparently Gunther was not arriving on his own.

Holding Johann's hand, Gunther walked beside Mr. Lang, who marched toward her as if someone behind him had a rifle aimed at his back. The man, whose good looks still caused her some unease, had very definite ideas. Gunther's head was lowered in obvious uncertainty. She hoped this solution would work for the boy.

Even as she tried to focus on the important task at hand, her unruly mind kept drifting back to phrases from her sister's letter.

I know you couldn't possibly live with our brother and his wife. It seems to me that Alice brings out all the worst in Randolph. Shouldn't love bring out the best in a person?

A very good question, Ellen thought. Was this evidence that her sister was maturing?

"Good evening, Miss Thurston." Mr. Lang greeted her as always, with that distinctive European style, making his respect for her plain. She noted that his blond hair waved around his ears, and he needed a haircut.

She forced a smile, reminding herself that Gunther needed her to make this work. "I see you've brought Johann, too."

"Yes." Mr. Lang looked stressed. "I thought he could help me watch the child while Gunther takes his lessons."

This surprised Ellen, but it shouldn't have. She

recalled how Mr. Lang had pitched in and taken care of William that night they'd found him. Because of that, she had expected Mr. Lang to side with her about keeping William. But he hadn't. Now, here he was offering her help, not lecturing her about her campaign to keep William.

An unusual and complicated man.

"A good idea," she replied.

As she looked at Mr. Lang and was reminded yet again of Holton, more of Cissy's words played in her mind. *I must say that I've been surprised by some of our oldest friends. They don't seem to welcome Holton as they should. Holton dismisses it as just small-town clannishness, but it hurts me all the same.*

Ellen hoped no one would tell Cissy the plain truth. Initially, when others noticed Holton switching his attentions from her to Cissy, she'd crafted excuses. She'd done it foremost to save face but then to protect her sister.

But maybe I shouldn't have. Perhaps I should have told Cissy the truth. But would she have believed me? Or put it down as jealousy?

Ellen forced herself back to the present. "Gunther, I thought we'd do our lessons in my quarters. Come in."

Soon she sat at the table with Gunther, and Mr. Lang settled in the rocking chair holding William. Johann played with a carved wooden horse, tapping its hooves on the half-log floor.

Accustomed to being here alone every evening, Ellen noticed a difference. The room felt as if it was happy to be filled with more than just her and William. *Foolishness,* she chided herself.

"Gunther, I am not going to be teaching you as a child, but as an adult student." She had given this a lot of thought and had rehearsed this speech in her mind. She looked directly into the young man's blue eyes, so like his handsome brother's. No wonder he'd gained Amanda's attention.

"Gunther," she began, "you have much to learn about English and American history and government if you are to be a knowledgeable American citizen. But I'm only going to teach you if you are interested in bettering yourself, preparing yourself to vote intelligently in the future. Do you want to learn?"

Gunther looked surprised. "I thought it had been decided already."

"I can present lessons," she said, "but I can't make you learn."

Gunther glanced at his brother, then lowered his gaze to the tabletop. Ellen waited while Gunther thought, and her mind drifted back to the letter.

Please write soon and tell me you're happy up there in the wilderness. If you aren't, we can bring you home where you belong.

Home where I belong. Holton's duplicity had robbed her of her home forever. Her emotions tumbled downward. Despair gripped her, but she wrenched herself from its grasp.

"What do you say, Gunther?" she asked more sharply than she'd intended.

The young man raised his eyes to her.

"Yes, I want to learn about this country's history, its government and I want to get better at English." Gunther's words tumbled out in a rush.

Relief rolled through her. "Yes, I can help you with speaking English, and also with reading and writing proficiently. And I will teach you American government and history—"

"That will not take long," Mr. Lang interjected, an edge to his voice. "This country is not a century old, even. Germany's history goes back over a thousand years."

Ellen heard the wounded pride in Mr. Lang's tone. He'd left his country behind. As a stranger in this new place, he was counted as less than others.

Gunther snapped, "I don't care about Germany. I want to be American. You brought us here. This is where I will live." Jabbing his chest with his thumb, he added, "Where I will take a wife."

Ellen thought of the Ashfords' low opinion of Gunther. Obviously Gunther hoped that gaining education would help change their minds. She hoped so, too. "Then shall we begin?"

Gunther nodded to her. "Yes, please." His tone no longer was angry.

"Since you mentioned it, I think we'll start with

helping you improve your pronunciation of English sounds." She began with the difficult "th" sound.

As she helped Gunther learn to position his tongue between his teeth to make this sound, she noted from the corner of her eye Mr. Lang and Johann silently mimicking her. So she would be teaching three, not one.

A strange feeling came over her, and she realized that sitting in her quarters and helping Mr. Lang and Johann and Gunther while Mr. Lang held William was close to how she felt when with Ophelia and Martin. This was a disturbing thought, which triggered a disturbing sentence from Cissy's letter.

You must plan to come home for a visit at Christmas. Holton and I will meet you at Moline and bring you home in our carriage.

She lost track of what she was saying to Gunther as the words rang in her mind. *Home,* Cissy had written. But she felt she would never go home again. She'd lost her parents to typhoid a year ago; her brother to his mean-spirited, pretentious wife and now her little sister to Holton.

Despair over these injuries weighed like lead shot in her midsection.

Then William gurgled in Mr. Lang's arms. The man smiled down at her child, and his expression touched her heart. She would leave the past behind and make her own family here. With William.

Oh, God, please make that come true.

Chapter Seven

Removing his hat, Kurt hesitated at the school door. Today after Sunday worship, everyone had shared a potluck picnic on the school grounds. Now the school board was going to hold a school dedication, an event new to him.

He found himself looking for Miss Thurston, as he'd been doing all day. And all day he'd overheard bits of conversations about her and William. No one approved of her keeping the child. Had Miss Thurston heard them, too?

Holding Johann's hand, Kurt entered the school and sat on their usual half-log bench at the back of the room. Johann was excited about something but when Kurt asked, the lad had just grinned. Kurt noted that the three men who'd been elected to the board—Mr. Ashford and Martin Steward and another man he didn't know—sat in the first row along with their families.

Miss Thurston, dressed as fine as a fashion plate, sat at her desk. She wore a stylish dress of some shiny dark blue material. With her bearing both graceful and striking, she overshadowed the other women in the room. He tried not to stare at the lovely picture she presented, something he found he was doing more and more these days.

On her desk perched the basket with the napping child. He watched as people kept looking at it and then looking away.

An air of expectancy hummed in the room, the scent of pine and cedar emanating from the newly cut, rough log walls. He liked that. How different the village school he'd attended had been, which had stood for centuries before he entered it.

He glanced around and glimpsed his brother sitting on the other side of the door. He noted a subtle change in Gunther. The boy still didn't sit up as straight as Kurt would have liked, but he didn't slouch quite as much, either. However, he was still gazing at the storekeeper's daughter. Kurt shook his head, wishing he could spare the boy the pain of coming rejection.

Mr. Ashford cleared his throat. "I'd like to welcome you all to the formal dedication of Pepin's first school."

Applause and foot-stamping broke out amid the crowd. Kurt sensed the pride the young town was feeling. They had worked hard and contributed much to see this school finished. Johann sat very straight beside him, still appearing eager about something.

Noah Whitmore asked everyone to stand and pray with him. The prayer came straight from the man's heart, asking God's blessing on the building, on the teacher, on the children and their families. At the end, a solemn and hearty "Amen!" swept the gathering.

At Mr. Ashford's request, Miss Thurston rose. She looked very elegant yet commanding. Her back straight, her chin lifted, but not so high as to challenge others. And he noted that she also wore a stylish hat with a feather today, not a bonnet like the other women.

"I have asked Miss Thurston to say a few words today," Mr. Ashford said.

The teacher turned to face the filled schoolroom. "Instead of speaking myself, my students have prepared a recitation for you in honor of this special day. Students," she said, "come forward as we rehearsed."

Her students—including Johann—leaped to their feet and hurried forward where, with a little jostling, they assembled in age order, the youngest students in the front.

"Johann," Miss Thurston said, "will you announce our recitation, please?"

"Yes, Miss Thurston," he replied in a loud voice, stepping forward. "We, the students of Pepin Community School, will recite the Preamble to the United States Constitution." Red-faced but proud, Johann moved back in line.

Noting that Johann had spoken with almost no accent, Kurt wondered if he'd been carefully rehearsed by the teacher. He also noted that he didn't know what "preamble" meant. He leaned slightly forward to hear it.

"We the People of the United States—" Miss

Thurston started the students in a clear, strong voice and then let the children go on without her "—in Order to form a more perfect Union, establish Justice, insure domestic Tranquility, provide for the common defence, promote the general Welfare, and secure the Blessings of Liberty to ourselves and our Posterity, do ordain and establish this Constitution for the United States of America."

Excitement and wonder raced down Kurt's spine, a tingling—an awakening. *We, the People.* Not the princes, not the lords, not the gentry—*the people* ordained and established. In some unseen way, he felt himself expanding, becoming more than he had considered himself before hearing these words. He inhaled deeply, letting this sensation sink in. He couldn't take his gaze from Miss Thurston as she stood so tall and so brave, without a bowed head or a voice of deference. *I love this country.*

A moment of silence and then everyone surged to their feet and applauded, some holding their hands high. The applause went on for over a minute, the parents glowing with pride. Kurt joined in. That Miss Thurston had chosen his nephew, the scorned immigrant, to introduce the recitation was not lost on him. How kind of her. How good.

No doubt awakened by the applause, William began to cry. Miss Thurston swiftly lifted him from his basket and he calmed immediately. Again, Kurt noticed everyone eyeing the teacher and the child.

"Well recited, students," Mr. Ashford pronounced, also with a sidelong glance at the teacher.

Kurt wished William hadn't called everyone's attention to himself. He knew how this would end but he wanted nothing to hurry along what would inevitably happen.

"Miss Thurston," Mr. Ashford said, "will you tell us if there is anything you need to do your job as teacher of Pepin Community School?"

Miss Thurston inclined her head. "I'd like the parents to ask their children each evening to share what they learned in school that day."

The parents around Kurt nodded in agreement and looked more pleased with each word the teacher said.

"Also, I ask that each child bring their own cup for water," Miss Thurston added. "I've studied modern sanitation and it is becoming accepted that using the communal cup, which hangs by the pump, is a way of spreading contagions."

The parents bent their heads together and discussed this startling announcement, seemingly impressed by Miss Thurston's knowledge. And when she thanked the parents for doing such a good job preparing the children to come to school, they all beamed at her praise. She was absolutely winning them over as their teacher. Kurt only wished that she could win them over in all matters, for her sake.

Mr. Ashford thanked the community for coming, and everyone applauded, rising to gather their families and head home. For some reason, Kurt found he couldn't leave. Johann had left his side to talk to friends outside and finally only he and Miss Thurston remained. She walked toward him, one brow lifted as if questioning him.

He could not provide a single, sensible reason for lingering. How could he say that he'd found it impossible to leave without speaking to her?

"Did you need something, Mr. Lang?"

Like an ocean swell, an answer came to him. He needed only to speak a few words to Miss Thurston. He had denied his growing interest in her, which was both inappropriate and doomed. But being in her presence, and speaking with her, had become a pleasure he couldn't deny himself.

"A very good dedication," he managed to say. "I had not heard that before. The preamble."

She gazed at him. "Thank you. I think the children did a good job. Did you notice how well your nephew pronounced his part?"

Kurt found his mouth had gone dry. "Yes. *Danke*—thank you." Since he couldn't trust his tongue, he simply smiled and bowed, and then took his leave as quickly as he could.

Outside, he called Johann and soon the three of

them were walking home together. As he listened to Johann's chatter, Kurt sternly took himself to task for giving in to his foolishness with regard to his feelings. Just as Gunther had no hope of gaining Amanda, Kurt had no hope of attracting Miss Thurston. The old wound twisted inside him like a sharp knife. The woman he'd proposed to had rejected him and at the worst possible moment, just after his father had lost almost everything and decided to take the coward's way out. In the end, that had pushed him to leave Germany.

Just as well. Just as well, he thought. And no one here must ever find out.

At school late on Tuesday afternoon, Ellen listened to the eldest students as they alternated reading portions of Longfellow's poem, "The Song of Hiawatha," aloud. The day had turned sultry, and she dabbed her face with one of her mother's delicate lace-edged handkerchiefs, one that she'd hidden from her sister-in-law, Alice. Alice thought that all of Mother's possessions should go to the wife of the eldest son, and the daughters should get nothing.

Ellen didn't like the way her thoughts stirred up irritation. Why was she thinking of Alice—of all people—now?

When the tall form of a man appeared in the doorway of the school, she thought one of the fathers had come early to take a child home. The sun shining behind him cast him in shadow.

"Yes?" she asked, shading her eyes to see.

"Ellen?"

It was her brother's voice! "Randolph?" She ran to him, and he opened his arms and let her hug him.

"What are you doing here?" Fear lanced through her. "Has anything happened—" She couldn't finish her question.

"No, nothing dire has happened."

Then why had her brother traveled three days north to see her?

She waited for him to continue, but he didn't. She stepped back from him and showed him in. He looked more and more like their father all the time—slender with wavy, dark hair and a distinguished face.

When she realized that all the children were gawking at Randolph, she mastered herself and said, "Students, this is my brother, Randolph Thurston. Please stand and say, 'Welcome to our school, sir.' "

The children rose as one and a slightly out-of-unison welcome rang through the schoolroom.

Randolph bowed slightly. "Thank you, children."

She glanced at the large wall clock. "Randolph, I still have some lessons to finish before the end of the school day. If you go through that door, you can wait in my quarters."

"Of course. I don't want to interrupt the children's studies." With a friendly wave, he strode up the aisle past her and through the door.

However, the children were distracted. She didn't blame them since she was distracted, as well. Finally she decided to let them go home early. Nothing was being learned and she found her agitation over her brother's presence growing moment by moment. Though she was glad to see him, she didn't want him to find out about William—at least not from anyone else.

After the last student hurried outside, she shut the school door and walked to the entrance to her room. To brace herself, she drew in a deep breath, crafted a smile and went through to her room. "Well, Randolph, this is a surprise."

He rose from the rocker. "Yes, I decided to come and see how you were situated myself. I left my overnight bag at the general store. The proprietor invited me to stay the night and directed me here."

Was this really a visit to make sure she was happy here? The brother she'd known before he'd married Alice would have done so, but not the man he'd become since.

"Well, how do you like my quarters?" She motioned with some pride toward her cozy room.

"It is simple compared to what you were accustomed to."

"Yes, but I like its simplicity." *And that it is my*

own place, with no one here to snipe at me. She tried to push away the volumes of hurt and anger Alice had created and which she still carried, thinking that she needed to get over Alice, forgive Alice her unkindness. "I'm not unhappy to see you, Randolph, but you must have a reason for coming."

"I came to see how you were faring here in the wilderness," he repeated, his evasion so clear that a first grader could have perceived it. "You've only written once since you left home," he scolded gently.

"And if my memory serves, dear brother, you didn't answer that one letter. Alice did," she teased him lightly in return.

"I've been very busy with business."

I moved to another state and began a new career, but I'm just a woman, therefore, what I'm busy with is not as important as what a man is busy with.

She decided not to voice this, knowing she didn't need to keep pestering him. Eventually he would have to tell her. This avoiding something he didn't want to do was so like Randolph that somehow it reassured her.

And she couldn't prevent him from meeting William. *Might as well face it.* She claimed her bonnet from the peg by the door and pulled on cotton gloves, determined to face the situation head-on.

"There is something I need to pick up just north of here. Will you accompany me?"

As she led her brother through town, she introduced him to everyone who came out to meet him. Finally they left town behind them and headed up the track toward the Brawley claim.

"What are you picking up?" he asked again.

"You'll see," she said, delaying. Better to be with the Brawleys when the truth came out. Their presence might temper Randolph's reaction.

Soon they approached the Brawley cabin. "Hello, the house!" Ellen called out.

Mrs. Brawley walked out with William in her arms. The woman's usual friendly greeting died on her lips at the sight of Randolph. Confronted by an unexpected guest, Mrs. Brawley automatically smoothed her hair.

"Mrs. Brawley, may I introduce my brother, Randolph Thurston? Randolph, this is Mrs. Anson Brawley."

Looking puzzled, Randolph slightly bowed and greeted the woman.

The moment of revelation had come.

"I wanted to surprise you, Randolph." Ellen lifted William from Mrs. Brawley's arms. "This is William. I'm adopting him."

Watching Randolph's shock rise through him like a geyser chafed her nerves. He would probably have much to say, like everyone else. Yet what could he do?

While Randolph silently grappled with her news, she chatted a few moments with Mrs. Brawley about how William's day had gone. All was well. Ellen thanked the woman. She shouldered William's sack of baby things but her brother gruffly told her to give the sack to him to carry. Was it just good manners or did it show concern for her? She pondered this as she led Randolph toward town.

As soon as they were out of sight from the claim, Randolph exploded. "What is this all about, Ellen Elizabeth Thurston?"

She drew in a deep breath. "The infant was left on my doorstep last week."

"What?"

She repeated the sentence.

"Surely someone else will take the child?"

"I am keeping him." Ellen kissed William's forehead.

"Nonsense."

"Did you notice what I named him?" she asked, hoping he would understand.

That shut him up. "William," he said finally.

"Yes, William."

They walked on in silence. Was Randolph remembering how he'd helped her care for their little brother? How they'd wept together when they'd laid him to rest?

Suddenly another thought intruded. Gunther would come for his session this evening, and

Randolph probably wouldn't like that, either. After supper at the Ashfords, she would try to persuade him not to come back to her quarters with her. She wanted to avoid the unpleasantness over her associating with "rude, ignorant immigrants," as she had heard her brother once say.

Mr. Lang was as far from rude and ignorant as a man could possibly be. And even in Gunther's angrier moments, he wasn't exactly rude. And Johann, well, he was a smart and charming boy.

She sighed, feeling frustrated that Randolph had intruded on the life she had built for herself. And still more worrying, she didn't know why Randolph had come.

Whatever the reason, she had a feeling that Randolph's visit was going to be a complicated one and might end with a confrontation—if he thought she was returning to Illinois.

Uneasy, Kurt stood by while Gunther knocked on the door of the schoolteacher's quarters. Though they'd all washed up before coming, he felt the effects of the uncomfortable heat, even this late in the day. When would cool autumn come?

Miss Thurston opened the door and motioned them inside.

"I brought you flowers, miss." Grinning, Johann shoved a handful of wilted brown-eyed Susans into her hand.

"Oh, Johann, thank you." She quickly put

them in a jar of water and placed them on the table.

And then Kurt glimpsed a well-dressed man sitting in the rocker—where Kurt usually sat. This must be Miss Thurston's brother, the one Johann had mentioned. Was this a good visit with family or had the man brought bad news?

"*Guten abend*, Miss Thurston." Irritation with himself rushed through him, hot and uncomfortable. Why had he greeted her in German?

The schoolteacher introduced Kurt to her brother. Kurt stepped forward and shook his hand, feeling the lack of calluses—this man didn't work with his hands. Though they stood eye to eye in height, the man managed to look down on him.

"Randolph, Gunther is an adult student of mine. He's bettering his English and preparing for American citizenship. I'll be busy an hour or more tutoring him. Perhaps you would prefer to go back to the Ashford's, after all?"

Her brother responded with a brief and disapproving smile. "I'll stay. Do you entertain students—" her brother eyed Mr. Lang up and down "—alone in your quarters often?"

Kurt felt a twinge of anger. Was the man insinuating that this was improper? Kurt nearly said something in her defense but contented himself with a pointed look at her brother. Surely he should know his sister would never do anything dishonorable or even questionable.

"So far only Gunther needs adult instruction,"

she replied stiffly. "Now we must begin so they can return home while some light still lingers."

Kurt caught the discontented tone in her voice. Her brother's visit evidently did not please Miss Thurston. Had Mrs. Steward, her cousin, written to her brother about the child and now he had come to forbid her to adopt William? No, there hadn't been time for a letter to reach Illinois.

Miss Thurston motioned for Gunther to take his seat at the table as usual. "Mr. Lang, why don't you bring my desk chair in from the schoolroom and be comfortable?" Then she began speaking to Gunther and looking at the assignments he'd done since their last session.

Gunther replied in a strained voice, no doubt unsettled at having a stranger present during his lesson. The lad had tried to hide his pride at successfully completing all his assignments. Kurt had praised him, and had been looking forward to thanking Miss Thurston for suggesting this teaching arrangement. The brother's presence had ruined the evening.

But Kurt obeyed her suggestion and brought the chair into the room, sitting opposite her brother and meeting the man's disapproving gaze, face-to-face.

Johann dragged his wooden horse from his pocket and approached the man. "My uncle made this for me."

The brother barely glanced at it. "Very nice."

Then he returned his gaze to Kurt. "How long have you and your wife lived here?"

Kurt knew immediately what prompted this question. Another twinge of anger. "I am not married. Gunther is my brother. Johann is my nephew. That is our family now."

The man looked more chagrined.

"Miss Thurston told us she is from Galena. Are you from Galena, too?" Johann said.

Kurt savored how easily Johann pronounced that pesky "th" sound now.

"Yes, I am" was all the man said.

Kurt tried to think of some topic of conversation, but realized he was content to sit in silence with the man rather than have to make conversation with someone who so clearly did not like immigrants. He listened to Johann tapping his horse's hooves on the wooden floor, and Gunther and Miss Thurston discussing his writing lesson.

Finally, Randolph Thurston fidgeted in the rocker and then rose. "Ellen, I am tired from my journey. I think it best I take your advice and return to the Ashford's since I accepted their hospitality for the night."

Miss Thurston swiveled to face her brother. "I'm sure you are tired. Get some rest. Mr. Lang lives close to Martin and Ophelia—I was going to have him tell them you are in town and invite ourselves to supper tomorrow after school. It wouldn't do not to see them while you're here."

"Good. I want to see their place, too." Mr. Thurston nodded toward Kurt. "Nice meeting you and your family. Good night."

Kurt heard the last sentence and did not believe it for one moment.

"I'll see you tomorrow then, Randolph." Miss Thurston dismissed him with a wave of her hand and turned back to Gunther.

The man left quickly.

Kurt heard the baby stirring in the basket. He went over and picked him up to find the child needed a fresh diaper. As he changed the child, he wondered not only what had brought Randolph Thurston to Pepin, but what it was about the man's presence that seemed to agitate Miss Thurston.

After the lesson ended, Miss Thurston rose and said, "You two go on. Mr. Lang will join you soon. I want to have a few words with him."

Kurt paused in the middle of her room. As the lads left, Johann chattering as usual, Gunther cast a quizzical look over his shoulder.

"Miss Thurston?"

She looked distressed. "I hope you weren't offended by my brother's . . . coolness. He is always a bit formal, but—"

"It is fine," he said, bending the truth.

"Very well, then." Her smile looked strained. "I will see you Thursday if not sooner."

After the long day, the schoolteacher's hair was beginning to slip from its pins. He found he was clenching his hands to keep from reaching out to touch the silken threads of gold that the summer sun had gilded in her light brown hair. The impulse caught him off guard and hurried him to the door.

"Yes, Thursday." He nodded, swiping his hat from the peg and heading outside. "Good night."

As he rushed to catch up with his brother and nephew, many thoughts swirled in his mind. Why had the brother come? Perhaps he'd come to persuade Miss Thurston to leave?

The thought of her being removed from their town felt like someone slamming a door inside him. The school had become the center of their community and Miss Thurston had brought such life to Pepin. He remembered the lift he'd felt when Johann and the other children recited the preamble, and thought of the change he'd already seen in Gunther after just a few lessons with the teacher.

Kurt, however, refused to contemplate just how much she'd added to *his* life. He must not think such thoughts. Even if, by some circumstance, he felt he could pursue her, he would simply cause trouble for her. Her brother's obvious disdain made that clear.

The thought hit him like acid, burning into his heart. The truth was, he was no good for Miss Thurston. And there was very little he could do about that.

Chapter Eight

Before supper that evening, Martin took Randolph outside to show him all he'd done on his land over the past year, leaving Ellen alone with Ophelia. As soon as the men were out of earshot, Ophelia exclaimed, "Did you know Randolph was coming?"

"No." Ellen held William and rocked the cradle with Ophelia's baby with her foot.

"Why is he here?" Ophelia was making gravy and busily stirred the contents of a large cast-iron skillet.

"I wish I knew."

"Do you think someone told him about . . ." Ophelia nodded toward William.

"The post doesn't move that fast and if you didn't write him, who would?"

"Well, you know I wouldn't have written a word to Galena about all this. I hope my mother doesn't get wind of it." Ophelia sounded really worried.

"Even if she does hear of it, she wouldn't dare say anything against my character," Ellen said, trying to sound convincing.

"Humph," Ophelia made the sound. "You witnessed the scene she enacted when she visited here only last year. Do you think your brother's worried about Cissy? I mean do you think there's some trouble concerning her and Holton?"

Since this unwelcome thought had occurred to her, Ellen frowned. "Cissy did say that some people were less than welcoming to Holton."

"I wonder why . . ." Ophelia turned her attention to her gravy.

Ellen shrugged, leaning down to kiss William's forehead. The truth was she missed him during the long school days apart. She didn't need to burden her cousin with the truth about Holton or discuss Alice. Ophelia knew Alice all too well already.

"Remember when Randy got too big for his britches," Ophelia asked, using her brother's childhood nickname, "and we all called him 'Boss' and played pranks on him?"

Ellen thought of her brother's disapproval of her choice to live here and teach school and felt that he probably still thought of himself as boss.

Ellen sat beside Randolph as he drove the wagon they'd borrowed from the blacksmith, with William asleep in the basket at her feet. They were on their way home. During dinner with Ophelia and Martin, Randolph repeated his excuse to their cousins for coming to Pepin. But tomorrow Randolph would head back to Galena and he still hadn't told her why he'd really come. By now, Ellen's nerves had been stretched tight enough to snap.

Finally in the dying light of day, she and Randolph approached the schoolhouse. He helped her down and lifted the basket, then followed her to her door.

She opened the door and inside, lit a lamp on the table. Then she turned to her brother. "Perhaps, Randolph, the time has come for the truth. You must have wanted something to come all this way and for such a short stay. What is it?"

After setting the basket down by her bed, Randolph put his hands together and worked them. She sat in the rocker and waited, listening to the crickets and cicadas outside.

He finally cleared his throat. "Ellen, it's time for you to give up this nonsense and come home where you belong."

His words sounded prepared and practiced, and Ellen heard Alice's voice in them. "My home is here now," Ellen said, keeping her tone light. "Please come to the point."

"Alice is expecting." He paused as if waiting for a response.

Looking her brother in the eye, Ellen said the only words she could. "I felicitate you."

"My wife needs family—needs you—home in this time of stress." Randolph dropped his hands.

They both fell silent.

"Is she having a difficult pregnancy?" Ellen finally asked.

"The doctor says she is merely suffering the usual discomforts."

"Then I fail to see why I am needed." Ellen waited.

Randolph's jaw worked as he evidently prepared to come to the point. "I'm afraid that Alice is having trouble keeping house help. The Irish girls can't seem to come up to the mark anymore. And with her feeling so badly . . . Ellen, it's your duty to come home and help out. Alice isn't strong enough to—"

"Alice is as strong as an ox," Ellen said blandly and rose. "I would suggest Alice learn to treat the Irish girls better and then she'll have no trouble keeping house help. Let me be clear, Randolph. I will not come home to keep house for Alice."

I have no intention of returning to Galena. Ever.

"Alice said you'd be difficult," he said, obviously disgruntled. "She wrote this note for me to give you." He handed her the letter, but wouldn't make eye contact.

She unfolded it.

Dear Ellen,
I'm sure you will refuse to come back, even though it is your duty as the unmarried sister to help your family. So let me just say this. Gossip is buzzing about Cissy and Holton. I don't know why people waited so long to

begin commenting about Holton switching his attentions from you to your younger and much prettier sister, but they did. I think your leaving town prompted a resurgence of the gossip. Cissy is finding all this talk distressing. I have done my best to put a good face upon the business. However, if you don't come home, I'm afraid I won't be able to carry this off. If you love your sister, you will come home and save her embarrassment.

Sincerely,

Alice

The letter and its veiled threat left Ellen aghast. She looked into Randolph's face, shadowed in the lamplight. The letter was dreadful but it might serve a purpose. Cissy had said it well— Alice brought out the worst in their brother. Maybe the time for revelation had arrived.

"Do you know what Alice has written me?"

"No."

She handed the note to him. "Here. Read it."

He accepted it reluctantly and then glanced down. Barely a minute passed as he read it. His face reddened in the low light.

"Randolph, you are my brother and I love you. But I don't think you realize that your wife shows a very different face to you than she does to me or even Cissy. Or the Irish girls who've left your employ."

Halfheartedly, he began, "You're reading something in this note that isn't—"

"No, Randolph, you and I both perceive the meaning plainly. And in your heart, you know that trying to bring me home now is selfish on Alice's part. That's why you've delayed and delayed telling me why you came."

Her brother sank onto the bench by her table, staring at the single page in his hand.

Ellen waited.

"I haven't wanted to admit it to myself," he said, not looking up. "But when you left so abruptly, Alice and I had an argument. A neighbor woman had said something sharp to me about Alice knowing why you'd left."

Ellen didn't reply. Randolph must work this out for himself.

"What am I going to do, Nell?" he at last asked. His use of her childhood nickname touched her. "After reading this, I can't deny it any longer. I've married a vain, selfish woman."

"I don't know what you can do except stand up to her. By ignoring it, you've been condoning her behavior."

He nodded slowly. "I'm sorry I didn't speak up when I first sensed matters weren't right between you and Alice."

"You are in a difficult position."

"And you are, too," her brother said, his voice becoming stronger.

"What?"

"What about this foreigner, this Mr. Lang?"

Ellen felt herself starch up on the outside and soften on the inside, an odd combination. "What about Mr. Lang?"

"I'd have to be blind not to notice how *friendly* the two of you are."

Ellen sent her brother a repressive look. "If you are implying that there is anything between us other than friendship—"

"Perhaps on your part, it's only friendship. I am a man and I know when a man is interested in a woman. Mr. Lang is interested in you."

Ellen half-turned from him. "Then he will be disappointed. I have no interest in romance now."

Her brother grumbled. "I know who's responsible for that."

"I don't want to speak of Holton—"

Randolph changed subjects. "You shouldn't have gone so far away, Nell."

"I am happy here. And now I have William."

"Martin told me that the town is against your keeping this foundling."

Her heart lurched but she answered calmly, "The town will get used to it."

Randolph sat a few more moments before he rose to leave. "My boat is expected early in the morning. I will write you when I get home. And don't worry about Cissy. I'll take care of everything." He turned.

She rose and threw her arms around him. "You can handle this, Boss." She used the old name to try to lift his mood. "Give my love to Cissy . . . and Alice."

He hugged her close. "We lost our parents too soon. Perhaps if they'd still been here . . ."

She choked back sudden tears. "I wish you traveling mercies."

After their farewells, she watched him drive up the track toward town in the moonlight.

Dear God, help my brother. He will need it to succeed.

Chapter Nine

Ellen stood by the school door, smiling as she watched the children enjoy their afternoon recess. She swallowed a yawn and leaned against the doorjamb, hoping William would soon sleep the night through. A stiff breeze played with the fringe on her shawl and her bonnet shaded her from the bright sunshine.

The first cool morning had come. A few leaves on the tallest maple trees had suddenly been trimmed in scarlet. The unusually long summer appeared to finally bow its head to autumn. She would have to start knitting warm socks and buntings for William.

"They're gonna take that baby away from the teacher," a boy's voice said.

The words, coming from around the corner of the schoolhouse, startled Ellen from her reverie.

"I don't know why. What's wrong with a teacher having a baby?" asked a girl.

" 'Cause teachers don't have babies. Or husbands. Only single ladies—old maids, like Miss Thurston—get to teach school."

"Oh, what do you know? Miss Thurston's not an old maid. She's too pretty—"

Ellen rang the bell, smiling as she shook inside. She understood all too well that children merely mimicked what their parents said at home.

From all over the schoolyard, the children ran to her as usual. She had recognized the voices she'd overheard but tried to forget who they were. Children weren't responsible for their parents' prejudice.

One thing was clear: it was time for Ellen to come up with a plan, or else risk losing William.

And that was something she had no intention of doing.

The school board meeting took place on the third Sunday afternoon of the month as usual. Sitting on the front bench in the schoolroom, Ellen had devised a way to distract everyone from William's presence in her life by giving them something else to talk about. It wasn't the best plan, but it was the only one she had at the moment.

At the front of the schoolroom facing the benches, the three men on the school board—her cousin's husband, the old preacher's son Micah and Mr. Ashford—had arranged themselves in a row. A few men and women clustered toward the back of the room to observe, but most people had gone home to enjoy a quiet Sunday.

Mr. Lang had not stayed for the meeting. Ellen found herself wishing that he had. She sat alone on the front bench facing the board, maintaining a calm expression and confident manner. Unfortunately, both were a facade. Her stomach swirled unevenly.

Martin, the board's secretary, was reading the minutes from the last meeting. "Miss Ellen Thurston asked the board to consider purchasing a wall map for the school. The suggestion was discussed. A motion . . ."

Listening, or trying to appear as if she were listening, Ellen waited for Mr. Ashford to ask if there was any new business. Then she heard William begin to cry in her quarters. Her jaw tightened. All three men on the board turned toward the door behind them. *Oh, please, not now, William.*

She'd hired Amanda to watch him so he wouldn't disrupt the meeting—she didn't want to call any attention to William right now. When he stopped crying abruptly, she found herself able to take a deep breath. *Thank you, Amanda.*

The board resumed their deliberations with Martin's notes being accepted unanimously. Next, Micah presented the treasurer's report. Then Mr. Ashford asked, as if merely a formality, "Is there any new business to discuss?"

Some people began to move, perhaps preparing to leave. In her room, William was fussing and the sound knotted the back of Ellen's neck. People stopped gathering themselves and looked askance toward the door to her quarters. Mr. Lang in contrast appeared at the door and took his place in the last bench.

His arrival and the negative expressions on the others' faces pushed her to her feet. "I have some new business to discuss with the board, if I may?"

The board members looked at each other and Mr. Ashford cleared his throat. "Yes, Miss Thurston, what is it?"

"I have come up with an idea I think will encourage our students to excel in their studies."

Those attendees who'd risen sat down again.

"What is it?" Martin asked.

"I propose our school prepare for and host a regional spelling bee here next April."

An astounded silence met her proposal. Unfortunately, Amanda's voice, as she tried to soothe William, filled it.

She pressed on, feigning a lightness far from

what she felt. "I know that there are schools in Lake City, Downsville and Bear Lake. All three are within an easy driving distance for a midday gathering here. I would write to the teachers of those schools and invite them to prepare their students for the spelling bee."

She took a deep breath and prepared to speak louder in order to cover William's continued whimpering.

"Then in April on the appointed day, the teachers and their students who have excelled in spelling will come here to compete with our best spellers. Also, I think two levels would give students in all the grades a chance to qualify to represent their schools. We could ask for a small donation from each school that participates to defray the cost of plaques for the winners."

She found herself breathless. Finally, William had quieted.

The board no longer looked surprised that she had spoken in the meeting; they looked pleased. Mr. Ashford glanced at the other board members.

"This sounds very interesting, Miss Thurston," Micah said.

"I can see that this would prompt all our students to work harder on their spelling lists," Mr. Ashford agreed.

"I also think it will add some zest to the school year, giving us a goal to work toward," Ellen replied. From the corner of her eye, she glimpsed

Mr. Lang nodding in approval. That lifted her spirit more than anything else. She tried to temper this but couldn't.

"Do we need further discussion?" Mr. Ashford asked.

The other board members shook their heads no.

"I make a motion that Miss Thurston contact the schools nearest Pepin and invite them to a regional spelling bee to be held in April, 1871 at Pepin Community School," Micah proposed.

"I second that," Martin chimed in.

"All in favor, say aye," Mr. Ashford said. After hearing the response, he said, "Motion passed unanimously."

A smattering of applause followed this.

"If that's all, I will entertain a motion to adjourn this meeting," Mr. Ashford said, starting to rise.

"Hold up!" A man in the rear stood. "I want to know when the board is going to deal with this baby left at the school."

Ellen froze where she stood. Her plan to distract everyone from William had just dissolved.

Mr. Ashford looked irritated. "That is not on the agenda for today."

"Well, the spelling bee wasn't, either," the man shot back. "Now, what are people from those other schools going to say when they come here and find that our schoolteacher has a baby? It won't look right."

"It's just not fittin'," another man agreed.

"Schoolteachers are supposed to be single ladies of good reputation."

Ellen straightened and turned to face her accusers.

Before she could speak, Martin rose. "I hope no one in this town is casting aspersions on my wife's cousin. Miss Ellen Thurston's character and reputation are spotless here and in Galena." Martin's aggressive tone charged the room with tension. "My cousin has even been received by the Grants in their own home."

A heavy and tense silence ensued.

"I wasn't castin' aspersions," the second man said in a calmer tone. "Everybody knows Miss Thurston is a fine lady. But it just isn't done."

The first man nodded emphatically. "He's right. Everybody says so and something must be done. We think it's mighty sweet that the schoolteacher wants to take care of the foundling. But it's just not fitting."

"I move that we table this discussion and hold a special school board meeting next Sunday," Martin said quickly.

"I second," Micah added.

"Ayes?" Mr. Ashford asked. Both men said aye and the school board meeting ended.

Shaken, Ellen turned and managed to smile at the school board members.

"Miss Thurston, the idea for a spelling bee is excellent," Micah said. She accepted this with a nod.

Amanda appeared in the doorway with William in her arms. "He wants you, Miss Thurston."

Ellen hurried forward and accepted the baby. She smiled down at the child who, for the first time, smiled back at her. Tears sprang to her eyes and she blinked them away. "Thank you, Amanda."

But Mr. Lang left without speaking to her and that stung.

Finally, only Martin remained. He followed her into her quarters. "Ellen, we know how much keeping this child means to you. Ophelia and I have talked it over, and we'll take the baby in. That way you can see him and be in his life."

Ellen was quite astonished by her cousin's offer, but Ophelia already had enough to do, caring for her own child. "That's very kind of you. But I plan to keep William. I don't think there is any law saying that I can't."

"It may not be against the law, Ellen, but you might have to choose between William and your job here. People apparently have very set ideas about single schoolteachers raising orphans."

Ellen held her tongue. She longed to refute what he said but couldn't. "I hope it won't come to that."

Martin patted her shoulder. "We'll see you Wednesday for supper, then?"

"Yes, thank you, Martin." Ellen saw him to her door. When he had gone, she sat in the rocker and gazed at the little child who had been entrusted to her.

She had a small inheritance in a bank in Galena, earning interest for the years far ahead when she retired from teaching. So while she wasn't penniless, she wasn't of independent means, either. She must work to provide for herself and William. She might be forced to choose between Pepin and William. She didn't like to think of moving and trying to come up with another way to make a living.

The thought of leaving tightened into a hard knot of pain. The school children had already become so dear to her, and she truly loved her work. The prejudice against her keeping William angered her, and she felt she might have a tiny glimpse into how Mr. Lang felt on a daily basis. She wondered why he'd come to the meeting and why he'd left without speaking to her. Her brother's words played in her mind. Was Mr. Lang interested in her? She hoped he wasn't but a tiny part of her hoped he was. She pushed this puzzle aside.

Why can't I keep this baby and teach? How can I fight this foolish prejudice against a teacher raising a child alone?

While Miss Thurston taught Gunther, Kurt sat glumly on the doorstep outside her quarters, thinking about what had happened at the school board meeting. The difference of opinion over the baby between Miss Thurston and the town didn't appear to be lessening.

He wanted to help her, and he didn't want to see this fine woman hurt. Perhaps he should be trying to persuade her to give in.

Beside him, the cause of all the commotion, William, lay kicking his feet and cooing in the cradle that Noah Whitmore had made as a gift. In the schoolyard beyond, Johann was swinging on one of two wooden rope swings Kurt had recently hung from trees, one for the girls and one for the boys. As Johann swung, the rope rasped against the tree branch, creaking.

Miss Thurston stepped outside and sat down beside him, a shawl around her. Coolness edged the evening air. He half rose and then sat again. As usual, she was dressed in a very fine manner with lace edging her high collar and cuffs. She looked completely at ease, as if she had no notion of the controversy piling up around her.

"Have you heard about the special school board meeting?" she asked abruptly.

Yes, he had, and hearing about it had made his stomach sick. "*Ja.*"

"I hear in your tone that you think they will make me give William up."

He turned his gaze to her. "*Ja.*"

She glanced down for a moment. "I honestly don't understand why anyone should care if I adopt William. He has not interfered with my school teaching at all."

"Yes."

"That's your third *yes*. You can't say it again without losing two points," she teased, suddenly grinning.

Her joke caught him off guard. He chuckled and shook his head. She was an unusual woman. "You make a joke but I do think they will make you give up William."

"If they make me choose between the school and William, I will choose William. I will leave Pepin."

"No." Kurt felt as if the word had been wrenched from deep inside him. "No."

She smiled with a bittersweet charm. "You've switched from *yes* to *no*."

He ignored her sally. "Where would you go?"

"Sunny Whitmore has told me of an orphanage south of here on the Illinois shore of the Mississippi. I might go there and see if they have need of another matron. It would be a good fit for me and William."

Kurt felt as if he had been caught between the jaws of some mighty animal and was being crushed. He nearly said no again, but stopped himself. He knew he never could be more than a neighbor to Miss Ellen Thurston, but that was better—much better—than losing her bright presence altogether.

He must try to persuade her. "Miss Thurston, I know better than you how it is to raise children alone. I have been father to Gunther since we lost our mother. I adopted Johann when my sister, Maria, died. Being father and mother to two boys—" He drew in a deep breath. "It is hard."

"I'm sure it is. But William was left at *my* door. I don't think it was random. I think someone wanted me to have him, to raise him."

Kurt watched Johann pumping his legs, swinging higher and higher. He loved the boy and wouldn't be parted from him. From behind, he heard Gunther softly reading aloud the Bill of Rights of the U.S. Constitution. Things had changed for the better between his brother and him, and Miss Thurston had achieved that. He was beholden to her.

Therefore, he must make her see the truth.

"You are a woman alone. A boy needs a father to learn how to be a man."

"I had hoped you were on my side, Mr. Lang." When he didn't answer, she continued, "A boy needs a mother to learn about women." She lifted her hands palm up. "How many children are raised in perfect homes?"

He snorted in derision. *I was not.*

"I had wonderful parents. But even with their guidance, life has taken unexpected twists and turns for my brother, my sister and me."

He thought about Randolph Thurston. The man

had not liked Kurt being around his sister—Kurt understood that. But her brother had not appeared happy in himself, either.

As his thoughts drifted, he noticed the fragrance of rosewater drifting on the breeze, and realized the lovely scent was Miss Thurston's perfume.

Kurt looked into the distance at the darkening horizon. Seeing that they'd stayed too long jerked him back to practicality. "Boys!" he called, standing up quickly. "We must go now. The sun is nearly set." He turned and gripped her hand. "Thank you again." He wanted to say more but he couldn't—what he had to say would be too personal.

Miss Thurston looked puzzled by his sudden departure but she said a polite good-night and then reached for the baby.

Soon the three of them were hurrying fast toward home. As darkness began to overtake them, the parting image of Miss Thurston holding William in her arms wouldn't leave Kurt. The terrible sensation of being forced to accept her fate pressed down on him.

I cannot let her leave Pepin, he thought. *Not after all the good she has done Gunther and the other students. This is about my duty to this community. It is not about how I may feel about Miss Thurston.*

Kurt turned his attention to the boys before he could acknowledge that he wasn't being entirely honest with himself.

Chapter Ten

Ellen had dressed with care for the special board meeting with a delicate balance in mind. She'd chosen a sober yet stylish dress of navy; she wanted to impress but not appear ostentatious.

As she looked around the room, she noticed Mr. Lang had not yet come in. Would he desert her? She cast this concern aside. She'd told Randolph she wasn't interested in romance and a thought like that was not appropriate. Whether he was here or not had little bearing on the issue at hand.

She'd chosen not to try to hide William this time. He napped in his cradle at her feet while she sat beside her desk before the schoolroom packed with citizens of Pepin, all of whom had come to address whether she could keep both William and her job.

She'd prayed about this, but her tension had not lessened. When Mr. Lang entered at last, she breathed a sigh of relief despite herself. He sat on the rear bench beside Old Saul in his wheelchair.

She had begun to know and like some of the people of Pepin. She recalled how hard it had been to come here to start a new life, and she was not anxious to venture into the unknown again. The very thought hollowed her out like seeding a melon.

Mr. Ashford looked at the clock and then at his own pocket watch. He loosened the tight collar around his throat and then he brought the meeting to order. After Noah Whitmore prayed for wisdom and guidance, Mr. Ashford rose and stepped to the front. "We have come here at the request of many parents and citizens to discuss whether our schoolteacher, Miss Thurston, should be able to keep the foundling and remain our teacher or not."

Ellen did not like the expressions of most of the men and many of the women. They telegraphed an aggravation with her as if she had affronted them in some way. She wondered where that came from, as it was a far cry from the warm welcome she'd initially received. Only Mr. Lang and Old Saul looked sympathetic.

Ellen rose and stood beside the storekeeper. She decided to be direct. "I would like to know why my taking in a foundling is a matter of public discussion."

"He just told you," a man from the middle said pugnaciously. "You're a teacher. You're not supposed to have a baby."

Mr. Ashford raised both his hands. "This is a school board meeting and there are rules to keep order. You can't just up and start talking. You must rise, say your name and then ask to speak."

Conceding this, Ellen nodded agreement and returned to her seat.

Another man, the father of twin girls she'd found precocious, rose. "I'm Isaac Welton and I'd like to say a few words, please."

Mr. Ashford nodded assent.

"We, my wife and I, think Miss Thurston is a bang-up teacher. Our girls love to go to school and at the supper table, can't wait to tell us all they'd learned. I just want Miss Thurston to know that our disapproval of her keeping this foundling has nothing to do with our respect for her as a lady and a teacher. That's all I—we—" he glanced at his wife "—got to say."

The man's words touched Ellen's heart. "Thank you, Mr. Welton." Her eyes sought Mr. Lang. He returned her gaze, not revealing anything. She looked away.

Another man rose. "I'm Jesse Canton."

Ashford nodded for the man to speak.

"Everyone knows Miss Thurston does a good job. But the thing is, a schoolteacher having a baby around, it just doesn't look right. I mean people, strangers, might get the wrong idea." The man looked uncomfortable. "If you know what I mean." Most everyone in the room nodded in agreement with his sentiment.

Ellen took a deep breath and rose. "I think I should reply to these comments, Mr. Ashford."

The storekeeper looked doubtful but nodded. "You have a right to a say." He sat down.

Already girded for battle, Ellen faced the room of disapproving faces. Her mind was made up, and she knew what she was going to do. She found herself looking to Mr. Lang again, and the kindness she saw in his eyes, even though it was a sad kindness, somehow gave her an extra bit of strength and courage to say what needed to be said.

Kurt had the sensation of the roof slowly lowering on him, closing him in, a feeling of imminent loss and pain. He'd known how this would go, but had no way of preventing or even slowing what was about to happen, and this helplessness was unbearable.

But Miss Thurston spoke evenly and forcefully, impressing him yet again.

"So far the only reasons given here have been that a schoolteacher doesn't usually have a child, and that when strangers see the town's school-teacher with a child, they might get the wrong idea of this community. But we live in America. We, as a nation, do things that others have not done before. I think the only question should be this —whether or not caring for this child prevents me or hinders me from doing my job well."

Another man near Kurt rose. "Joe Connolly."

When he'd been acknowledged, he continued, "Those are not the only considerations. A child needs a ma and a pa. Everybody knows that. This child won't have a pa." He sat down among approving murmurs.

Kurt, having already tried this argument and failed, knew exactly what she was going to say.

"I agree that having a mother and a father is the ideal situation," the schoolteacher replied. "However, how many children are fortunate enough to reach adulthood still having both parents? I myself lost both parents to typhoid. And where will this child go if I don't care for him? Mrs. Whitmore has suggested that orphanage south of here. Yet if we send William there, he will have neither father *nor* mother."

A man stood, red-faced. "But a schoolteacher isn't supposed to be married or have children. It isn't done!"

"Why?" Miss Thurston asked, eyeing the man.

Mr. Ashford sent a warning glance to the man for not following procedure. He sat down, grumbling to himself.

Kurt had to keep his lips pressed together. He wanted to stand up and tell them all to be quiet or they might lose this fine woman. And then where would the town of Pepin be? They had no idea what a treasure they'd be losing.

Martin Steward rose. "I really think this meeting has gone on long enough. Ophelia and I have offered to take the child and raise him as our own. There is no need for this public upset."

Kurt hadn't known that. The perfect solution. The tension in the room ebbed amid murmuring.

Miss Thurston turned to him. "Martin, I appreciate the offer, but as I've already said, I'm keeping William. He was entrusted to me. And if the town doesn't want the two of us—"

Kurt's heart thudded against his breastbone. She was going to go through with it. She was going to tell them she would be leaving.

Miss Thurston faced the crowd. "If I can't keep this child and remain your teacher, then I plan to—"

"I am Kurt Lang," he said, surging to his feet before he even recognized what he was doing. His mind scrambled for words. Now more than ever it was important that he spoke correctly. He had to, for her sake. "I am new in this country." He swallowed down his nerves. "Many things here are different than in the old country. This is a free land. I see more than you, you who are born here. Why can't a teacher raise a child alone? Isn't every mother a teacher? And every teacher a mother?"

Everyone had turned to him, gawking.

Sweat trickled down his back as he continued, forcing his voice to sound strong and sure. "My mother taught me much. And I am both father and mother to my nephew, Johann. Would you take him from me because I am not married? Should a farmer be allowed to raise a boy by himself?" He took a breath, one final thing to say coming from deep within. "Miss Thurston is a good person. William will be lucky to have her as a mother."

He sat down abruptly. He wanted desperately to wipe his perspiring forehead with his handkerchief but felt it best to continue to look his surprised neighbors in the eye. And then he looked at Ellen, and saw a combination of shock and gratitude on her lovely face.

The people had been silenced.

Probably they couldn't believe that he—a man who spoke with an accent and wasn't even a citizen—had spoken up in a public meeting. He could hardly believe it himself.

The old pastor touched his arm. "Will you push my chair to the front?"

When Kurt complied, everyone turned at the sound of the wheelchair. A few men who had risen—no doubt to contest what Kurt had said—slowly sank back to their seats. When he reached the front, Kurt turned the chair so that the older man faced the gathering.

"I have listened to all the opinions voiced here this evening," Old Saul said. "And I can see merit in all of them. But in this case, what mere men think doesn't amount to much. Yes, a child should be blessed with a mother and father. Yes, it is unusual for an unmarried schoolteacher to raise a foundling alone. Yes, no doubt people who visit here may think it out of the ordinary. However, only one fact matters."

Everyone sat forward, listening carefully so as not to miss a word.

"I don't believe the child was left on Miss Thurston's doorstep by accident. I think William's mother meant the lady to have him. And more important, God meant for Miss Thurston to have this child. I have prayed about this, as I'm sure Noah has." Old Saul glanced at Noah, who nodded solemnly. "And each time, I have received peace about Miss Thurston keeping the child."

Kurt swallowed, trying to grasp what the man's opinion could mean for Miss Thurston's future.

"I don't think we should meddle in this." The older man's voice strengthened. "William was given to Miss Thurston, not anybody else. He is being well cared for and the children in school are being well taught by a fine woman. We should be satisfied, don't you think?"

Uneasy silence filled several moments, then Noah spoke, "I thank Mr. Lang and Old Saul for clarifying this situation." He nodded to each in turn.

"I must agree with Old Saul. And I'll add that I was pleased when Mrs. Brawley stepped forward to help with William, and when Martin and Ophelia offered their help. In a way, this child has been given to all of us."

This last statement seemed to affect everyone in the room. No one rose to counter Noah.

Mr. Ashford talked quietly with Micah and Martin, then stood beside Noah and Old Saul. "If no one else has anything further to say, I think Noah should close with prayer and we can all go home."

Kurt bowed his head during the prayer. The crisis had passed and had left him dumbfounded. He'd been sure Miss Thurston was going to leave him . . . leave their town, that is. But there had been a complete turnaround. And he had helped make it happen.

A welter of emotions cannonaded within him. Had he done right to defend her? What would people think? More important, what would *she* think?

Mr. Lang had turned the tide in her favor. Why? Ellen hadn't expected that at all and was even more surprised when many people came forward to shake her hand and peer down at William, who'd slept through it all. She now knew what the Bible meant about going through the crucible and being refined by fire. She felt as if that was exactly what had just happened to her.

The town's attitude toward her and William had changed in just a few moments. What had prompted Mr. Lang, who had been concerned about her desire to keep William since the very night they'd found him, to speak on her behalf? She couldn't help but stare at him from across the room, where she was pleased to see people speaking to him. She hadn't realized until this very moment that usually he was ignored. Her heart seemed to swell for him.

Had the world tilted on its axis?

"Well, you won," Ophelia said, giving her elbow a squeeze. "But raising a child alone won't be easy. You know that, right?"

Ellen wrenched her gaze from Mr. Lang. "I don't expect it to be easy, Ophelia. But I do expect that we can help each other over the coming years."

Ophelia threw her arms around Ellen. "You are truly my dearest cousin." Then Ophelia lowered her voice. "Did Randolph ever tell you why he'd come here?"

"He did," she said, as she stepped out of their hug. "I will tell you about that another time."

Ellen saw that Noah had taken the handles of Old Saul's wheelchair and was preparing to leave. She hurried forward, offering her hands. "Thank you, sir."

He grasped her hands with his, which were gnarled and wrinkled. "God has entrusted you with a child. I will pray you are given the grace to carry this forth."

His words brought unexpected tears. She couldn't speak so she squeezed his hands and then stepped back so his son could push the old preacher outside.

People moved around her, offering their

farewells, and she replied politely. But as she waited for Mr. Lang to come and speak to her, she realized that hc had left without a word. A lost feeling filled her that she couldn't quite explain.

When she was finally alone again, she shut the school door and secured it. Then she dragged the cradle into her quarters. William, as if on cue, stirred and began whimpering.

"Right on time, young man." She mixed the Horlick's for him and then carried him to the rocker where she hummed to him as he took his night bottle. Suddenly, fatigue overwhelmed her. "We'll sleep well tonight, William."

She closed her eyes and once again saw Mr. Lang rise to his feet in her defense. What had changed his mind? Warmth for him welled up within her but she took herself firmly in hand. Her path had been set.

She had always resolved to pursue an education, not marriage, as most women did. But Holton had somehow weakened or made her forget that for a brief time. Perhaps after losing her parents she had been vulnerable. But now she was herself again. She taught school in Pepin, and a child had been entrusted to her. Therefore, she shouldn't, and wouldn't, interpret Mr. Lang's defense of her as anything more than a change of mind expressed by a caring and sympathetic man. Because she would never be foolish over a man again.

Once had proven to be quite enough, thank you.

Chapter Eleven

In the quiet amber of twilight, Kurt and Johann stood over the outdoor wash basin, cleaning the supper dishes. As they worked, Kurt wrestled with a question: Should he and Johann go with Gunther to the school this evening or not? What did Miss Thurston think of his speaking up for her after he'd held the opposite view to hers? How would she react toward him? Would she want an explanation?

When he recalled his speaking in Miss Thurston's defense at the meeting, his heart flipped up and down like a hooked fish. He'd tried to convince himself that he'd spoken up for her, but in reality, he had to admit that he'd done it because he didn't want Miss Thurston to leave.

The feelings he had for Miss Thurston brought back memories of his broken engagement with Brigitte, making him recall the cause of their breakup. He and Brigitte had been childhood sweethearts. His father's gambling had turned her family against him, but she had remained true.

But when his father had lost everything and then taken the easy way out, the shame had been too great. Like a metal file, the memories scraped against his peace, shredding it fragment by fragment, leaving him raw and bleeding.

He was becoming enamored of Miss Thurston, though he knew he had no business forming any attachment—spoken or unspoken—to a woman so far above him. Overhead a crow cawed, mocking him.

I must remember who I am here and what I am now.

But even as he thought this, something chafed at him, something that wouldn't let him consider the matter settled. He was a newcomer here, a foreigner, but this land with all its freedom was loosening the old ways of thinking in him.

Gunther stepped outside. "Are you done with the dishes?"

Kurt noted with pride and some apprehension how carefully Gunther was speaking each word. His brother's motivation could not have been more transparent—he wanted to be accepted here, wanted to be American. He wanted to court Amanda Ashford.

Kurt had tried many times to warn Gunther against this distant hope. But why? Maybe Gunther was young enough to lose his accent, to become acceptable to the Americans, to win the Ashfords' approval. What was possible for Gunther might not be possible for him.

"Gunther," Kurt said, his decision made. "I have things to do this evening. I will not go with you."

Kurt looked down at Johann, denying the cold loss this brought him. "Will you go to help with little William? Can I trust you to know what to do?"

Johann stood very straight. "I can take care of William. I know how to rock him and hold the bottle." He pulled his wooden horse from his pocket. "And he likes my horse, too."

Kurt let the corners of his mouth rise, let his tension ease. He had two good lads. He looked to Gunther. "You don't need me there, do you?"

"No, but I thought you liked to go with me." Gunther looked puzzled.

Kurt studied his brother's face. Had Gunther noticed his preference for Miss Thurston?

He shrugged as if the matter was of no importance. "I have worked hard today. I need to sharpen my tools." He forced himself to sound convincing. "You are young. It is long walk. You have more energy."

Gunther still looked puzzled but merely lowered his head as if bowing to his brother's decision.

Johann quickly dried the final pan and hurried to Gunther, who had secured his books on a strap hung over his shoulder and was waiting to leave. Kurt watched them go down the path. Part of him strained like a horse at the starting line, strained to follow them. He clamped his lips tight so he didn't call out he'd changed his mind.

Instead, he dragged out a chair and began doing

what he'd told Gunther he would do. He began sharpening his tools. The shrill noise of the small grindstone filled his ears and grated his nerves. He suddenly saw himself sitting at home in his village using this same grindstone.

Home . . .

A sorrow he could never voice seized him tightly and twisted him, as if wringing him. An image he would never be able to banish flashed in his mind, his father's lifeless body, hanging in their barn. He rubbed his eyes, willing the pain away. Would a time come when thinking of home didn't bring piercing, wrenching pain?

The answer rushed to him. When he was with Miss Thurston, the pain was forgotten. Her sweet voice soothed him like no other. The temptation to be with her was a dangerous one. He must be wary or spoil the delicate balance of their friendship. And they were friends. If anything he did or said hinted at courtship, she would withdraw from him. He must watch himself, his words, his manner when with her. But to deny himself the pleasure of being with her was impossible.

"The colonists had no representation, no member in Parliament," Gunther explained earnestly, sitting at the table in Ellen's quarters. "They believed they shouldn't have to pay the taxes England demanded."

Across from him, Ellen tried to keep her mind

149

on Gunther as he explained taxation without representation. Behind her, Johann knelt by the cradle, entertaining William with a stream of chatter about the wooden horse. But neither Gunther nor Johann seemed able to command her complete attention. Why had Mr. Lang stayed away this evening? She'd been so looking forward to thanking him properly for what he'd done.

Had she offended him? Did he regret defending her?

Why did his absence bother her?

Mr. Lang's excuse of being tired and needing to stay home was perfectly natural and understandable. But now she was forced to confront the fact that she had begun to look forward to their evenings together.

I cannot allow myself to slip again. I miss seeing Mr. Lang because we've been thrown together so much, that's all.

A jumble of emotions rioted within as she calmly asked Gunther, "And how did England respond to the colonists' argument?"

"Parliament, the English congress," Gunther replied with an eagerness she loved, "said that the colonists had virtual representation, that Parliament represented all of England and its territories."

Gunther's English had improved so much in such a short time. Though she knew he was not pleased that his accent lingered, his progress lifted her mood. "Exactly right, Gunther. Do you think that made sense?"

Gunther paused to prepare an answer as her mind went back to the question of Mr. Lang. Was her disappointment actually about his absence? Or was it merely that after dealing with children all day, she looked forward to adult conversation? Of course, she spoke with the Ashfords at supper each evening, but she didn't exactly count them as friends.

Mr. Lang is my friend. A startling idea.

"No, it didn't make sense," Gunther answered finally. "I think it was just a way to make a good-sounding excuse. I don't think the men in Parliament thought much about the colonies. They were so far away."

As she nodded in agreement, she wondered, could she consider a man a friend? Single women rarely had men who were friends, not suitors.

But why couldn't she consider Mr. Lang a friend? Just because they were both unmarried didn't mean they couldn't be friends, did it?

Somewhere in the back of her consciousness, a warning bell faintly rang. She ignored it.

On Saturday morning, Martin had come with his pony cart and fetched Ellen and William so Ellen could help Ophelia with the fall canning. Ellen had worn her oldest dress and an older apron. Now Ophelia and she were outside in the quickly warming morning. With a large, long-handled, slotted spoon in hand, Ophelia was dipping tomatoes into a pot of boiling water and setting them to cool on the table outside. Ellen was coring the stems and then slipping the skins off the warm scalded tomatoes and then dropping them into a large pot in preparation for making catsup.

Several feet away on the wild grass, Johann entertained William, who lay on a blanket, kicking his feet vigorously. Johann also kept Ophelia's cheerful toddler, Nathan, from crawling too far away with the help of the Steward's dog. Johann had walked over by himself as planned.

Ellen found herself about to ask her cousin if Mr. Lang would be coming over, too, but she nipped off the thought. Mr. Lang had his own work to do.

"I'm so glad you offered to help," Ophelia repeated, perspiring as she leaned over the boiling water.

"I can see why you needed me." Ellen glanced at the bushels of ripe tomatoes sitting around them. The sight inspired Ellen with a desire to lie down and nap.

"I know it's a lot of tomatoes." Ophelia smiled tartly as she had when they were girls together and up to some mischief. "But I have a bumper crop this year and that might have to stretch over two years. One never knows," she said airily, "what the next harvest will bring. We might have a drought and no tomatoes."

Though grinning, Ellen smothered a sigh. For some reason she couldn't identify, her normal zest for life had diminished over the past week. Everything she did seemed heavy like a chore.

"Ellen, are you all right? You seem down in the dumps." Ophelia slid another two tomatoes into the boiling water and watched them closely.

Ellen tilted her head. She could fool everyone but Ophelia. "You know me too well."

"I would think you would be happy now that it's been decided you can keep William." Ophelia turned the tomatoes and then scooped one up, letting water drain through the spoon.

"I would think so, too." Ellen didn't look up from the basin in her lap where the red skins fell. "Sometimes I can't believe I won. I don't know. Maybe it's the letdown after all the turmoil over my effort to keep him."

Maybe it's because you haven't seen Mr. Lang since the meeting, a voice whispered in her mind.

Ellen ignored it and forged ahead. "Does that make sense? Perhaps a reaction to all that stress?"

"Perhaps." Ophelia flexed her shoulders but didn't look up. "You never told me why Randolph came north."

Yellow-and-black finches twittered and flew from branch to branch, as if gossiping about the

153

two women. "You guessed, didn't you, that Alice sent him?"

Ophelia glanced at Ellen, her face twisted with apprehension. "What did Alice want?"

"Me. She's expecting and has managed to get such a bad reputation that no Irish girl will work for her."

Ophelia made a hissing sound of irritation. "That woman. So you told him no?"

"Of course I did." Ellen went on to reveal how Alice had tried to blackmail her into returning to Galena.

Ophelia was suitably shocked and aggravated. "That woman! Makes me remember why we would never play with her when we were kids. Spoiled crybaby."

Ellen agreed with a nod and then shooed away a fly. "Well, I haven't heard anything since from my brother so we'll just have to wait and see."

At that moment, Johann made a neighing sound as he held his wooden horse above William's face, and the baby gurgled in excitement. As Ellen watched the two, her question about Mr. Lang simply slipped right out of her mouth, as if she had no say in the matter. "Johann, what's your uncle doing today?"

"Harvesting corn with Gunther, miss," Johann called politely while running after Nathan, who was crawling fast toward the surrounding forest.

Of course Mr. Lang was harvesting corn—every

man and many women were. She vented her irritation at herself on the tomato in her hand, squeezing it until it spit seeds up onto her cheek.

Ophelia chuckled and handed her a clean rag. "What's that? The tomato's revenge?" she said.

Grinning ruefully, Ellen wiped her cheek and shook her head, frustrated at her foolishness. She remembered such foolishness all too well from when she'd allowed feelings for Holton. She wanted no part of it now.

But the trouble was, it seemed that she no longer had any say in the matter. Mr. Lang refused to leave her mind.

As the morning wore on, the women continued their work. A few times the Stewards' dog rose to its feet and barked. Once it started to head toward the fields, but halted when Ophelia told him to stay. He whimpered on and off, staring toward the distant field where Martin was picking corn. Maybe he just missed his master.

When the first batch of tomatoes was finally simmering outdoors in a large pot, Ophelia glanced at the sun directly overhead.

"I wonder why Martin hasn't come for lunch. He knew I'd be serving a cold meal." She turned to Johann. "Will you run and tell Mr. Steward that I'm going to put out our lunch?"

Johann nodded and jogged away, the dog racing after him.

"He's such a nice boy," Ophelia said, leaning backward, stretching her spine.

Ellen tried not to let her mind drift to his uncle, who was nice, too. She had barely washed her hands and taken off her tomato-smeared apron when Johann came running back.

"Mrs. Steward! Your husband needs you. He can't get up!"

Ellen flew to William, and snatched him from the blanket as Ophelia scooped up Nathan. The two women pelted after Johann toward the farthest edge of the cornfield.

Martin was lying at the end of a row, flat on his back. A large muslin bag filled with corn lay beside him, its contents scattered.

Despite the noon-high sun blazing on her shoulders, the sight of Martin on the ground chilled Ellen.

Ophelia dropped to her knees beside him. "What's wrong? What happened?"

Martin panted. "I don't know. I was picking corn. I heard a noise and turned too fast, I guess. Something snapped in my back. The pain . . . I couldn't stay on my feet. I fell. I must have lost consciousness. When I came to, I tried to get up, but I can't get up by myself, Ophelia." Fear shuddered in each of the last few words. "I tried to call out but couldn't."

"I will get my uncle!" Johann called over his shoulder, already running back toward the cabin and the trail beyond.

Ellen took charge of both children while Ophelia ran to get thirsty Martin some water to drink. The dog lay next to Martin, his large brown eyes worried. Fear rattled Ellen as she pressed William to her and talked nonsense to Nathan who crawled to his father and sat, patting him.

Then Ophelia appeared with a dipper and a bucket of cold spring water. She knelt beside her husband and gently lifted his head and helped him drink. Then they waited.

Both women were relieved to hear the sounds of men running through the field sometime later. Johann appeared with Mr. Lang and Gunther, and Ellen felt her fear and tensions relax, giving way all at once at the sight of Mr. Lang.

She knew he would be able to help. He was that kind of man.

"Martin is hurt? How?" Kurt asked, panting from running. He focused on Martin, not Miss Thurston, schooling his eyes to obey him with effort.

"I did something stupid," Martin replied, sounding as if merely forcing out each word caused him pain. "I had a full sack of corn. I heard something and twisted. I must have passed out—I came to on my back. Kurt, I tried to get up but the pain . . ."

Kurt dropped to his knees beside Martin, ignoring the nearness of Miss Thurston, who stood within a few feet of him. "Can you move your hands and feet?"

Martin complied, gasping as if the movements caused him pain.

Kurt rested a hand on the man's shoulder. "This is good, Martin. You have not caused injury to your spine. You have only pulled a muscle, I think. It will heal with time."

"Listen to Mr. Lang, Martin," Miss Thurston murmured, just behind Kurt. Her voice so close shivered through him. He quelled his quick reaction, forbidding himself even a glance at her.

Martin moaned, sounding both upset and in pain. "But it's harvest. I can't be laid up, flat on my back."

"You do not worry," Kurt said. "Right now we need to get you to your cabin. You cannot spend the rest of the day lying here in the sun."

Martin tried to get up but failed, stifling a groan.

"No," Kurt commanded sharply. "You must stay still or hurt yourself more. We will move you." Kurt looked to Mrs. Steward. "I need a strong blanket."

Ophelia leaped to her feet and ran toward the house.

"I'm so glad you came, Mr. Lang," Miss Thurston said. "There was nothing we could do for him."

"I am glad to help." Kurt rose but did not look at her. He had stayed away from her this week as if doing a penance. He'd hoped his pleasure at being near her would ebb with distance and time, but as he lifted his eyes to hers, he knew that it hadn't. Seeing her now awakened him as if he'd only been half-alive while away from her.

He just hoped it didn't show.

Mrs. Steward ran toward them with a folded navy blue wool blanket in her arms.

Gratefully, he turned away from Miss Thurston to the task at hand. With quick directions, he and Gunther lifted Martin onto the blanket. Using it as a stretcher, they carried him through the cornfield to the cabin.

Inside, Kurt eyed the rope bed. "I think he will be better on the hard floor on a few thick blankets." Ophelia quickly arranged a pallet of blankets and then he and Gunther lowered Martin to the floor.

Martin's face had gone from white to gray, probably from the pain of being moved. "Thank you," he said, panting. His wife dropped to her knees beside him and wrung her hands. Kurt hated to see her so distressed. "You are not to worry, Martin. We will harvest your corn."

Miss Thurston moved closer to him. He wanted to distance himself from her, but couldn't. Everyone had gathered into a circle around the stricken man. The dog lay down again beside his master, whining with what sounded like sympathy.

"How long do you think Martin will be laid up?" Mrs. Steward asked Kurt.

Kurt remembered himself and drew off his hat. "Maybe a week, two weeks."

Martin groaned. "Who will take care of the animals?"

"I will come and stay here," Gunther announced.

"Gunther!" Miss Thurston exclaimed with obvious surprise. Kurt and everyone else turned to look at him, startled.

Gunther reddened at the attention. "Mrs. Steward will need help with her husband. I can lift him and I can do his chores," Gunther said in a tone that announced he would not be deterred.

"Oh, Gunther," Mrs. Steward said, springing to her feet to clasp Gunther's hand. "Thank you. Thank you."

Kurt couldn't press down the pride rising in him. Gunther had been changing over the past weeks and now the difference was unmistakable. His brother had lost the chip on his shoulder, and Kurt and Gunther both had Miss Thurston to thank for that.

"That's very good of you, Gunther," Miss Thurston said with a look of obvious approval. Kurt couldn't help but smile at her then, and she smiled back. Gunther was turning into a fine young man. The fact that Miss Thurston saw it, too, was nearly overwhelming for Kurt.

Miss Thurston moved toward the door, asking

Johann to come with her to watch the children. "I must keep working on the catsup. Everything will spoil and be wasted if I don't."

"Ellen, as soon as I see to Martin, I'll bring out the lunch. Mr. Lang, I have enough for all of us."

Kurt watched as Miss Thurston laid William in the cradle outside and Johann set Nathan down on the grass. For a brief moment he watched her stirring the simmering tomatoes and let himself imagine what it would be like if she were . . . his wife. And a mother to Johann, and even Gunther.

He shook his head to clear his thoughts. He had much work to do and he wasn't needed here. "Can I help?" Kurt asked, saying exactly what he hadn't intended to.

Miss Thurston looked surprised. "What?"

"I am the cook in our house," he said. "Perhaps I can help?"

I should leave now. He didn't move.

She dipped the thermometer into the simmering tomatoes. "It's the right temperature. We need to ladle the sauce into the Mason jars." She gestured toward the line of clean jars covered with clean dishcloths on a bench near the cabin.

He nodded. "I will hold the pot, you will ladle the sauce and seal the jars."

Soon the two of them were working side by side. As they wiped the jar rims with clean rags and then capped them with lids, he was careful not to accidentally brush against her or touch her hands. This trying to keep apart tortured him. Mrs. Steward soon came outside, carrying a tray of sandwiches. Miss Thurston hurried to her side. "How is he?"

"Resting." The wife set the tray on the table and sat on a bench as if the action had taken the last of her strength. She bent her head into her hands. "We didn't need this."

The woman's morose tone moved Kurt. He knew how unexpected disaster dashed hope.

Miss Thurston patted her cousin's back. "We will manage. Gunther has offered to stay and help you. Mr. Lang will harvest your corn. I'll come every evening to do what I can. You're not alone, Ophelia."

When Kurt realized Mrs. Steward was weeping quietly, he stepped away to give her privacy. As he looked at the Steward's cabin, Kurt had to acknowledge that though he had planned to distance himself from Miss Thurston, circumstances had thrown them together once again.

What could this mean? Was he being tested to see if he could keep within the boundaries that separated them? What would happen if he couldn't?

After the long day of labor at the Steward's had been completed, once more Kurt held out his hand to help Miss Thurston onto Martin's pony cart to take her home. He didn't know what to say so he slapped the reins and started down the path. Darkness cloaked them, though a nearly full moon lit their way. Turmoil over sitting beside her again unsettled him.

William lay asleep in his cradle in the back. Exhausted to his marrow, Kurt wished he could lie down and sleep, too. In addition to helping with canning what they called catsup, jars and jars of the red sauce, he'd shown Gunther how to help Martin move, and he'd brought in several bags of corn and stored it in the corn crib to dry, all after working since dawn.

Crickets chattered, unseen. A mourning dove cooed overhead. Yet the human silence stretching between Kurt and the schoolteacher wasn't the pleasant kind they had begun to share during Gunther's lessons. Tension vibrated between them.

"I can't believe this has happened," Miss Thurston finally said. "Right in the midst of harvest. Martin kept trying to move till you insisted he was making his condition worse, not better. Thank you." She glanced at him sideways. "Thank you, Mr. Lang, for all you have done today."

"Gunther and I will get Martin's crop in. You need not worry."

"I promised Ophelia I'd dig potatoes next Saturday." She sighed, exhaustion in her voice.

"You would dig potatoes?" he asked with surprise.

"My mother always had a kitchen garden. I used to help her with it. I like growing things and picking things. I've never dug potatoes, though. But since I'll probably be invited to eat many of the potatoes Martin has grown, I better be ready to dig some," she added, evidently trying to lighten the mood.

He tried to make the image of Miss Thurston digging potatoes fit, but couldn't. "America is a strange country."

"Why do you say that?"

He shook his head, still baffled. "In Germany, no lady digs potatoes."

She glanced at him, but the low light merely cast her elegant profile in stark shadow. "I am considered a lady because I am of good reputation, nothing more. Ophelia is a lady, Mrs. Whitmore is a lady. If they can dig potatoes, why can't I?"

He shrugged, unable and unwilling to voice his discomfort with this idea. "I hope I am not seen as pretentious," she added. Her tone had stiffened.

"What does that word mean?" he asked cautiously, afraid he had offended her.

"*Pretentious* describes a person who is self-important, a show-off."

"No, you are not pretentious," he said, sounding out the word new to him. "But you are a lady—a fine lady."

She appeared to give thought to his words. "I think I see what you're trying to say. But this is America. That very first day, when you drove me home, you and I talked about the Grants. Remember?"

"I remember." *How could I forget that day?*

"In the past, Mrs. Grant was the wife of a man who ran a leather shop with his father. Now she is the wife of the president. Here, people aren't constrained by society to stay in one place or one rank. We can occupy many different stations in one life. What matters is what we can do, what difference we make in this world."

He didn't respond, torn between the hope that her startling words, this new idea, ignited in him, and the conviction that they did not apply to him. *Maybe that is true of Americans, Miss Thurston, but they will never think of me as anything but a foreigner.*

"You are new here and people look down on you because of that." He sensed her leaning forward a bit to see him better. "But it won't always be that way."

Swinging around to face her, he voiced a sound of disbelief. "No?" Even he was surprised by the sarcasm that laced the word, trickling sourly through him.

"No," she repeated with emphasis, ignoring his tone. "Look at Abraham Lincoln. He was born in a log cabin, worked as a farmer, then a lawyer, then became president. So you weren't born in this country—so what?"

"You are kind, but that I was born in another county will never be forgotten."

"You are building your reputation here in this country every day, Mr. Lang," Miss Thurston said, sitting straighter. "Don't you see that? You've been given a brand-new start."

He'd left Germany exactly for that purpose, yet somehow, inside, he had yet to change, heal. He looked at Miss Thurston beside him, and for a brief moment, he actually considered telling her about what had happened at home, what had driven him to leave his country.

But he knew he could not. She would never look at him the same way again.

He faced forward again and fell silent. The hope that had been warring inside him with despair folded inward, unequal to the contest. Hope only set one up for pain.

Chapter Twelve

Sunday morning had come. Ellen's back and arms ached from the day of making catsup. She finished dressing William in a baby shift Ophelia had made for him and looked at herself in the mirror to check that she was presentable. She felt a pang over how tired she looked, and found herself thinking of what Mr. Lang would see when he looked at her.

She turned hastily away from the mirror and walked into the schoolroom for worship. There, she paused. She usually sat with the Stewards, and now realized everyone would notice their absence. She must be tired, or else she would have considered that already. Would she be the one to give the bad news?

She couldn't resist glancing toward the back to see whether Kurt and Johann had arrived this morning. Perhaps they stayed home to help Gunther with the Stewards. Or perhaps she had somehow offended Mr. Lang last night.

She approached Noah Whitmore as he prepared for the service. "Are you aware of Martin's accident?" she asked in a low voice. At his dismayed denial, she told him what had happened yesterday.

Noah looked shocked. "I'll ask for prayer. Thank you for telling me, Miss Thurston." Then he glanced at the wall clock. "I need to begin."

Ellen settled down beside Sunny Whitmore, who had obviously overheard Ellen. But she said nothing to Ellen as her husband opened the worship service.

Unhappy over Mr. Lang's absence, Ellen let William nap on her lap. She patted him, noticing how he was becoming chubby. For a moment, her heart sang with silent thanksgiving for him.

She held in all the blessing of being given this wonder, this child.

The service progressed to the end, when at last Noah opened the time for intercessory prayer. He announced the news about Martin and a collective sound of dismay went through the congregation.

"What can we do to help?" Gordy Osbourne, the church deacon, asked.

"He'll need help getting in his crop," Noah began.

Ellen rose. "Pastor, Kurt Lang has already volunteered to bring in Martin's crop. Since he is the nearest neighbor, he's the one who came to help us with Martin."

An odd silence followed, a prickly momentary pause as Ellen sat again. Then Gordy brought up another need. "Ophelia, that is Mrs. Steward, will need help with chores and such."

Ellen raised her hand, her mood lifting. "Gunther Lang volunteered to stay with the Stewards and do Martin's chores, as well as help with his care. I think the Langs must all be at the Steward's now, helping my cousins. That's most likely why they are not here this morning."

Another pause came, filled with some ominous meaning Ellen couldn't read.

"I'm glad to hear that," Noah said. "The Langs are the closest neighbors to the Stewards—"

"But they're foreigners," a man in the back

objected. "Do the Stewards want them around?"

Anger ignited and blazed within Ellen, nearly consuming her, tying her throat into a knot. She was astounded. And yet, given the conversation she and Mr. Lang had had just last night, she should not have been. In fact, she should have expected this.

Noah looked distressed, his head tilting down with disfavor. "The Langs have always been good neighbors to the Stewards and I don't know what being foreign has to do with one Christian helping another. The Langs have never missed a Sunday at worship until today. In fact, Kurt helped build this very school that you are sitting in now," Noah said, gesturing to the walls around them. "I think as we pray today we need to remember that in God, there is no Greek or Jew, slave or free, man or woman. To him, we are all loved and valued the same. He sees no difference between us." He held up both hands. "Let's pray for the Stewards and the others who can't be with us today."

The fire of Ellen's anger began to die down, thanks to Noah. She hoped his words would give the good people of Pepin something to think about. Because their words had certainly given her something to think about.

She'd told Mr. Lang the community would come to accept him. Now she hoped she'd told him the truth.

• • •

Sitting at the Ashford's table for Sunday dinner, Ellen tried to keep her mind from wondering how Ophelia and Martin were faring today. After the meal, she intended to walk out and see for herself. Maybe Amanda would watch William for her. Right now her little one lay on a blanket nearby, trying to roll over.

Mrs. Ashford finished loading the table with dishes and removed her apron. The delicious aromas of bacon in the green beans and butter melting on corn bread started Ellen's mouth watering. Mr. Ashford said grace, and then his wife motioned for him to start passing the bowls. She glanced at Ellen.

"I'm so sorry to hear about Martin's unfortunate accident. But I was surprised to hear the Stewards had become thick with the Dutch."

Ellen's fork stilled as she stared at the store-keeper's wife.

"Miss Thurston, I'm glad you told everyone about Gunther volunteering to help the Stewards," Amanda said, glancing sideways at each parent in turn. "People are so mean to him just because he wasn't born here. What does that matter?"

Both Amanda's parents reacted with deep disapproving frowns. Mrs. Ashford shook her head, her nose elevated. Something snapped inside Ellen.

"Yes, Amanda, and they're mean to Mr. Lang

and Johann, too. Why? Just because they speak with an accent?"

Mrs. Ashford replied stiffly, "It's because they aren't Americans."

"Gunther is going to become an American citizen," Amanda piped up. "He's studying with Miss Thurston so he'll be ready to take the test to be a citizen."

Both her parents looked at Amanda with startled disapproval.

Ellen's heart beat faster for the girl. To distract the parents, Ellen rushed on, "My great-grandfather, Patrick, came from Ireland as an indentured servant just before the Revolution. I'm sure he faced the same prejudice as immigrants now. But we are not ashamed of him."

"You're part Irish?" Mrs. Ashford said, sounding surprised. The unchanging prejudice against the Irish was particularly sharp.

"Yes, I am." Ellen had lost her appetite but she forced herself to begin eating.

"But he was your great-grandfather," Mr. Ashford pointed out. "That's a long time ago."

Ellen sighed inwardly. Maybe she had indeed misinformed Mr. Lang last night when she suggested that the people of Pepin would come to accept him. Would these people ever give Mr. Lang or Gunther or Johann a chance, or would the Langs carry the burden of this unreasonable bias for the rest of their lives?

She wanted nothing more than to find a way to help the community see how sweet Johann was, and how Gunther was growing into a fine young man . . .

. . . and what a wonderful, generous person Mr. Kurt Lang was. As she thought of him, his handsome face came to mind, wearing one of his endearing smiles. She thought of how when she'd walked through town with William recently, people hadn't frowned at her as before but they hadn't come up and cooed over him like they did over the other babies in town. But Mr. Lang always greeted her and tickled William's chin to make him grin. His kind nature always came through to her.

Mr. Lang and his family didn't deserve the shoddy treatment they usually received. Perhaps it was time she came up with a plan.

Several days later, Ellen stood at the front of the schoolroom, a tad buoyant. She had some good news for her students that she couldn't wait to share.

"Children, do you remember when I told you about my desire to have a spelling bee in the spring? Well, I have received a letter from the school at Bear Lake." She held it up. "The teacher writes that their school will participate in our spelling bee."

The children applauded, and their excitement cheered her.

"Since we now have one school committed to the spring spelling bee, today we will formally begin practicing. To prepare us for competition, we will form two teams and spell against each other. Starting with Amanda, count off by twos, please."

Amanda announced, "One!"

The boy beside her counted off, "Two." The separating count ended with the first row where Johann sat among the first graders.

"Now number ones go to my right and number twos go to my left. Stand against the opposite walls." She motioned with her hands. As the children went to their places, Ellen overheard one boy say to another. "Bad luck. We got the Dutch kid on our team. You watch. We'll lose."

The words hit her and she experienced the strange feeling of being drawn back like stone in a slingshot. She opened her mouth to reprimand the boy, but telling people how they should think or feel never worked well. A better idea quickly came to mind, which would send a strong message without her having to say a word to him.

"The captain of team one will be Amanda Ashford. The captain of team two will be Johann Lang."

A few members of team two groaned. She cast them a wordless scold and they lowered their chins, and then gazed directly at the boy who had made the rude comment about Johann. He, too, looked at the floor.

She opened her copy of *Webster's American Spelling Book* as she explained the rules. "If a team member misspells a word, he or she will sit down. The team with the last person standing wins. I'll begin with team one. Amanda, step forward, repeat the word I give you, then spell it, and repeat the word, please. Your word is *zeal.*"

Amanda stepped forward, standing very straight. "Zeal. *Z-e-a-l.* Zeal."

"Correct! You may shift to the end of your row." Ellen smiled and tried to look cheerful and not too serious. This should be fun, too. She turned to Johann. "Your first word is *kin.*"

Johann chewed his lower lip. Finally the girl standing next to him shoved him forward. "Kin," Johann parroted, staring at the floor. "*K . . . i . . . n.* Kin."

Ellen's heart lifted with pride as well as relief. Johann's face beamed. "Correct! Please move as Amanda did," she said, trying to sound as neutral as possible.

She noticed that many in Johann's row looked startled. *We'll show them, Johann.* How she wished Kurt—Mr. Lang—were here to see his nephew's victory. She could practically hear his deep musical voice congratulating Johann.

Unable to stop from smiling, she turned to the next student in team one and pronounced the next

174

word as she wondered if perhaps this spelling bee had even more potential than she realized.

On Saturday, Kurt paused where he stood on Martin's land, listening to the voices around him. Miss Thurston had indeed come to dig potatoes. Since just after noon, he had been picking Martin's corn and stewing over what he must say to Miss Thurston.

Nearby, Johann and Mrs. Steward also dug potatoes. The storekeeper's daughter had brought lunch and then stayed to care for the children. She sat on a blanket with the babies in the shade, close to where Gunther was picking corn. Kurt hadn't missed their frequent exchange of glances. Or the girl's innocent blushes.

Fleetingly he recalled being a child, so care-free, so unaware of tragedy. An innocent time in life. Or it should be. He thought of Johann, who faced challenges here that Kurt had never had to face. And he was concerned that Johann being captain of a spelling bee team was only going to make things harder for him.

Kurt had hoped for a few moments to speak to Miss Thurston but no opportunity had presented itself. He twisted off another rough cob of corn and dropped it in his nearly full sack. When could he get her to himself for a moment?

Then his wish was granted. Gunther excused himself to go check on Martin. When Mrs.

Steward rose to go along with him, Amanda called Johann to watch the children while she prepared a bottle for William. Johann ran to the shady spot, eager to play. Kurt saw his opportunity and forced himself to walk over to Miss Thurston.

She sat back on her heels and looked up. "Mr. Lang, what can I do for you?"

She had a smudge of dirt on her nose and across one cheek. In spite of this, and though wearing an old dress and apron, she appeared as elegant as ever. He wrapped up all his foolish feelings and put them away.

"Miss Thurston, I am glad you choose Johann to be captain, but . . ."

"But?" she prompted.

"Maybe people will not like this and make trouble for Johann."

She rose to face him, a militant gleam in her eye. "What kind of trouble?"

His inability to put his thoughts into words chafed his nerves. Or perhaps it was merely the nearness of her. "They will call him names" was the best he could mutter.

She tilted her head and considered him. He felt his face warm.

"Mr. Lang, that will only happen if he does a poor job spelling. If he does a good job, quite the opposite will happen. He will rise in their estimation. I suggest you go over his weekly spelling list every evening. I know this is harvest but before bed—"

"We do already," he said somewhat gruffly. Why did he have to notice how her hair had slipped down the back of her neck, and how, from her working in the sun, two tiny golden freckles had popped up on her nose?

"Then I don't think you have anything to worry about." She smiled. "Johann is doing quite well."

Evidently she was unaware that Johann doing well might only make others sharpen their claws. He didn't want to point this out, spoil her faith in her students. Without another word to her, he turned to carry his bag of corn to the corn crib near the cabin.

His head was full of worry for Johann—till he heard a girl's giggle. Uneasy, he halted at the point where the cornfield gave way to the clearing and scanned his surroundings.

To his right, just in the cover of the surrounding forest stood Gunther and the storekeeper's daughter. She pressed her back against the tree and Gunther rested a hand above her head, leaning toward her.

Aggravation and alarm vied within Kurt. He had ordered Gunther to put Amanda Ashford out of his mind. He was too young, and her parents would make a big noise if they heard about their daughter and that "Dutch" boy. Kurt nearly called out to Gunther, but something stopped him.

Things with Gunther had been much better at home. Did he want to risk this new harmony just because Gunther was stealing a moment with Amanda?

At that instant, Mrs. Steward solved the problem by coming around the cabin toward the fields. She waved to him. "I'm bringing water for us!"

He walked to meet her. Out of the corner of his eye, he noted the young couple separate and disappear, probably to reappear far from each other in a few moments. "Good. I will just add this to the crib and be right back."

Mrs. Steward halted and poured him a cup of water. "Wait. After you dump the corn, would you drop in on Martin? I think he'd like a man to talk to."

Kurt downed the cold water in a single draft and, refreshed, handed her back the cup. Though he wanted to make every working minute count —who knew when rain would come and make the fields muddy and the corn wet?—he nodded to her request. He understood loneliness, since he lived with it daily. The least he could do was go talk to Martin.

He dumped his sack of corn into the crib and then secured its door against scavengers. He walked to the cabin, his muscles still warm from the work. Sitting down would feel good.

He stopped in the open doorway, sorting

through his thoughts, choosing something safe to discuss with Martin.

"Kurt," Martin greeted him with evident pleasure. "How is the harvest coming?"

An easy subject. "I think you have a fine yield. The soil is good here."

Martin grinned, moved slightly and grimaced. "I'm sorry to make double work for you."

"It is no trouble. You would do the same for me."

Martin nodded. "How's Ellen?"

"Ellen?" Why had Martin asked him that? "She is digging potatoes."

"I see. That's all you have to say about my wife's pretty cousin?"

Kurt stared at Martin.

"You think Ophelia and I haven't seen how you look at her sometimes when you think nobody is looking?"

Kurt tried to deny this but his tongue tangled up and nothing to the purpose came out.

"Don't be so shy. I know Ellen has declared that she isn't interested in marriage, but . . ."

When Martin's voice trailed off, Kurt studied him. "But?" he prompted finally.

"Sometimes a woman gets swept off her feet by a man with a glib tongue," Martin said, not enlightening Kurt very much. "I think Ellen is getting over . . . something like that. I probably shouldn't be saying anything. It's her business, not mine." Martin appeared pained by his suggestion.

A man with a glib tongue? That gave Kurt some idea of why Ellen held herself aloof sometimes. "I understand," Kurt said, though of course he really didn't. "I think another two days and I'll have your corn in."

Martin looked relieved at the switch back to farm talk.

Soon Kurt excused himself and headed back to the cornfield, turning over in his mind Martin's words about his cousin. Kurt had thought Martin would be against his interest in Miss Thurston, but he hadn't sounded unsympathetic. What should Kurt make of that?

Why did life have to be so complicated? All he wanted was to raise Gunther and Johann and live a quiet life, free of gossip and conflict. What was wrong with that?

Well, to start with, in all honesty, that *wasn't* all he wanted.

Before turning his attention to getting in Martin's corn, he looked across the field to where Miss Thurston was digging, giving in to bitter-sweet temptation.

Chapter Thirteen

The Sunday worship had finished and outside people were chatting, or climbing into wagons and carts to head home. Kurt had brought Mrs. Steward and little Nathan with him, and now he waited for them alone beside his wagon. After the closing prayer, Mrs. Steward had been surrounded by people who wanted a firsthand and detailed report on her husband's recovery.

Johann mingled with the other children. Since today was the Sabbath, none of them could run or play or swing but they could talk and tease quietly. Kurt couldn't see Gunther, which of course made him think that Gunther was with Amanda.

"I wonder why Miss Thurston doesn't put that Dutchman in his place." A woman's sharp voice from the other side of his wagon hit Kurt like an arrow through his heart.

"Maybe she doesn't realize that he's making up to her," said another woman.

"Humph. No woman is that naive. You heard him speak up about that baby she'd taken in. I think she encouraged him. Why else would he have done that?"

Kurt cringed. What he had most feared was

happening. His association with Miss Thurston was harming her reputation.

"I wonder if that's why she chose his nephew to head up one of the spelling teams at school."

"Maybe that's just for practice, not the competition. I'm sure she wouldn't put a foreigner forward at the big spelling bee in the spring, would she?"

The other woman sighed. "Who knows what she would do."

For a moment, Kurt hoped they wouldn't see him as they came around the side of his wagon. But as they came abreast of him, they glanced his way and shock registered on their faces. In return, anger boiled up inside him. Covering this, he nodded slowly at the women, touching the brim of his hat as their faces reddened. They flashed him false smiles and gathered their skirts to hurry toward their husbands and their wagons.

His body radiated heat like a torch. *People are talking about me and the schoolteacher.* Hadn't he been flogged enough by gossip and whispering in Germany? Must he also endure it here?

He'd been right to be concerned that people would gossip about Johann being chosen as captain. And he was right to fear that Gunther's infatuation with Amanda would soon be noticed and spark more gossip. But never in his worst nightmares had he thought people would link him with Miss Thurston in a romantic way. Being coupled with him would surely do her no favors.

As Miss Thurston approached him with William in her arms, Kurt suddenly felt as if every eye around the clearing was on him.

"I'm going home with Ophelia," she said.

He knew Miss Thurston was waiting for him to help her up onto the bench yet he found he couldn't touch her.

"Let me get Johann," he said sharply, stepping away from her. He hated himself for such a display of poor manners, but he had no idea how else to save her reputation.

"Johann," he said as he approached the boy, "it is time we leave."

Johann looked unhappy but, waving to his friends, he joined Kurt. "My team is studying spelling. We are going to win again."

Kurt glanced at his nephew's shining face. *My team. We are.*

Dismay and gratitude warred in his heart. Was it possible Miss Thurston was right, and that Johann was being accepted? *And I left her standing by the wagon.*

They arrived back at the wagon and found Mrs. Steward and Miss Thurston already seated on the wagon bench. Gunther sent Kurt a confused look. "I helped the ladies up."

"*Danke.* Thank you, Gunther." Kurt walked around and got himself up on the bench without looking at the women while Johann climbed in back with Gunther. Kurt untied the reins and started the team off toward home.

As he drove, he couldn't help but wonder if the two women he'd overheard were saying what everybody else in town was already whispering. He swiped at his perspiring forehead with his sleeve. He knew exactly what he must do to silence the gossips. He hated the very thought of it, but he'd been left with no recourse but to gently distance himself from Miss Thurston.

He owed her that much.

On Tuesday afternoon, Ellen was standing at the front of her classroom, listening to the second graders reading aloud from *McGuffey's Reader*, so happy for just another routine day. Then Mrs. Ashford burst through the school doors.

"We need Johann!" she shouted. She grabbed the boy by the hand and yanked him to his feet, dragging him behind her like a kite tail. "It's an emergency!"

Half the students also jumped to their feet.

"What is it?" Ellen called to the woman's back, her pulse racing suddenly.

Mrs. Ashford didn't reply, holding on to Johann and running outside.

"Amanda!" Ellen said, halting the girl who looked ready to follow her mother. "Come forward! Children, stay where you are and do whatever Amanda tells you to. Disobedience will

184

not be tolerated." Ellen swished past as the girl moved quickly to the front of the class.

What could possibly cause Mrs. Ashford to require Johann? Ellen reached the town's street within minutes. A Conestoga wagon sat in the middle of the street, oxen drinking at the water trough in front of the General Store.

The blacksmith and Mr. Ashford stood beside the wagon looking troubled. Ellen approached them, trying to calm her breathing. "What's wrong?"

"It's a bad business," Mr. Ashford replied. "We've sent for the preacher, but you go on inside and help my wife, please. The . . . woman is distraught."

The woman? And why the hesitation? She tried to peer into the wagon, but Mr. Ashford forestalled her with a raised hand. "Don't look."

His words pushed her back as if he'd shoved her. He was clearly shielding her from something he thought unfit for a lady. She hurried inside and found Mrs. Ashford sitting by the cold stove, patting a weeping woman's hand. Three boys like stair steps huddled behind the weeping woman.

Johann was in the center of it all, speaking to the stranger in German.

Ellen tried to still her qualms and sat in the chair opposite the woman. "Mrs. Ashford, what's happened?"

"I'm afraid that this poor woman stopped for

help. Her husband was ill. Mr. Ashford couldn't understand her but she took his hand and drew him outside. When he climbed into the wagon, he found that the poor man had already expired."

From what she'd seen outside, Ellen had anticipated something like this but still couldn't hold back a gasp. "She doesn't speak English?"

"Barely any. That's why I came for the Dutch . . . for Johann. I didn't know how to tell her."

Ellen hated that a seven-year-old boy had been given the task of informing a woman that her husband had succumbed to death. But necessity often forced youngsters to accept responsibilities they were too young to carry. How was the boy?

Ellen noted his unusual crestfallen expression. She touched his arm. "Johann, tell the woman that the town will help her. Mr. Ashford has sent someone to fetch our pastor."

"Yes, indeed. We must help her," Mrs. Ashford agreed, wiping her own eyes.

Ellen realized that the storekeeper's wife was feeling the woman's suffering. Some things cut across the barriers of language and nationality. "What is her name?"

"She is Mrs. Bollinger," Johann said, "Marta Bollinger from Switzerland."

"Where was she bound?" Ellen asked.

Johann asked the woman and then replied, "New Glarus."

"Why, that's way southeast of us," Mrs. Ashford exclaimed. "They should have gone east when they reached the Wisconsin River."

Johann translated this. The widow sobbed, rocking in her misery. Her children huddled closer to her.

"Johann, I think it's better not to ask her any more questions," Ellen instructed. "Mrs. Ashford, I think some chamomile tea might calm the lady."

"Of course!" The storekeeper's wife leaped to her feet. "And I'll bring some food down, too. Won't take me a moment."

Ellen was glad she'd come. She would make sure no one said anything unfeeling or unkind to the poor woman. Johann talked gently to the children in German, but the three boys said little in return. The eldest looked to be only around the same age as Johann. Moving nearer, Ellen patted the woman's back, praying for her.

Soon Mrs. Ashford bustled in with a large tray of tea, thick slices of fresh bread, pale butter and golden honey for the family.

"*Danke*" was all the woman said, tears still washing down her face. She tried to nibble at the food. The boys murmured their thanks, too, and they ate as if starved. Mrs. Ashford had just returned with another tray with sliced apple cake when Noah Whitmore arrived.

And Kurt Lang, just behind him.

Ellen's heart leaped at the sight of him. Kurt would be able to comfort the woman.

"Is this the new widow?" Noah asked gravely, doffing his hat.

"Yes," Mrs. Ashford said, looking truly saddened. "You brought Mr. Lang with you."

Ellen was pleased to hear the obvious relief in Mrs. Ashford's voice.

"Kurt says he will translate for me. I think it's better to have an adult address this sensitive situation."

"Of course." Mrs. Ashford wiped away a tear herself. "It's just so sad."

At this moment, a woman with a basket over her arm entered the store, jingling the bell, startling them. Mrs. Ashford hurried to steer the customer away from the knot around the cold stove. Ellen stepped back also but stayed nearby because she didn't want the woman to be surrounded only by men. Johann moved to stand with the three little boys.

Noah sat on one side of the widow and Kurt on the other. "Has she been told her husband is dead?" Noah asked Johann.

"No," Johann said, sounding scared. "I thought it better for my uncle to tell her. He would know what to say. Her name is *Frau* Marta Bollinger."

Ellen looked at Kurt. When he met her gaze, she wanted to reach out and comfort him. The task before him was an dreadful one. But she knew he had the strength and heart to do it. And apparently, so did other people in Pepin.

Kurt nodded to Johann and then grasped the woman's hand. "*Frau* Bollinger, my name is Kurt Lang," he said in German. "I came to live here this spring. This man is Noah Whitmore. He is the pastor here. I am very sorry but I'm afraid your husband is dead."

The woman bent her head into her hands, sobbing. "*Nein, nein . . .*"

Noah gently claimed her other hand. "Tell her we'll take care of everything. And she isn't to fear being in want. She has our deepest sympathy."

Kurt translated this and patted the woman's hand. He was aware of Miss Thurston hovering nearby, her sympathy evident in her expression. He wished he could turn to her to help him comfort this stranger. She would know just what to say. But he had promised himself he would not do anything to add to the gossip about them.

"What will we do now?" *Frau* Bollinger asked Kurt, near hysteria. "I have no idea how . . ." She shut her mouth, obviously trying to stay in control.

Kurt did not know how a burial was handled here. He knew how death was dealt with when one had a church and a churchyard, a home and a family. He turned to Noah. After Noah reassured Kurt that all would be done as it should be, he rose and went out to talk to Mr. Ashford. Miss Thurston took Noah's place beside the woman, her pretty face drawn in deep concern. She murmured soft, comforting words to *Frau* Bollinger.

To witness Miss Thurston being so kind to this woman reminded him that he must keep his distance from her. Kindness could move any heart and he needed to keep his own far from Miss Thurston. He focused his attention on the widow as they began to help her calm herself to face her husband's final resting. Bad memories of funerals flowed through Kurt's mind, stirring up a pain too deep for words. He noticed behind him that even Mrs. Ashford spoke to the customer in hushed tones. His sympathy went out to this woman, a stranger in a strange land.

After all that had taken place since Mrs. Ashford had come running into her school, Ellen felt dazed. Noah and the Ashfords had sent for people, and the poor man had been laid out and buried on land Mr. Lang offered. Now Ellen, the Ashfords, the Langs, the Stewards, the Whitmores with the Bollingers stood on the gentle green hillside where they had laid Joachim Bollinger to rest. Around them the maples blazed scarlet, bright spots amid the sorrow.

Ellen had already decided what she would do, and now was the time to announce it. "I'll take Mrs. Bollinger and her sons home with me."

Everyone turned toward her.

"But you don't speak their language," Mrs. Ashford objected.

"I was hoping that Mr. Lang would permit Johann to stay with me to translate. That would make it easier for her sons, too."

As everyone simply stared at her in disbelief, a host of melancholy black birds swooped skyward, their strident calls filling the air.

"I'm offering," Ellen said, raising her voice, "because staying with someone unmarried will be easier for her, and because I have plenty of room." This was true since most families lived in one-room cabins with a loft; adding another family would crowd any host family.

Ellen glanced to Mr. Lang but he looked away. This cost her more than she wanted to acknowledge. She suddenly realized that throughout this trying incident, he'd kept his distance. She wondered why, and was this just because of this situation or something else?

"Well," Noah said, "in light of the language barrier, if Mr. Lang was married, I would suggest he host them. But yes, I think you're right." He paused, probably to see if there were any other offers. None came. "Kurt, would you tell the widow that Miss Thurston has offered her a place to stay. Unless she has some objection."

The woman, looking only half-alive, listened to

Mr. Lang. She merely nodded and murmured, "*Danke.*"

Ellen moved closer and gripped her hand, trying to comfort her without words. *God, help this woman.*

In worship that Sunday, Ellen didn't sit in her usual place beside her cousin. She sat with her houseguests, the widow and her children, wanting to help them through this crucible of being on display. All too well she recalled her first few weeks here when she endured being the center of attention. Not a pleasant memory.

With William asleep on her lap, Ellen sat on one side of Marta Bollinger and Mr. Lang sat on the other. Gunther sat on the other side of Ellen, then Marta's three sons and finally Johann. People continued to gawk at the widow and her sons. Ellen wished people here would behave in a more mannerly way. Didn't they know staring was impolite?

Marta had donned mourning, and the black of her dress set off her very fair skin and flaxen hair. Several times over the past few days, the woman's beauty had overwhelmed Ellen. For some reason, Marta's beauty pinched at her, and Ellen was not proud of that.

From the front of the room, Noah brought his sermon to its end. Then he glanced toward the rear bench.

"I'm sure you've all heard about the widow and her sons. Miss Thurston has told me of the many kindnesses shown this bereaved family. I want to thank everyone who has brought food to the schoolhouse for them. And a special thanks to the Ashfords, and to Miss Thurston."

Mr. Lang translated what Noah said to Marta, who whispered back to him. Mr. Lang rose. "Mrs. Bollinger says thank you everyone for your kindness in her loss. She told me her husband has a cousin in New Glarus. That was where they were headed. She still wants to go there. I think she will need someone to go with her." Mr. Lang sat down.

The thought that he might volunteer stung Ellen, and she wrestled her feelings under control.

"Thank you, Mr. Lang. Please tell Mrs. Bollinger we'll figure out who will go with her—"

Gunther surprised Ellen by rising. "I can take her. I speak her language." The young man reddened as he spoke.

"Thank you for offering," Noah said. "We will discuss this with Mr. Lang and Mrs. Bollinger. Let's pray."

Soon everyone had spilled out into the schoolyard to enjoy the sunny October day and to tender their condolences to Marta. Ellen stood near the widow. She couldn't stop herself from watching Kurt translating for Marta. The two stood so close. Ellen tried to quiet her edginess. What was it she was feeling? Could it possibly be . . . jealousy?

Finally, everyone finished offering sympathy through Mr. Lang. The Ashfords had invited Ellen and her guests to Sunday dinner. Kurt and Gunther headed home. Though stung over Kurt leaving without speaking directly to her, Ellen walked with her guests to the General Store and up the familiar back staircase.

When they entered the upstairs quarters, Mrs. Ashford called for Ellen to help her. Ellen left Johann with the Bollingers and entered the kitchen. "How can I be of help?"

Mrs. Ashford motioned for her to come close and whispered into her ear, "I have come up with the perfect solution for Mrs. Bollinger and her sons."

"Oh?" Ellen whispered, too.

"Mr. Lang should propose to her."

Ellen gasped, shards of surprise shooting through her. Her first instinct was to insist that it was a terrible, terrible idea. But she found she could not utter a word.

"I know it's not the usual. But just think—when will another Dutch woman come to Pepin? Mr. Lang would have a wife who understands him and three more sons to help with the work."

Ellen, reeling from this unpleasant shock, turned her back to Mrs. Ashford. She knew it was rude but without a word, she went to the dining table and sat.

The meal went by in a blur. Ellen struggled against the ugly undertow of jealousy, her cheeks flushed and warm. She'd experienced this same resentment and shock the first time Holton had come calling and taken Cissy out for a stroll instead of her. And now she faced it again.

Why am I feeling this way? I don't intend to marry. Mr. Lang has made no advances toward me. This is too foolish for words. I refuse to feel this way.

Her turbulent emotions paid absolutely no heed.

"Did you notice how Gunther offered to help Mrs. Bollinger?" Amanda asked.

Ellen came back fully into the flow of conversation. Amanda's parents had pokered up so Ellen replied, "Yes, Gunther is very thoughtful."

"Yes, he is," Amanda stated with emphasis.

Then Marta spoke to Johann, and Johann turned to everyone and said, "Mrs. Bollinger would like to know if there is any way she could travel south on the river with her wagon and team. It would be quicker and safer than by land. I can tell," Johann added, "she wants to go to her family soon."

"That's understandable," Mr. Ashford said. "Tell her that barges dock here sometimes. She must be packed and ready."

"Does she have funds for the fare?" Mrs. Ashford asked.

The widow replied that she had some funds left.

The rest of the dinner passed with conversation about the weather, the rising prices, the news of unrest in the South between blacks and whites. Would the trouble between North and South ever end? Ellen tried to participate in a normal fashion but couldn't concentrate. Images of Mr. Lang leaning close to Marta bedeviled her.

Afterward, Johann and the boys went outside to wade in the shallows near shore, looking for shells. Claiming William, Marta settled into the rocking chair—holding the baby seemed to soothe her sorrow. And Ellen saw Amanda slip away, having a good idea of whom she was going to meet. Gunther.

As Ellen helped Mrs. Ashford by drying the dishes, the storekeeper's wife wore a deep frown. Ellen surmised she was worried about Amanda and Gunther, too. But her next words took Ellen by surprise.

"I know you think my idea of Mr. Lang marrying this widow is foolish, but it isn't."

Ellen nearly dropped the gilt-edged china plate she was drying. "Why would you think she would remarry so soon?"

"I know she is recently bereaved but marriages of convenience happen all the time. I mean, when will another Dutch woman come through for Mr. Lang to marry?"

Ellen startled herself by speaking her mind.

"You think then that no English-speaking woman would marry Mr. Lang?" Heat flashed through Ellen at her own words. *Why did I say that?*

"Well, most American women don't want to marry foreigners."

Ellen struggled, holding back words.

"I mean, yes, he is very good-looking, but that accent." Mrs. Ashford shook her head as she scrubbed another dish within an inch of its life.

"I don't think Marta has any desire to marry anybody." In the midst of her own upheaval, Ellen tried to say the words as unemotionally as she could.

"Well, I will tell you my mother's story. She was orphaned at only thirteen when both her parents died," Mrs. Ashford said. "She had three younger brothers to provide for. When a neighbor much older than she offered marriage and a home for her brothers, she accepted. Sometimes a woman does what she must for her family."

Ellen heard the fierceness in Mrs. Ashford's voice. "She was very brave."

"Yes, and the marriage turned out to be a good one. I loved my father and my older uncles. You may think I'm unfeeling but life isn't always pretty and polite."

Ellen touched the woman's shoulder. "You're right, of course. Life throws us surprises, both pleasant and unpleasant." The words vibrated in Ellen's mind.

"I just hope that Amanda comes to her senses. Ned and I see how she moons over that Dutch boy."

"His name is Gunther." Ellen maintained a calm tone. "And don't girls fall in and out of calf love many times? She's only fourteen. Surely you've seen how Gunther is turning into a fine young man."

Mrs. Ashford paused in her scrubbing. "I hope you're right."

Ellen bit back all she wanted to say in favor of Gunther. She knew that telling people what they should think and how they should feel never prospered. Besides, given all the turmoil she was experiencing herself this afternoon, she was in no position to lecture anyone.

She wondered what Mr. Lang would think of the possibility of a marriage of convenience with Marta Bollinger. She closed her eyes in denial. The very thought of it caused her stomach to clench.

Chapter Fourteen

For late October, the Monday was golden and balmy. Ellen even had a few of the school windows open. So unfortunately for her state of mind, she could hear Mr. Lang and Marta speaking German as he helped her load the wagon with her belongings. The sound of them chatting in a language she couldn't understand grated on her nerves. She hated this evidence of weakness and worked hard not to reveal it. After everything that Mrs. Bollinger had been through, she deserved kindness, not jealousy.

She brought her attention back to the third graders, who were practicing adding and carrying over on their slates. "Add 12 plus 19," Ellen instructed. "Raise your hand when you have the answer." Johann coughed and then sneezed in the first-grade row.

Tomorrow morning, early, Gunther and one of Old Saul's grandsons would travel with the Bollingers to New Glarus. With the weather getting colder, Marta had decided not to wait upon the chance of a barge arriving. Ellen was furious with herself for being glad that the widow was leaving. Jealousy was such a lowering emotion.

Johann coughed again.

"Dorcas, please tell us the answer." Ellen glanced out the window as Mr. Lang and Marta, both smiling, tried to fit one more thing on the wagon. They were smiling. She swallowed down her unworthy response.

"31?" Dorcas, the daughter of the new homesteading family replied.

"Yes. Now, children, 27 plus 18." The sound of chalk on slates gave sound to the irritation she was experiencing over Mr. Lang helping Marta.

Johann coughed a third time, and she glanced his way and paused. He appeared flushed. She didn't want to call attention to him, but a faint worry nudged her. "Johann, come here, please."

He obeyed.

She touched his forehead with the back of her wrist and felt heat. "Johann, you may have a fever. Did you feel warm this morning?"

He shook his head. "No, miss." He coughed again.

She was irritated with herself. *If I had not been concentrating on my own ridiculous emotions, I would have noticed this earlier.* "Go sit on the far side of the room, please."

"Did I do something wrong?" he asked.

"No, Johann, but you may be contagious."

He looked confused, but went to sit on one of the empty benches. The children in the room became restless. Ellen decided to assess the situation. She went from child to child, touching their foreheads. Three other children, including Marta's oldest son, also felt warm. A presentiment of coming trouble draped itself over her mind.

All the students looked worried now, glancing to brothers and sisters.

To avoid igniting fear, she must be firm. "Children, I need to take the temperatures of these students. Please work quietly on the assignments I gave your class for this evening."

The sound of worried whispering followed her as she walked swiftly into her quarters. From her trunk, she brought out a large, leather-bound book, a medical dictionary of symptoms and treatments. She located her medical kit and turned back toward the schoolroom.

"Miss Thurston?" Mr. Lang had halted just outside the door to her quarters. "Is something wrong? You look worried."

She gazed at him, wishing he had spoken to her not only because she must look fearful. When had he stopped talking to her as a friend? She pushed down this reaction and her alarm. "I'm not quite sure yet." She moved swiftly back into the classroom, acting as if she weren't aware that Mr. Lang had followed her to the connecting door-way. On her desk she set up the thermometer and poured alcohol into a glass vial in a metal stand.

She spoke to the isolated children. "I am going to take your temperatures. Have any of you seen a thermometer before?" She held it aloft.

All heads swiveled to see it.

"What does it do, miss?" Johann asked, sounding fearful.

"First of all, a thermometer tells what a person's body temperature is. If a person's temperature is above 98.6, that means a fever. Now, I am going to slip the glass cylinder into your mouth and under your tongue and wait five minutes. It doesn't hurt. Just make sure you don't bite it."

"I should go home," Dorcas said, rising. "My mama told me to come right home if anybody got sick in school. I don't want to catch anything—"

"Sit down!" Ellen ordered as others rose, too. "I am merely taking temperatures. There will be order here."

The children sat down, but the atmosphere became agitated with worry.

Ellen proceeded to take Johann's temperature, watching the wall clock tick toward a full five minutes. She forced herself not to glance toward Kurt, still standing in the connecting doorway, silently observing her every move.

After the longest five minutes in her recent history, she withdrew the glass stick and read the rainbowlike mercury—100.2 degrees. Not allowing her dismay to show, she shook down the thermometer, immersed it in the vial of alcohol, and then went to the next child.

By the time she'd finished, she'd become completely and dreadfully certain that some contagion had invaded her classroom. She forced her lungs to inhale and exhale evenly. Yet she couldn't regulate her galloping heart.

She looked at all of the feverish children. They were coughing, had runny noses and inflamed eyes. Could this be just the common cold? She moved to her desk and opened the large medical dictionary she'd brought with her. The near silence magnified the dry ruffling sound turning each page caused.

She opened to the section of childhood illnesses and read quickly through the various collections of symptoms. Mr. Lang moved into the room just behind her and stood watching the children, supporting her decree for order.

After reading, she walked back to the isolated children. "Johann, will you open your mouth, please?"

Small red spots dotted the inside of Johann's mouth, and the mouths of the others. Dread sent gooseflesh up her arms.

Measles.

There was no doctor in this town. And even if there had been, no cure for measles existed. She tried to make her worried mind focus. What should she do next?

"What is it?" Mr. Lang from the front of the room asked.

"I'm afraid that we have an outbreak of measles," she said as unemotionally as she could.

Dorcas popped up from her seat and ran toward the door.

"Stop!" Ellen commanded, racing after the girl. She caught her shoulder just before she escaped.

"Mama told me if any sickness came to school, to run home," Dorcas insisted once more, trying to pull free.

"Dorcas, everyone here has already been exposed to measles. If you run home, you might give it to your parents and your two little brothers. Now come back and sit down."

"Mama said!" The little girl pulled away and dashed through the door.

Ellen tried to catch her but the child escaped. Feeling her pulse throbbing in her temples, Ellen stood at the door to prevent more children from fleeing. Mr. Lang had moved to guard the other doorway. He looked very concerned, just as she must.

Her head spun with all the questions. The children had all been exposed to the disease but it might take days for symptoms to appear. "Children, if I let you go home, you might spread the infection to your families. You could bring hurt to them," she explained to the strained faces beseeching her.

"Will we be in quarantine?" Amanda asked, sounding frightened.

Quarantine, a terrifying word. How could she quarantine all these children here? She couldn't care for a roomful of sick children by herself. Her petty concern over Mr. Lang and Marta shamed her.

I should have been concentrating on my students. Did I miss something this morning that I should have caught? Dear Lord, what should I do?

"Miss Thurston," Kurt said after several moments of heavy yet restless silence, "I will go tell Noah Whitmore and Mr. Ashford. They will help."

The schoolteacher looked at him, her hands clasped tightly together. "Thank you, Mr. Lang. An excellent suggestion." The relief evident in her voice commanded his sympathy.

"I come back soon." He turned and shut the door, hurrying through her quarters and then outside. Briefly he told Mrs. Bollinger what had happened. She exclaimed and, shutting the tailgate of the wagon, hurried inside, saying she would help the kind teacher.

Kurt went straight to the Ashford's store. He burst inside and found the proprietor helping two women he recognized vaguely from church. His agitation spurred him but should he speak in front of others?

He removed his hat and nodded politely to the ladies. "Mr. Ashford, may I speak with you a moment, please? The matter is urgent."

The two women gave him a look as if he'd spoken out of turn, and moved to look at fabric together. Kurt ignored them and strode forward and motioned to the storekeeper to come closer.

"What is it, Lang?" Mr. Ashford was clearly annoyed that Kurt had interrupted a sale.

Kurt lowered his voice. "I have come from

school. There is sickness. Miss Thurston needs help."

"Sickness? What kind?"

"The teacher says maybe measles." Kurt didn't know the German word for this illness but Miss Thurston had looked as if it were a bad disease.

Ashford's face fell and he whispered, "Measles can be deadly, or cause blindness. It is very dangerous."

Kurt's insides turned to ice and a roaring swelled in his ears. Johann could die?

The storekeeper turned and said, "Ladies, you must finish your purchases and then I'm closing up."

The women turned to the proprietor in surprise.

"Miss Thurston thinks there has been an outbreak of measles at the school," the man explained.

The women gasped. Kurt was frankly surprised that Mr. Ashford had been so plainspoken about the situation.

"Mr. Lang and I will head over to the preacher's to decide whether quarantine is necessary. I will be closed for the rest of the day."

The transactions were tied up quickly. The ladies held handkerchiefs over their noses and mouths as they rushed from the store.

Ashford locked the door and flipped the sign to read "Closed." "We'll borrow the blacksmith's nag and cart. Let's go!"

He paused, then hurried to the bottom of the

rear staircase. Quickly he shouted the facts to his wife. "Go to the school and help Miss Thurston! I'll get Noah Whitmore!"

Within a few minutes, they were heading as fast as the rough trail would allow them, soon rounding the bend to the Whitmore place. Kurt recalled Miss Thurston's grave expression and how the women in the store had gasped and hurried away.

What *was* measles? Was Gunther in danger as well as Johann?

And what about Miss Thurston? The thought of anything happening to her was more than Kurt could bear. He snapped the reins, encouraging the horse to go faster.

By the time Ellen glimpsed Kurt, Noah and Mr. Ashford coming through the trees, a few parents already had gathered outside the school door. Had Dorcas told everyone she met? Regardless, the word had spread.

They had to decide whether to quarantine the students or not. She was grateful to see the others arrive. She didn't feel up to making that decision alone. Mrs. Ashford stood beside her in quiet support.

Noah hurried forward. "Miss Thurston, are you sure your students have measles?"

Grateful for his calm tone, she held up the hefty medical dictionary. "I brought this so I would be prepared for the inevitable. Wherever children gather, contagion can spread. According to this, it certainly sounds as if they have measles."

"Then our main priority is deciding how to handle this outbreak. Ordinarily we would quarantine any child who showed symptoms. Miss Thurston, does that book tell how long it takes for symptoms to show?"

"Ten to fourteen days. And the disease usually takes the same time to run its course. Also, stricken children should be kept away from the sun or bright light to protect their eyes." Ellen clasped the heavy book to her as a shield. Mrs. Ashford patted her arm.

"We want to take our children home," one mother spoke up. "If they stay here with the sick children, they *will* get it."

Noah's deep concern and uncertainty showed on his face. Ellen had the sudden urge to weep. Evidently the panic around her was seeping into her own emotions. Or was it something more? Images from the past . . . a fevered baby in her arms, struggling for breath . . .

No, no. That is in the past. She wrenched herself back to the present, forcing herself to gain control. She, like everyone else, waited to hear what Noah would say.

"I think each family should decide for themselves whether to leave their child here at school or take the child home," Noah said at last.

"No!" Ellen objected. "Each parent should consider their younger children. The younger the child, the more chance of . . ." Fear clogged her throat. She couldn't go on. When she looked at the faces around her, she realized she didn't need to say more.

"But you cannot care for so many alone," Mr. Lang protested.

"Kurt is right," Noah said. "If anyone decides to leave a child here at the school in quarantine, one of the parents or an older sibling must stay to nurse that child."

"And I suggest we close the school for regular classes till this has run its course," Mr. Ashford said. "Personally, I've had the measles so I will keep my store open, but only come if you are in real need of something."

Noah and the other men nodded solemnly. And then Ellen heard, "That's what we get for letting foreigners into our town."

Ellen recognized the speaker as one of the men who had opposed her keeping William. She knew people would think what he had just said, though she'd hoped no one would say it aloud.

"We live in a river community," Noah said in an even tone. "We may never know how this disease came here."

"Well I for one think it's clear how the disease came here," the man said, staring at Mr. Lang. Ellen watched as he met the man's gaze dead-on.

"Mr. Lang," she said. "Will you get William for me?" She sensed a ripple move through the assembled crowd. Even Kurt himself looked surprised that she would make such a request after what the man had just said. "He has already been exposed. Tell Mrs. Brawley what's happened and that I'll be keeping William home for the foreseeable future. Tell her I'm sorry." Her voice died in her throat. The thought that she might have infected the Brawley baby crushed her.

The sympathy on Mr. Lang's face nearly brought her to tears. "Miss Thurston, you are not to blame for any of this," he said.

She couldn't trust herself to respond to his kind words.

"I will get William and supplies then return to be with my nephew. Noah, please tell Gunther to stay home."

Ellen heard the anxiety in his voice. She wished she could reassure him, offer him hope. But she could not mouth false platitudes in the face of this thing that had come against them all.

"Those of you with no children at school should go home now and stay there," Noah said. "Don't come into town until this is passed. Miss Thurston, if you need me, send for me." Then he began to pray aloud. "Heavenly Father, help us. Preserve the lives and sight of our children. All of us. Amen."

"I'm taking Amanda home," Mrs. Ashford said.

"But I'll bring food and medicine by suppertime."

Ellen nodded but she was more aware of Kurt as he hurried off to bring William home to her. She was touched by his willingness to help others—to help her.

Given permission to claim their children and take them home, people milled in front of the door and consulted one another. The unclaimed children fidgeted inside the schoolroom, looking out the door and windows, waiting while their parents decided what to do.

Their worry flared palpably. If they decided the mother would stay, the parting of husband and wife and child at the schoolroom door touched Ellen's heart. Especially heartbreaking to watch fathers say goodbye without touching their children.

Ellen struggled against cold waves of fear coursing through her. She tried to pray but no words came.

Chapter Fifteen

Word continued to spread and by evening, all children had either been taken home or remained in quarantine with their mothers. Kurt watched as families dealt with the crisis and tried to face it as bravely as they could.

The quarantined group at the school included Marta's children, Johann, little William and three mothers who stayed with their children in hopes of protecting their toddlers, staying safely at home. An unnatural hush hung over the school.

As the sun set, Kurt helped these women make pallets on the opposite side of the schoolroom floor from those who were already ill. He pumped and carried water in for tea and washing. All the while he tracked Miss Thurston, aware of the fear she masked.

He wanted nothing more than to offer her comfort, but he knew he must keep his distance, especially in such close quarters. His mind kept going back to the way she'd stepped in when one of the townspeople had all but accused him of bringing measles to Pepin. She was an extraordinary woman. There was no doubt.

Standing outside Miss Thurston's door, Mrs. Ashford handed him a large kettle of pork and beans, and one of thin oatmeal for the sick children. Amanda handed in a pot of hot willow bark tea for the fevered.

For once, Mrs. Ashford didn't have much to say and she and Amanda left quickly.

Just before dark, Kurt brought in more wood to keep the low fire burning in Miss Thurston's fireplace and in the large Franklin stove that sat against the wall between the schoolroom and teacher's quarters. Eventually, once everyone was settled for the night, he took a seat at Miss Thurston's desk.

He woke in the dark with a start sometime later. What had wakened him? How long had he been asleep?

The school door stood open, letting in a wedge of moonlight. Cool air rushed in. One glance told Kurt that only Johann's pallet was empty.

Kurt moved quickly to the open door. Looking outside, he glimpsed nothing but the trees surrounding the school. Fear grabbed the back of his neck. He shut the door and raced to Miss Thurston's room to see if Johann had gone there. He leaned inside.

Miss Thurston looked up from the rocking chair. "What is it?" she asked softly, urgently.

"Johann. He isn't inside."

She leaped to her feet, laying her child in his cradle. She hurried to him and clutched his arms. "We must find him. The night air will do him harm."

She whipped on her shawl, lit a lantern and let herself out her door. He hurried after her, closing the door silently behind him. In the midst of the schoolyard, she stood in a shaft of moonlight, turning her head slowly, scanning the woods. The wind ruffled the leaves, but he could hear no other sound.

Dear God, help us find him. Johann could have wandered anywhere. If they didn't find him . . .

Terror for his little nephew turned his empty stomach. He swallowed down dry heaves.

Miss Thurston picked up her lantern and began searching the circle of trees around the clearing. She halted and motioned for him to follow her.

"Do you see him?" he asked, keeping up with her.

"No, but this is the path the children sometimes take to the creek that leads to the river. I think he might go this way out of habit."

He hadn't thought of that danger. The Mississippi River was so near.

Miss Thurston began nearly running and he edged in front of her. *God, help. God, help.* With each step, his mind chanted this.

The trees thinned so near the river flats. Ahead, Johann's white shirt glimmered in the creek. "Johann!" Kurt thundered.

Miss Thurston grabbed his elbow. "He's delirious. Don't agitate him. He's not really awake."

The boy mumbled something as Kurt waded into the creek, shivering from the cold water. Panic surged within him, a bellows being pumped hard and fast. He lifted Johann and carried him out of the creek, dripping cold water.

"Is he breathing?" Miss Thurston asked, hurrying to him.

"I don't know." He couldn't think.

She leaned close, putting her cheek next to

Johann's mouth. "He's breathing. Let's get him inside. Quickly!"

The two of them raced back to the school. The schoolteacher reached the side door first and swung it open wide. He ducked inside.

"Lay him in front of my hearth and strip him," she whispered. "I'll find something for him to change into." She went to her trunk and began rummaging.

Kneeling, Kurt stripped off Johann's clothing, tossing the sopping wet pieces to the floor.

Then she was at his side again, pushing a dry towel into his hands. "Dry him." She used another towel on Johann's face and hair. "Rub his skin as you dry him. It will bring the blood to the surface."

He did as she said, grateful to see the white skin turn ruddy under the friction. Finally, they had him dry and dressed and wrapped in a blanket.

"*Was ist los*?" Marta had risen from the bed.

Kurt explained what had happened as he laid Johann on the floor in front of the hearth.

Marta exclaimed her distress, picking up the sodden clothing and hurrying outside, saying she would wring them out and hang them on the clothesline.

Kurt knelt beside his nephew. "Why did he do it?"

Miss Thurston pressed her wrist to Johann's forehead. "Sometimes a high fever causes delirium. Or he might have instinctively sought the water to cool his fever. He likes the creek. He goes there during recess often."

"But being chilled could kill him." Just saying the words shook Kurt.

"His fever is down," Miss Thurston said calmly. "We will just keep him warm and hope this hasn't made matters worse." She laid a warm brick at Johann's feet to ward off the chill.

"I shouldn't have fallen asleep." He rested his forehead in his hand. "*Dummkopf.*"

She gently took his hand away from his head, and he was forced to look at her. "You fell asleep because you were exhausted. You woke and we found him. We are only human."

"I can't lose him." *I can't bear to lose anyone else.* His mind went to Gunther. How was he? Was he sick and alone?

"Don't worry about Gunther," Miss Thurston said as if reading his mind. "Ophelia and the Whitmores will check on him. Now strip off your wet shoes and socks before you come down with this, too."

He wanted to argue but he knew Miss Thurston was right. He eased back and did what she'd asked. A shiver shook him and he didn't know if it was from his sodden shoes and socks or from terror. He was too frozen even to pray.

Two days of nursing the children passed in a blur.

Night had fallen once more and most of the sick were dozing restlessly. Two of the children who had remained had come down with the illness, and one more child had come with her mother to enter the quarantined school.

In her quarters, Ellen sat in the rocker, nearly paralyzed with fear. William, so small and helpless, lay on her lap. Last night he'd begun sneezing and she'd discovered the telltale red spots in his tiny mouth.

I could lose him, this child who was entrusted to me for safekeeping, this child I love.

The fire burned low and William's fever burned higher. By firelight, she saw how hard the tiny infant fought for each breath. She'd been afraid to give him the willow bark tea Mrs. Ashford had brought over which sat on the table nearby. Would it help or hurt such a small child?

Since she'd first noticed William's symptoms, this fear had been trying to wrap itself around her lungs and choke her. She'd held it at bay, but now the terror conquered her.

Why did I think I could raise a child?

She began to weep, each sob wrenching her.

Then, before her eyes, William began to convulse. Her little brother had seized like this before he died. All those years ago, Dr. Litchfield had said that no one could have saved him. Remembering her brother only increased her suffering. Instantly ice went through her in horrifying waves. She rose and cried out word-lessly.

Please, God, help. Help my William.

Unable to fall back asleep, Kurt was sitting in Miss Thurston's chair again, keeping watch over the sleeping children and mothers, when someone cried out. He peered into the gray moonlit room, listening. The sound had come from behind him.

Ellen.

Panic sliced his heart. William—was he worse?

Hoping not to disturb the others, Kurt rose and raced on tiptoe to her quarters. Ellen sat in her rocking chair holding William, horror on her face.

He moved swiftly to her. "What is it?" he whispered.

She looked up, tears spilling from her eyes. She tried to speak but could only weep. Kurt knelt beside her. In a shaft of moonlight from the window, he saw the child flushed with fever and breathing with difficulty. Then the child shook violently and gagged.

Instinctively, Kurt snatched up the infant into his arms and turned him on his side. The thought of the child choking shot like lightning through his mind. He unwound the blanket and ran to the door. He stepped outside into the cooler air.

The child convulsed once more, then lay quiet, lying over Kurt's arm, panting.

Ellen hovered beside him. "Won't the night air harm him?"

Kurt found he was panting, too, the emotional reaction causing him to feel as if he'd just sprinted across a finish line. Finally he managed to say, "Perhaps not. Just a few minutes. We let him cool down and see."

When William appeared to cuddle closer as if seeking warmth, Kurt turned and gently urged Ellen inside. He silently shut the door behind them and halted by the fireplace. Ellen stood opposite him, gazing down at the child. Everything else receded from Kurt's mind. There was only Ellen, the child and him.

"You are worried," he whispered so inadequately.

She nodded, shaking with renewed but silent weeping.

He had no more words. He laid William in the cradle at her feet. Then, not letting himself pause to consider, he did what he felt compelled to do. He drew Ellen into his arms.

"You must not fear so," he whispered into her ear. "He is sick but I think the bad part is done."

They shared the same fear. This evening, Johann had been so feverish he had not recognized Kurt.

At first, she stood straight and stiff in his arms, and then she gave way, leaning into him. "I should have let them take William from me. He wouldn't have become sick, then," she murmured brokenly.

"You don't know that," he replied. "You cannot know that."

"I can't stop remembering losing my baby brother. He could barely breathe." She sobbed against him, not making a sound as she shook in his arms. "He shook like that, too. And then . . ."

"This child will live," he whispered, forcing certainty into his voice.

She shook her head no against his chest. "My baby brother died in my arms."

At these heartbreaking words, he wrapped his arms tightly around her and let her hushed sobs beat against him. He absorbed her anguish as best he could. But Ellen's desperate state ignited his own alarm. He'd survived what had happened in Germany. *He would not see Gunther and Johann taken from him now.*

He realized those words were whistling in the dark, as death hovered at their elbows, always ready to snatch life from them. But he would not give in to this despair, nor would he let Ellen.

He focused on the sweet woman in his arms. Here, in this dark room while all slept, he could comfort her. Had he ever known a woman with a kinder, more caring heart? He buried his face in her soft hair, allowing himself to breathe in her natural scent and a trace of lavender.

Minutes passed. He let himself float, without thought or worry, just holding her close.

Comforting her comforted him. Was that wrong? He knew in his heart it was not.

Finally, she drew a long, shuddering breath and straightened herself. "I'm sorry I gave in like that," she whispered.

He tried to think of words but none came to mind. Then, as if someone else were in control of him, he leaned forward and kissed her forehead. "William will not die."

She tried to smile but failed, her lips quivering with more sobs. She bent and lifted the baby out of the cradle and back into her arms.

Kurt waited there, not sure what to do. He knew he shouldn't have held her like that, but it was done now. And if he was honest with himself, he didn't regret it.

"Do you think I should try some of the willow bark tea?" she asked.

"I do not think a spoonful will hurt," he said. "I'll get it."

He poured out a spoonful of the tepid brew, and then tickled William's chin, waking the child. He trickled the tea into the baby's mouth. When he was done, he gave Ellen a smile and turned to go back to his uncomfortable chair.

"Kurt," she murmured, "thank you."

She said my given name.

Kurt didn't turn, afraid for her to glimpse his reaction. "*Guten nacht*," he murmured and walked softly back to the classroom, trying to ignore the thrill he was feeling at the sound of his name on her lips.

He moved to the pallet where Johann tossed and turned, mumbling in his fevered sleep. With the inside of his wrist, Kurt tested his nephew's forehead. Would the fever never break? Kurt didn't even have the energy to walk back to the desk and sit. Instead, he lay down beside Johann on the bare half-log floor and fell asleep almost instantly, the last thought in his head of Miss Ellen Thurston and how right she had felt in his arms.

Chapter Sixteen

Standing outside the school in the chill morning air, Kurt felt as if he'd aged a decade over the past two weeks. The worst of the measles outbreak had passed. A few children remained at home, still recovering from the illness. But after today's thorough cleaning had been done, the school would no longer serve as a hospital, but return to its true purpose. He hoped people would come to help them get it ready, but it was possible that they might still be afraid to come.

He rubbed his eyes with both hands. After two weeks of little sleep, he wondered if he'd ever feel rested or normal again.

Pale and thinner, Johann came outside and

leaned against him. Kurt patted his bony shoulder. "Tonight, we go home."

"Good. I want to see my kid," Johann said, referring to his beloved pet, a baby goat. "Do you think he missed me?"

"I'm sure he missed you." An image of Johann, delirious and floating in the cold creek, flashed through Kurt's mind. *That night I thought I'd lose you, little one.*

Movement at the edge of the trees snagged Kurt's attention. Gunther appeared in the clearing. Kurt's heart clenched and then expanded. One glance and the young man raced to them. Throwing down a bucket, he wrapped his arms around Johann and lifted him off his feet.

Kurt didn't know how it happened, but soon they were hugging each other as they never had before. Then he realized Gunther was crying hard, wetting Kurt's shirt. He held his brother close. In a way he couldn't understand, Gunther's tears were washing away the fear and cleansing him, too.

Finally, Gunther drew back and lowered Johann to his feet. "I missed you, little guy."

Kurt had expected Gunther to speak in German as they usually did when no one else was near. But he'd spoken in English and with so faint an accent that he'd almost sounded like someone else. For the first time, the knowledge that his baby brother would soon be a man lodged solidly inside Kurt.

"I missed you, too, Gunther," Johann said.

From inside the school, a child called to Johann.

"Be right back," Johann said, leaving them.

The two brothers gazed at each other. "I thought we might lose him," Gunther admitted and then swiped his wrist over his moist eyes.

Kurt couldn't speak. He hadn't thought Gunther would fear what he feared. *He is growing up fast, too fast.*

"I thought I might lose you, too." Gunther looked down then, not meeting Kurt's eyes.

Kurt could think of no reply to this. When trying to keep Johann from succumbing after his cold night swim, he'd given little thought to his own vulnerability to illness.

"We had a rough time in Germany." Gunther leaned back and folded his arms. "But here we have a new chance."

Kurt drank in each of Gunther's words of hope. "Life is getting better," he said. Kurt thought of Miss Thurston, of how deeply he'd allowed her into his mind, his heart.

Gunther stared down at the step. Finally, he just nodded.

As if Kurt had summoned her merely by thinking of her, Miss Thurston stepped outside. "Did you come to help us sanitize the school, Gunther?" Her words were warm and her smile also.

All too well, Kurt recalled the sensation of

holding this lovely lady close. Now, every time he saw her, he had to fight the urge to put his arm around her and draw her near. Not a wise idea.

"Yes, I brought cleaning things," Gunther said, picking up the bucket he'd dropped and rattling the contents.

"Good." Before she could say more, a wagon rocked into sight. The old preacher's daughter-in-law, Lavina, sat beside her younger son, Isaac, who was close to Gunther in age. She waved, announcing, "We brought my laundry tub to boil water for the cleaning!"

And then more wagons jostled into the schoolyard. Kurt was relieved to see that at least some people had turned out to help, after all.

Kurt helped move the benches and all the other furniture in the school and Ellen's quarters outside. Though he kept busy, Ellen would not leave his mind.

I will do the work here and then I will go home and I will not think of her.

An inner voice replied, "Not think of her? Who do you think you are fooling?"

Ellen welcomed those who'd come to help disinfect the school with pure joy. The fact that the town of Pepin had made it through the measles and not lost a soul was surely something to feel good about.

Soon she was sweeping out the schoolroom

while outside others filled the laundry tub to begin heating water. Kurt seemed to be everywhere she looked, helping everyone with everything. She tried to stop herself from noticing him, from responding to the sound of his deep, sure voice. But since the night when he'd comforted her with such tenderness, she seemed to have no control over herself. The man had lodged in her mind. And her heart. She had not a clue what to do about him.

People on their hands and knees began scrubbing the floor and walls with the hot water and lye soap. Marta was polishing the windows with pungent vinegar water and newspaper. The potent mix of odors made Ellen's eyes water. She decided to work outside, away from the fumes and away from Kurt Lang.

There, with a stiff-bristled brush in hand, she scrubbed down the benches. Amanda, recovered now from her own bout with measles, watched the children—including a healthy, happy William —outside in the sun. Ellen noticed that except for Lavina, the Whitmores and her cousins, those working to disinfect the school were those whose children had recovered from measles.

Evidently, much of the population would steer clear of the school building for a time. She couldn't blame them. But it brought her a worry. She wished most of all the Brawleys had come to help today. How had they weathered the measles outbreak? No one had mentioned them yet.

Mrs. Ashford worked nearby. Something about the dejected way the storekeeper's wife moved and sighed again and again put Ellen on alert. Finally. Ellen asked in an undertone, "I think you should sit down for a while. You've helped so much already, bringing food even after Amanda came down with the measles."

Mrs. Ashford's face crumpled. Ellen drew the woman to sit on a more private bench behind her quarters. "What's wrong?"

The woman continued to cry. Finally, with a hiccup, she asked, "Have you seen Amanda's face?"

Ellen stopped to think. "From a distance. What's happened?"

"Her eye, her right eyelid droops," the woman said in a hushed, hopeless tone. "It makes her look squinty."

Ellen considered this. "That's a possible after-effect from measles, I think. Yes, the medical dictionary warned that could happen. The muscles in the eyelid are weakened."

Mrs. Ashford muffled a wail in a handkerchief pressed to her mouth. "It gives her a very off appearance. How will we ever find her a decent husband?"

The words sent anger flaring through Ellen. She called on her self-control, not letting out any of the words rushing through her mind. When she could command herself, she said, "Amanda is intelligent, kind and hardworking. Any man with sense at all would find in her a wonderful wife."

Mrs. Ashford sniffed. "You're sweet to say that, but men always want a pretty wife."

"Some men make that mistake," Ellen said, recalling how much prettier her younger sister was than she. "But others look under the surface. Besides, Amanda always presents herself well. What is a droopy eyelid after all is said and done?"

"Ned says it could have been worse. She could have caught small pox and been dreadfully pockmarked."

Or she could have died.

Ellen patted the woman's arm. "Why don't we leave Amanda's future husband up to God?"

Mrs. Ashford rose with a pronounced sigh. "Of course, you're right. I don't know why I'm being so foolish."

Before the measles outbreak, Ellen knew she would have responded inwardly that this woman *was* foolish. But Mrs. Ashford had worked tirelessly to help Ellen and the other mothers tend their sick children, and Ellen saw her differently now. She patted the woman's back, trying to comfort her. "Let's go back and finish those benches."

As they rounded the corner, Ellen saw that the yard had emptied of workers except for Amanda, who was watching toddlers near the swings. And Gunther.

Gunther leaned forward and tenderly kissed Amanda's right eye.

As she heard Mrs. Ashford's sharp intake of breath, Ellen braced herself, awaiting in dread for the onslaught of scolding. But she waited in vain.

Mrs. Ashford took Ellen's elbow and hurried her back to where they had been.

Ellen obeyed the silent prompt not to let the young couple know they'd been observed, but was confused. Hadn't Mrs. Ashford seen Gunther kiss Amanda's eye? If she had, why hadn't she reacted in her usual manner? Ellen sent her companion a questioning look.

"I didn't want to embarrass my daughter," the woman confided, obviously touched by the tenderness she'd just witnessed. "It seems you were right about Gunther, Miss Thurston. Perhaps he is a fine young man after all."

Astounded by Mrs. Ashford's change of heart, Ellen looked back at the young couple. For a moment, her mind recreated the image she'd just seen. Only this time, she—not Amanda—sat with William in her arms, and Kurt was kissing her, starting a warm current swirling through her.

Red-faced, Ellen quickly turned away from

Mrs. Ashford as if the woman could somehow know what she was thinking.

By the first week of November, Kurt was once again helping work with Marta outside the lady teacher's quarters. Once again they were packing up the Bollinger's possessions for their impending trip to New Glarus. School had resumed now, and the horror of the town's measles epidemic was behind them.

Because all the windows were shut tight against the advancing cold, Kurt could hear Miss Thurston's voice inside the school but he couldn't make out individual words. Still, he couldn't stop himself from listening.

Since the night he'd held her, the feelings he had for her had become harder—much harder—to conceal. He'd been trying to keep his distance from her, but it had done him no good. In some ways, it had probably made the situation worse. Absence did make the heart grow fonder.

Marta carried out the final box and set it into the rear of the wagon. "That is all except for the bedding." The woman sighed and leaned against the lowered tailgate. "Why are you alone?" she asked him suddenly.

Her question startled him. "What?"

"Why aren't you married?"

He couldn't hide how shocked he was. "I have Gunther and Johann to care for."

"You should have brought a wife with you."

The memory of Brigitte's horrified face flew into his mind. His father's act had horrified everyone at home, and with the horror had come repulsion. No one wanted even to look at Kurt or Gunther or Johann. Bitterness choked him, his heart hardening.

"I would never have come here unless my Gus wanted us to. And now he will never see New Glarus." Marta appeared to be fighting tears, her lips quivering. "I don't understand why this has happened. Every step of the way we prayed and now I'm here alone to raise our sons."

Pushing aside his own tragedy, Kurt rested a hand on her shoulder. "You have suffered. But God hasn't forgotten you. Gus died but your son didn't succumb to the measles."

"I know. I don't want to sound ungrateful. I'm just speaking what's in my heart to the only adult here who can understand me."

He comprehended that, too. So many times he had felt left out when people spoke rapidly or when they addressed him as if he were hard of hearing. And he was unable to express himself as clearly, as thoroughly in English as he could in German. Talking to Marta was a relief in that way. But she wasn't the one he really wanted to speak to.

"Why don't you come with us to New Glarus?"

Her question startled him so, he jerked backward. "Leave?"

"Yes, New Glarus is Swiss but we are German-speaking Swiss. You would be with people who understand you and know Europe, not just this lonely, raw land." She cast a glance about her.

"Leave?" he repeated, taken aback.

"Yes, you would be among those who are like us, not these people who think they are better than we."

All the rude words and misconceptions that had been hurled at him over the past months streamed through his mind, sparking a fire in him. He hadn't realized that he'd stored them up.

This woman only spoke the truth. But he didn't know what to say in reply.

"You think about it," she urged him. "I could delay leaving to give you time to gather—"

"No," he said, speaking more sharply than he wanted. "I have worked too hard to leave. Gunther is doing better and Johann has a good school with a good teacher."

Marta shook her head at him. "I see how you look at the schoolteacher. But if you think she will marry you, *a foreigner*—" she said the word in English "—you are deluding yourself."

Kurt's insides twisted with denial and shock. "I am not so unwise." He swung away from her.

Marta caught his arm and stopped him. "I'm sorry. I just don't want you to be . . ."

He turned back, his hot anger dwindling by the second. "I know." He held up a hand as if to make peace. "Gunther and I will come just after breakfast tomorrow to start your journey."

Marta murmured her thanks and released him.

Kurt was glad he'd walked to town. He had more than two miles home to work off his spleen.

The idea Marta had planted resisted his efforts to uproot it. Life would be easier if he went to a German-speaking village.

But my home is here.

And of course, Miss Thurston was here, too. The thought of never again seeing her elegant features or hearing her gentle, cultured voice left him bereft as if a dark veil descended over his heart.

For that reason alone, he should leave with Marta.

In the crisp November dawn, Ellen carried William as she and Kurt walked to town with Marta. It was not lost on Ellen that Marta walked between her and Kurt. Ellen was grateful for the distance, and she also resented the distance. Both reactions irritated her.

Dawn gold still hung in the eastern sky. Behind them, Gunther, with her three boys jabbering excitedly to him in German, was driving Marta's wagon into town. There he would pick up the old trading road along the Mississippi and head south. Marta had preferred to walk into town.

Ellen worried about William and the Brawleys. The husband hadn't wanted William in the first place. And in the days after the outbreak ended, Mrs. Brawley hadn't come for William. Letting the uneasy matter lie, Ellen had accepted Marta's offer to watch him during school hours. But today with Marta leaving, Ellen had to go through town on her way to leave William for the day.

Marta said something in German to Kurt, pausing in front of the store. Ellen only caught "Mrs. Ashford." She looked to Kurt for the translation.

"She would like to thank the Ashfords," he replied to her unspoken question, and then turned toward the store.

But before he could enter, Mrs. Ashford came out, followed by her husband. "I thought you'd be leaving early," the wife said.

Marta hurried forward, speaking in heartfelt German as Kurt translated. "Thank you, Mrs. Ashford, for all you and your husband have done for my family. We were strangers and you fed us. We were sick and you helped us. You are true Christians. Thank you."

Marta curtsied.

Mrs. Ashford blushed at the praise. Her husband replied, "Mr. Lang, you tell Mrs. Bollinger we were happy to help. And that we hope she and her sons will prosper in New Glarus."

Marta shook hands with both Ashfords as

Amanda came around the side of the store and approached Gunther. The lad tied up the reins and climbed down to meet her.

Ellen was watching the Ashfords observe the young couple, wishing each other farewell. Marta came to her and tearfully shook her hand. *"Danke. Danke."*

Ellen drew Marta close and pressed her cheek to hers. The woman had become a friend and now they must part. "God be with you, Marta."

Kurt helped Marta up onto the wagon bench next to Gunther. Her three boys sat at the back of the wagon, looking out over the raised tailgate and waving their farewells.

"You stay safe, Gunther!" Mrs. Ashford called out.

The lad looked shocked, but responded with a polite bow of his head, "Yes, ma'am, I will."

Ellen maintained a straight face. Mrs. Ashford constantly presented yet another facet of human nature. Though Ellen sincerely doubted a drooping eyelid would keep Amanda from marrying, Mrs. Ashford obviously was not going to risk alienating a possible suitor.

In Ellen's arms William fussed a little as if he were aware that friends were leaving. Ellen rocked him close and hummed to him as she stood beside Kurt. Together, they watched the wagon turn and head southward along the trail that followed the Mississippi, that mighty river, all the way south to the delta at New Orleans.

When she could no longer see the wagon, Ellen started walking toward the Brawleys. Kurt fell into step beside her. She didn't understand why Kurt was walking with her, but she was glad of his company. Each step weighed upon her. She hadn't heard anything from the Brawleys since the measles outbreak.

It was difficult for her to admit it, but having Kurt by her side made her cares easier to bear. He was the kind of man who could help solve any problem, any issue. In that way, he was invaluable.

Actually, she was beginning to realize that Kurt Lang was invaluable to her in many ways. The question was, what was she going to do about it?

"You are worried?" Kurt said, unable to keep the words back. After the wagon had disappeared around a bend, he'd also been unable to make himself turn and walk home as he should. This morning, Ellen had some magnetic force he couldn't break free from. Which, to be honest, was no different from any other morning in his recent memory.

"I am worried," she admitted.

"Tell me."

She shook her head. "A waste of words. And most of what we worry about never happens."

He chewed on this idea, appreciating how she did not give in to worry, an unusual trait. Crows, fat with pilfered corn, sat in the bare trees and mocked the two of them. Overhead, geese flew in a long V against the gray sky. Crumpled red and amber leaves and golden pine needles littered the path beneath their feet. Somehow walking beside this special woman heightened his wonder at the beauty all around them and gave him a simple joy.

As they approached the Brawley cabin, Kurt noted that Ellen straightened as if she were bracing for something.

When Mr. Brawley stepped outside the cabin and folded his arms, she didn't seem surprised.

However, Kurt didn't like the man's hostile stance.

"Miss Thurston, I'm sorry but my wife won't be watching your foundling anymore. We can't take the chance of you bringing disease from the school to our house."

Kurt bristled at the man's tone. This was not how he should speak to a lady like Miss Thurston. He took a step forward then halted. Ellen would not want him to make a scene.

Ellen stopped short. "I understand. Give my regards to your wife."

Kurt sent the man a disgruntled look and turned with Miss Thurston, impressed with her aplomb.

When they were out of sight of the cabin, she looked at Kurt. "Unfortunately, my worry proved to be warranted this time. What am I going to do with William during the school days?"

He wanted to say, *I'll keep him.* But of course, he couldn't. He, too, had work to do, and more than usual with Gunther gone for at least a week. "I will take him to Mrs. Steward today. She will watch him."

Ellen let out a long sigh. "Thank you, Kurt. I can always count on you."

She had said his given name again. Delight shimmered over him and then caution rattled a warning. He recalled Marta's words about how Ellen would never choose to be with a *foreigner.* He refused to allow himself to consider what her use of his given name meant, pushing his joy away.

In front of the General Store, they paused.

"I'll walk Johann home after school," she said. "Please tell Ophelia I'll come and pick up William then." She transferred William and his sack of necessaries to Kurt. "Thank you so much."

Kurt nodded and turned with a wave. He strode down the path toward the Stewards', troubled by thoughts he had no right to be thinking. And all because she'd called him by his given name, an act that had much more meaning to him than she could possibly know.

For a brief moment, Kurt allowed himself the pleasure of wondering what it would be like to be able to talk to Miss Thurston exactly as he really wished to, to tell her what he thought of her, not to hold back anything. He wished he could just walk with her in an evening, just the two of them . . . and as more than friends. He thought of brushing her pale cheek with the back of his hand and burying his face once more in her fragrant silken hair. He tamped down the feelings these errant ideas sparked. Oh, Ellen . . .

Chapter Seventeen

Weary, Ellen sat at the table in Ophelia and Martin's cabin, trying to think of someone to replace Mrs. Brawley. She sipped her tepid coffee and rested her elbow on the table, not caring that it was unladylike, as little Nathan crawled around William's basket, chattering baby talk.

Ophelia was washing the supper dishes in a tin tub on the table. Ellen drained her cup and handed it to her. "I really appreciated your watching William today. Are you sure you can care for him tomorrow?" Ellen asked.

"Yes, and I'm going to keep him here tonight," Ophelia insisted, shaking out the damp dish towel. "You need one night of completely uninter-rupted sleep. I see how dragged out you are. And pale."

If you only knew, Ellen thought.

This afternoon, as she was teaching, the realization had dawned on her that she had begun thinking of Mr. Lang as Kurt. She'd even accidentally referred to him as Kurt several times, and wondered if he had noticed. She tried to convince herself that this was merely a sign of their growing friendship but she was too honest to let herself get away with that fib. Kurt Lang had become special to her, very special. And she tried not to make more of this than she should. Memories of Holton had faded. Holton and Kurt were cut from very different cloth, very different men.

Then she heard Kurt's voice outside, greeting Martin, who was finally up and about, and able to tend to his animals.

"I'm glad when Kurt brought William this morning, he offered to drive you back in our cart to save you the long walk home. You look exhausted."

Ellen didn't have the strength to argue with her. Something beside her fatigue was weighing her down. But what? Kurt's handsome face flickered in her mind. She closed her eyes as if this would make the image go away.

"Miss Thurston?" Kurt entered, his hat in hand. "I am ready to drive you home."

His voice sent chills up her arms, a feeling she hadn't ever experienced before, not even with Holton. She rose with a practiced smile in place, spent a moment smoothing William's bedding and whispering good-night and then donned her bonnet and shawl. The evenings became cooler and cooler. Winter would come all too soon, she feared.

Ophelia stepped outside to wave goodbye, shutting the door behind her to keep their cabin warm.

As she took her place on the seat of the cart, Ellen's arms felt empty. For a moment she almost jumped down to run back for William. But she gripped the hard bench under her, hanging on as Kurt started the pony up the rutted, bumpy trail.

For a moment, she had the impulse to lean her tired head on the broad, substantial shoulder just inches away. She sighed at herself. *I'm merely exhausted, not just physically but mentally. That's what this is all about.*

But tonight, because of Ophelia's kind offer, she would be able to sleep and begin to recover from the stress of the past few weeks. Her mind returned to the first time she'd sat beside Kurt on this pony cart. He had driven her home and they'd found William in a wooden box on her doorstep. Could that only be a few months ago?

Neither of them spoke as amber evening turned to black-velvet night. A chilling half-moon lit their way. She snuggled deeper into her wool shawl and felt her chin bobbing. She tried to open her eyes wide but it was too much work.

She sighed, letting the veil of sleep soothe her.

A bump jolted her and she woke with a start and realized she'd fallen asleep on Kurt's broad shoulder. "Oh," she breathed.

"No worry. You were sleepy. It is all right."

She blushed and was grateful for the shadows cast over them from the moonlight. Better to say no more. She straightened herself and faced forward, letting herself enjoy sitting near this man, even enjoying the rocking over the ruts in the rough road as they made her slide closer still. She nearly rested her head on his shoulder again.

And then Kurt turned from the trail to the narrow track into the schoolyard, and Ellen sat up straighter.

Someone had lit a lamp in her quarters.

Kurt jerked up sharply on the reins. He glanced sideways, the shadows hiding his expression from her.

"You are expecting someone?" he asked. When she shook her head, he said, "I will come to the door with you," and started the wagon on its way again.

Ellen didn't demur. With strong hands, he helped her down from the cart and they walked together to the door. She paused there.

Who was waiting for her? Had Randolph come again, bringing bad news from home?

She refused to let fear get a toehold. She turned

the knob and pushed the door open, but pausing, not entering immediately.

Cissy turned to her, the glow from the lamp and low fire lighting her pretty face and strawberry-blond curls.

"Cissy!" Ellen ran forward. She had no other words to say.

"Oh, Nell," her sister wailed and threw herself into Ellen's arms.

Kurt cleared his throat. "I will go now. After school tomorrow, I will bring William when I pick up Johann."

Ellen gently nudged her sister away. "Thank you, Kurt—Mr. Lang." She blushed over the slip of her tongue. She must not call this man by his given name. "Please tell Ophelia that my sister has come for a visit."

"I will. Good night." He bowed himself out and shut the door behind him.

"Who is that?"

Her thoughtlessness pained Ellen. Why hadn't she made a proper introduction? Now Kurt probably felt that she didn't think he was worthy of meeting her sister. "I'll introduce you tomorrow. That's Mr. Kurt Lang. He's a close neighbor to Martin and Ophelia. I ate supper with them and he drove me home." She heard herself babbling, but couldn't stop. Her mind was racing, streaming with questions she couldn't put into words.

But it seemed that Cissy wasn't quite listening. She sat in a straight chair and looked away from Ellen. She was the picture of dejection.

Ellen covered her eyes with her hands and tried to rub away the tiredness. She sank into a rocking chair. After many moments of silence, she said, "I'm happy to see you, Cissy. But you are obviously distressed. Why have you come?"

Cissy buried her face in her hands and began weeping.

The sound buffeted Ellen, as if a straw broom were slapping her, trying to break her thin, protective shell. In her haze of exhaustion, Ellen missed the signs of hysteria until Cissy began to have trouble breathing.

Ellen leaped up and pulled her sister to her feet. "Cissy! Cissy!"

Her sister slumped against her as if she couldn't get her breath. Ellen reached past her to the pitcher of water on the table and managed to fill a dipper half-full. She splashed it into Cissy's face.

Her sister gasped and then collapsed against her, shaking.

Ellen realized two things simultaneously. Her sister had worked herself up to a state beyond reason, and she herself was too tired to do anything about it.

She half-dragged Cissy over to her bed, letting her down gently. Then she removed her sister's shoes and loosened her corset stays and covered her. Ellen dressed for sleep, blew out the lamp and slid in on the other side of the bed.

Her last thoughts were selfish ones. She had felt so happy riding with Kurt. And now this. Why did her sister have to come now? *I can't face another crisis.*

Kurt drove slowly home in the nearly complete darkness. The precious moments alone with Ellen had affected him. When she'd fallen asleep on his shoulder, he'd felt as if it were the most natural thing in the world. But he'd hated to see how upset Ellen seemed upon finding her sister waiting in her quarters. He knew the shock had made her forget to introduce him. Perhaps it was just as well. Would this sister trouble them as that brother had? Her family obviously didn't bring happiness to Ellen. Why couldn't they stay in Illinois where they belonged?

Drowsy morning dawned after a restless night. Ellen lay in bed, not wanting to open her eyes, to wake completely. Cissy was lying beside her like they had at home as girls. However, they were no longer girls.

If she opened her eyes, she'd have to face another crisis, one that most likely involved Holton. Unfortunately, waking to the sensation of phantom bricks stacked upon her chest had become all too familiar. What had happened to cause Cissy to come north, and more important, alone?

Her sister suddenly jolted upright. "Holton, no!"

Ellen sprang upward herself, and caught her sister. "Cissy, you're fine. You're here with me."

Her sister fell back, breathing hard.

Ellen took her hand. "Cissy, what's wrong?"

Her sister rolled away from her. "Everything."

Glancing at the small bedside table, Ellen glimpsed her pendant watch. The dial read 8:37 a.m. Could that be right?

She threw back the covers and leaped out of bed. "I must get up! My students will be here in less than a half hour. You rest more, and I'll make us some tea."

Soon she was dressed and brushing the tangles out of her hair. She'd been too tired to brush and braid it last night. All the while, she watched her sister lying in bed, staring at the fire. She prepared tea and set a cup on the table. "Cissy, come and drink your tea."

"I'm not hungry." Cissy sat up slowly as if she were ninety years or more.

Ellen decided kindness was not working. "I know you're very upset but not eating will help nothing. Get dressed and make yourself some toast." She heard voices outside. "The children are arriving and I must begin my day. We'll see Ophelia later and you'll meet my little William." To soften her words, she went over and kissed her sister's forehead. "And then you can tell me what's happened."

Cissy accepted thc kiss but said nothing.

Ellen crossed to the door and then halted abruptly, what she'd seen catching up with her. When she'd leaned close to her sister, she'd glimpsed a yellowish tinge around her left eye. As if the eye had been bruised.

Memories of an Irish maid who'd been beaten by a boyfriend bubbled up in her mind. She turned and looked back at her sister who had not moved from the bed.

"Cissy, is there anything wrong?" Ellen asked tentatively. "Anything you need to tell me?"

"No," Cissy replied, not turning to look at her.

The reply did not satisfy Ellen, but what could she do now?

And she realized then as much as she wanted to know, she wasn't sure she could handle it. Too much had happened over the past year in her life—grieving her parents, losing Holton, defending William, battling the measles. How much more could she take?

Though she knew she should go back to her sister, the sounds of more children arriving in the schoolyard propelled her forward. *Oh, Lord, what has caused my sister to run to me?*

That evening, Martin, Ophelia, Ellen and Cissy sat around the table in the Steward's cabin, outwardly calm, inwardly tense. The reason for Cissy's unexpected visit had yet to be broached, though Ellen knew she was not the only one who'd noticed the slight bruise on her sister's face.

As usual, Nathan crawled under the table. William, still thin after his bout with measles, lay in Ellen's lap as she sipped her coffee. She patted him and savored the last bite of the sweet yet tart apple brown betty with fresh whipped cream Ophelia had made.

"You're really becoming a good cook," she complimented her cousin, trying to put some life into the anxious mood of the room.

"Yes," Cissy agreed in such a dispirited tone that even Martin noticed.

He rose and kissed Ophelia on the forehead. "Another outstanding meal by my lovely wife. I have to see to the stock for the night." And he escaped the danger of impending feminine emotions.

"All right," Ophelia said, taking this pretty bull by the horns, "what's wrong, Cissy?"

Cissy shook her head.

The time for hesitation ceased in Ellen's opinion. "How did you bruise your eye?"

One sob escaped her sister's mouth. "Holton struck me."

Despite the fact that Ellen had already suspected this in her heart, she gasped so hard she almost choked.

Ophelia leaped to her feet, hurried over to Cissy and put her arm around her. "No. Oh, no."

Ellen found she couldn't move or say a word." It was the last straw," Cissy declared. "As soon as I was sure I could hide it, I packed up and left him."

"Why didn't you go to Randolph's?" Ophelia asked. "It's his place to deal with your husband. A woman's family protects her, if necessary."

Cissy shook her head and sent a searing look toward Ellen.

Ellen's initial shock was wearing off. She recalled how her sister could hold on to a wrong, how hard it was to break its hold over her. "What, Cissy? What happened? What led up to this?" *What aren't you telling us?*

Cissy sprang to her feet. "You dare to ask me that? After what you did?"

Ellen's mouth dropped open and she gaped at her sister. *After what I did?*

Before Ellen could respond, the door opened and Kurt and Martin came in. Ellen found herself wishing she could simply leave with Kurt before she had to hear Cissy's answer to her question. She wanted to sit beside him and draw strength from his presence.

"I can take you ladies home now, Miss Thurston," Kurt offered, his hat in hand.

Gazing at him warmed her, steadied her. "Cissy, this is Mr. Kurt Lang, a good neighbor.

Mr. Lang, this is my sister, Mrs. Holton Rogers."

Kurt bowed his head to Cissy, "Mrs. Rogers."

Cissy merely nodded, lifting her chin with a touch of haughtiness. Ellen knew that Cissy was taking her grudge against Ellen out on Kurt. She wished they were girls again—she'd pinch Cissy.

Martin helped Cissy with her shawl as Ellen wrapped William up in a warm blanket to go home. Ophelia forestalled her, taking William into her arms. "I think I'll keep him one more night. We'll be coming in the morning for the workday at school. You need sleep." And she covertly nodded at Cissy as if to say to Ellen, *Find out what's wrong with her.*

Ellen wanted to object. Watching William sleep had become one of her sweetest pleasures, but she knew Ophelia was right. "Thank you." Ellen kissed her cousin's cheek.

Kurt helped her with her shawl, his strong hands brushing against her. Then he opened the door and she and Cissy walked into the chill early-autumn twilight. She tightened the shawl around her. Kurt paused at the two-wheeled cart. It only sat two on the bench, and the driver had to get on first and balance it.

"I'll ride in the back," Cissy said, giving Ellen an unreadable sidelong glance.

Ellen didn't try to decipher it. She waited while Kurt took his seat and Cissy settled herself in the rear. Then he reached down and pulled Ellen up beside him. The desire to keep her hand in his swept through her. Instead, she moved her grip to the bench. "Hold on, Cissy."

Kurt agreed as he turned the cart and headed toward the sinking sun, its rays filtering through the golden trees and evergreens.

Martin waved and went inside. And envy swept through Ellen. Ophelia had married wisely and now she had a snug cabin, a baby, a busy happy life with a good man.

Were those things within her reach? She'd been so certain when she'd come here of what she wanted, now she wasn't so sure.

As the cart rocked over the bumpy trail, Ellen experienced the strangest sensation. It was as if invisible bands connected her to Kurt, tugging her toward him. She fought against the pull, but soon she found herself sliding closer to his solid, comforting body, inch by inch. Only her most rigorous effort at control prevented her from leaning against him.

The world around her receded till she only perceived the two of them. In the lowering light, she studied his hands gripping the reins, the golden stubble on his chin, the way his hair curled around his ears. She forced her gaze forward, trying and failing to stop looking at him, very aware that her sister sat only inches behind them.

All too soon they reached the schoolhouse and

her door. "Don't get down," Ellen told him. She slid from the bench. "Thank you, Kurt."

Cissy hopped off the back without a word.

"Good night, ladies." He touched the brim of his hat. "I will wait till you are safe inside. Mrs. Rogers, it was very nice to meet you."

Cissy did not acknowledge that Kurt had spoken to her as she made her way to the door. Ellen sighed and gave Kurt an apologetic smile before she hurried after her sister, the chill nipping at her heels.

"Kurt?" Cissy asked archly before Ellen could even close the door, her hands on her hips. "You called that Dutchman Kurt?"

"I believe we have more pressing matters to discuss than Kurt Lang, Cissy," Ellen said, feeling her face redden. "Would you care to tell me what you meant at Ophelia's?"

"I'm tired, Ellen," Cissy replied. She turned her back on her sister and began preparing for bed.

Ellen warmed bricks on the hearth and then with only light from the low fire on the hearth, dressed herself for sleep and slipped into the warmed bed beside Cissy. She would eventually get the whole story from her sister. Cissy was hiding more than being struck, though that was bad enough. Cissy was nursing another wrong in her heart, something her little sister was prone to do, her one character flaw in Ellen's opinion.

But Ellen found that she was having a difficult

time being as sympathetic to her sister's plight as she thought she should have been. Perhaps it was the fact that she'd lashed out at Ellen earlier. But more likely, it was the way she'd treated Kurt, as if he were not worthy of common courtesy.

Ellen couldn't think of a man more worthy of common courtesy than Kurt Lang.

Tomorrow was another day. She would put aside her anger and insist her sister tell her the truth, and get to the bottom of whatever had happened with Holton. Holton had hurt her, but she didn't see him as a man who would hit his wife. But Cissy wouldn't have told them a lie. Regardless, something was not the way it should be between her sister and her husband.

Please, Father, help me to be the sister that Cissy needs.

Chapter Eighteen

On Saturday, the next morning, Ellen sat in the knitting circle on benches inside the schoolroom with her sister. She realized she was biting her lower lip, her sister's moody presence casting a pall over her. Cissy sat to her right, occasionally stitching on a quilt square while Ellen knitted a pair of mittens, her wooden needles clicking.

Everyone in the circle had welcomed Cissy, and

her sister had risen to the occasion and appeared fine to the casual observer. Ellen was not a casual observer, however. And she was dreading hearing the rest of the story from her sister, guessing that her sister held Ellen responsible for some portion in her problem. She found it impossible to relax.

The women of the community had come together to knit, quilt and sew today while the men built the school's woodshed. Outside, the men were enlarging the school clearing by cutting down trees and then chopping the wood to stack and dry. Winter was coming—the brisk wind that buffeted the windows announced that.

Ellen's stomach knitted itself into knots. The news that Holton might have struck Cissy was not the only cause. She knew there was more, and since it was being held back, Ellen was certain it would be worse. Although what could possibly be worse?

"I'm so grateful to everyone for donating yarn and for knitting socks, hats and mittens. My son Isaiah will be so happy," Lavina said, sitting across the circle from Ellen. Her son helped at the Ojibwa reservation in far northern Wisconsin, and they were knitting items to donate to his mission work.

"I thought he'd come home for good by now," Mrs. Ashford said. "He's been up there with those Indians almost a year."

"He is needed at the mission. And he loves it," Lavina said mildly.

Ellen could hear the men's voices outside over the noise of saws, hammers and axes, and she realized she was actually listening for Kurt's voice. This caused her to blush, and she bowed her head over her work so no one would notice.

"So have President and Mrs. Grant been home to Galena, Mrs. Rogers?" Mrs. Ashford asked Cissy.

"No," Cissy said, not looking up from her quilt square. "I believe they are quite busy in Washington."

Mrs. Ashford waited for more of a reply, but none came. Ellen's neck muscles knit themselves tightly together. Her sister seemed to have drifted back into her sullen rudeness. Ellen felt she needed to make some excuse for her, but didn't quite know how.

"What do you think of your sister taking in a foundling?" The archly asked question came from one of the women whom Ellen didn't know well.

Cissy looked at William lying in his cradle at Ellen's feet, exercising his legs and arms and gurgling as toddlers crawled around him playing with blocks and clacking jar rims. "My sister has a tender heart—too tender sometimes."

"Everyone knows how sweet your sister is," Sunny Whitmore agreed.

"Yes, Ellen is *always* thinking of others,"

Cissy replied with an ironic edge to her voice.

Ellen pricked up her ears and gave her sister a sharp look. What on earth was she referring to? As soon as the knitting circle was finished, Ellen intended to get to the bottom of it. She couldn't put it off any longer.

As Kurt entered the schoolhouse behind Martin, he couldn't stop himself from immediately directing his attention to Ellen. To him, she stood out from all the other women. He tried to not let this show. But he couldn't help responding in kind to the welcoming smile she sent him.

"It's lunchtime, isn't it?" Martin asked, taking off his leather gloves as the other men began coming in, clapping their chilled hands together.

The women rose from their handwork and the men began moving the benches into rows and noisily setting up the rectangular folding tables Noah Whitmore and Gordy Osbourne had built. The women set out the food on the table in the teacher's quarters. Soon Noah had blessed the food and the work the community had come together to do, and everyone settled down to good food and to enjoy the gathering.

Kurt found himself sitting beside Ellen, across from the Ashfords. The teacher's sister sat beside Mrs. Ashford, not talking to anyone. He'd gotten the impression she didn't like having an immigrant nearby. However, he wasn't about to leave Ellen's side. He'd realized that Ellen, under her smile, did not look happy and he suspected her sister was the reason.

Just then, the door opened and Gunther walked inside. "Hello! I see I arrived in time for a good meal!"

Amanda leaped up as if to go to him, but instead she remained beside her father, smiling and clasping her hands together.

Kurt was surprised and pleased by the warm welcome Gunther received. People called out, "Welcome home!" A few of the men even rose and slapped him on the back.

Soon, Gunther sat near Kurt with a heaping plate of food, telling everyone about the trip to New Glarus. "Mrs. Bollinger's cousin has a fine farm at New Glarus and he welcomed her," Gunther said between bites. "Of course, everyone was sad about her husband's death, but her cousin will look after her. It was odd to be someplace where everyone was speaking German." He shook his head. "I've gotten used to English."

Amanda smiled at him and he grinned back.

"Amanda," Mrs. Ashford said, "why don't you go to the dessert table and choose something for Gunther? The desserts are nearly picked over."

Amanda looked startled, but moved to obey.

Kurt was also quite surprised by Mrs. Ashford's instruction to Amanda. Then he felt the lightest touch glance his hand under the table. Looking sideways, he caught the briefest smile as it flickered over Ellen's face. The intimacy of this wordless communication nearly withdrew all the air from him. He struggled to appear normal while his heart did somersaults.

"I think I'll go, too," Ellen said, rising. "May I get you something, Mr. Lang?"

"Yes, thank you, Miss Thurston," he replied, sounding much more normal than he actually felt.

When Amanda and Ellen returned with desserts in hand and set them in front of Gunther and Kurt, Ellen's sister got up, her chin lifted defiantly. "Ellen, I have one of my headaches. I'm going to lie down." Then she left, walking stiffly through the crowded room as if she'd been offended somehow, looking neither right nor left.

"I am sorry your sister does not feel good," Kurt said.

"Me, too," Ellen murmured, sounding worried.

"We should remove what's left of the food from your quarters," Mrs. Ashford said, "so we don't disturb her."

Ellen rose and the two of them disappeared through the connecting door. Amanda asked Mr. Ashford's permission to go outside with Gunther to "talk."

Kurt watched in amazement as the man nodded his permission. After the young people left, Mr. Ashford looked at him. "I'll admit, Mr. Lang, that we didn't have a very good opinion of your brother at first. He seemed to have a chip on his shoulder. But he has helped many without being asked. And Amanda tells us he is studying hard and plans to become a citizen when he's able."

"Yes," Kurt said, astonished by both the burst of pride within him and Mr. Ashford's words.

"You're doing a good job with your charges."

Kurt nodded, dry-mouthed. "*Danke.*" In a daze, he got up and went to help the ladies move the food out of the teacher's quarters. When Mrs. Ashford left the room with her hands full, he leaned over to whisper in Ellen's ear. "What has happened with the Ashfords?"

Ellen merely looked him in the eye and raised both eyebrows, giving him a pleased smile.

"So, Ellen," Cissy snapped, reminding him that they were not alone. "You left me behind with Holton and are already interested in someone else. A foreigner, to boot."

Ellen turned to her sister, appearing incredulous.

Kurt mumbled a few quick parting words and hurried outside, shutting the side door behind him. What was going on? Who was Holton? His head spun with questions.

He quickly donned his jacket, went outside and picked up where his work had stopped along with the other men congregating around the finished wood shed. Swinging an ax to make firewood would be easier than trying to figure out what was happening inside between the two sisters.

• • •

Ellen gaped at her sister. "Now? With the whole town in the next room, you decide to tell me what's going on *now?*"

"Yes, now!" Cissy exploded. "Why didn't you tell me the truth about him, Ellen?"

Surprise buzzed up Ellen's spine. "About whom?"

"I'm not a child! Why do you keep treating me like one, Ellen?" Cissy jumped to her feet.

Reeling, Ellen sat down on the stool by the hearth. "I have no idea what you are talking about."

Cissy glared at her. The expression brought back memories of trying times with Cissy as a stubborn little girl and the times when Cissy had behaved like Ophelia's mother, making something small into a crisis. All drama.

Two women came in to retrieve the last of the plates, and the dish tub and towels. One glance at the sisters and they vanished within a minute, shutting the door behind them.

"I'm ready to listen," Ellen said evenly.

Cissy sank to the side of the bed. "Why didn't you tell me about you and Holton?"

Hearing the question out loud—the question she'd avoided even thinking about. Now she was unsure of what to say, of how to handle the situation.

"Why didn't you tell me he was making up to

you before I came home from school?" Cissy stamped her foot, angry again.

Finally, Ellen came to herself. Now, when she recalled her brief interest in Holton, she didn't feel the same hurt she'd felt before. Why was that? Could it be, perhaps, that her feelings for Kurt had shown her what she had really been looking for when she'd allowed Holton to become part of her days? She nearly blushed, just thinking of what it would be like to have Kurt call upon her and treat her as someone special.

"Holton did take me out walking and escorted me to a few functions before you came home last summer." Ellen didn't add anything about his flattery and marked attention and the way he'd kissed her hand at each farewell.

"Why didn't you tell me?" Cissy demanded.

"I . . . I . . ." How could she say the truth?

"Because I'm your little sister and you didn't want to hurt me?" Cissy asked with withering disdain.

Ellen gave her sister an apologetic shrug. "Because I love you and you were so taken with him and happy."

"Oh, Ellen," Cissy said, the starch going out of her. "Was that really a kindness? How could you let me fall in love with a man you thought untrustworthy?"

Cissy's words struck Ellen like lightning. "I never thought that. I just thought that like most men, he wanted you because you . . . because he preferred you. I didn't think him untrustworthy . . . not as far as you were concerned."

Men always want a pretty wife, Mrs. Ashford's voice echoed in her mind, recoiling from them.

"I wrote you about the gossip after you left," Cissy continued. "I didn't believe it at first, but then Alice told me it was true and that you left because you couldn't bear to live in town with me and Holton together. Then Ophelia's mother had to come and enact one of her scenes in my parlor about how I'd stolen Holton from my own sister." Cissy's tone had become dramatic as if mimicking Aunt Prudence.

"Oh, dear," Ellen said with real sympathy, neglecting to mention that Cissy's recent behavior had put her in mind of Aunt Prudence.

The two sisters sat, mute. Ellen didn't know what to say. *What was I thinking?* And why had Holton struck Cissy? He'd never seemed that kind of man. *Did I unwittingly cause my sister to marry an unworthy man?* The possibility devastated her.

"Cissy, I need to know how you got that bruise. How did it happen?" Ellen insisted.

"I told you. Holton struck me." Cissy's tone was pouty and she turned away.

Ellen wanted to press the issue but knew this could only stir her sister to more melodrama. And most of the town was still so near them. *The truth will out,* she told herself, *in time.*

• • •

There was only one person Ellen wanted to go to—Kurt. She realized he couldn't change anything. He didn't even know about Holton and her and Cissy. Still, at the end of the day, Kurt had lingered after everyone else had left. Was he hoping to speak with her?

Wrapping her shawl close around her, Ellen stepped outside, leaving Cissy to mope alone. At the far side of the clearing, Johann was gathering woodchips into a sack for kindling. Kurt was working on the new woodshed, testing the swing of the double doors. She approached him. "Kurt?"

He turned, startled. "Ellen."

Every fiber of her being drew her closer and before she could talk herself out of it, she was resting her head against his chest. Oh, the comfort of being near him.

After a moment's pause, his arms closed around her. "You are upset, *ja*?"

"*Ja*," she whispered.

"Your sister has troubles?"

She nodded against him.

He patted her back and murmured, "*Liebschen*."

She didn't know what the word meant, but it sounded nice. "I don't know what to do."

"You are wise. You will sort it out."

She shook her head against him, again feeling the thick flannel of his shirt rub against her cheek. She had thought when she'd kept quiet over

263

Holton's sudden interest in Cissy that she had acted in Cissy's best interest.

Now she might have let her sister be swept into a possibly disastrous marriage. She felt this guilt pulling at her.

Was that true? She wanted to lie down on the cold ground and weep until she ceased to think. "Kurt, sometimes I just want to pack up William, get on a riverboat and run away." Even as she said the words, she knew they weren't entirely true.

She didn't want to leave this man.

Unable to lie to herself any longer, she pulled away from him and looked into his eyes. *I have feelings for this man, deep feelings.*

The thought stunned her.

"I know how that feels, but we both ran away already. Didn't we?" Kurt asked gently.

Over Kurt's shoulder, she glimpsed a familiar figure entering the clearing. Ellen wanted to pick up her skirts and run. "Evidently, I didn't move far enough," she said with an ironic twist.

"What?" Kurt turned.

Ellen's brother was striding toward them.

Instant irritation swept away Ellen's low mood. Did the whole family have to troop to her door?

Randolph strode toward them. "Ellen! Is Cissy with you?"

Ellen recognized that tone of voice. It was

Randolph's "I'm the big brother; I know best" tone. "Yes, Cissy arrived yesterday."

"Where is she?"

"In my quarters." She motioned toward the door behind her.

Randolph paused to kiss her forehead. He turned to Kurt and raised an eyebrow. "You're that Dutchman who lives near Ophelia?"

"My name is Kurt Lang, Mr. Thurston," Kurt replied formally. Neither man extended his hand in greeting.

Randolph looked back and forth between Ellen and Kurt, his silent questioning what Kurt was doing alone with his sister plain.

Ellen forced a smile. "Cissy's inside. Please go in quietly. William is napping."

Randolph lingered another few moments, eyeing Kurt, and then her brother marched to the door and went inside.

"*You* may have moved far enough from home," she muttered to Kurt, "but I am still just a few days away by boat." She sighed. "Thank you . . ." What could she say—*thank you for comforting me, for understanding . . . for holding me?*

"You do not owe me any thanks," Kurt said to her gently. Then he called to Johann, who started to run to him.

Ellen knew she should move away, but she couldn't.

Johann reached them and held open the bulging

cloth sack. "See all the kindling I picked up?"

She smiled and complimented him on his hard work.

After a pause, Johann looked back and forth between them, evidently sensing something.

Finally, Kurt smiled and said, "Good day, Miss Thurston." He pulled at the brim of his hat, and he and Johann walked away.

Ellen waited till they had disappeared around a bend. She'd hoped he would turn for one last look her way, but he didn't. She stood there, feeling again his strong arms around her, wishing she hadn't been forced from his embrace.

"Ellen?" Cissy called from the doorway. "Aren't you coming in?"

Ellen stifled her desire to make a run for it and turned back toward her door. "Yes, Cissy, I'm coming."

Hoping to soothe everyone's nerves, Ellen made a pot of coffee and set out cake that had been left for her while Randolph paced and Cissy sat gloomily on the side of the bed. William woke and Ellen changed his diaper and prepared him a bottle. Then she sat in the rocking chair with him.

A log crumbled on the hearth, bringing Ellen back to waiting for Randolph to come to the point. Perhaps she would now finally understand what had happened to Cissy.

Randolph poured himself a cup of coffee and cut a thick slice of the brown sugar cake. He sat down and ate hungrily. "The food on the boat was atrocious."

"Did you come alone, Randolph?" Cissy asked.

Ellen sincerely hoped so.

"Yes. Alice is expecting and Holton couldn't leave the bank. I told everyone that Ellen had invited us to visit before winter set in and the river froze." Randolph looked directly at Cissy. "What were you thinking, running away like this? Do you want to plunge our family into scandal?"

Cissy stood with fury on her face. "Did you know that Holton made up to Ellen before I came home?"

"The whole of Galena knew, Cissy," Randolph said, taking another bite of cake and washing it down with coffee. "No one was surprised that he changed his mind. You're prettier than Ellen and younger."

Ellen gasped.

"No offense, Ellen, but it's the truth, so why deny it?" Randolph continued chewing in between words.

Ellen steamed in silence.

"Then why didn't anybody tell me?" Cissy demanded.

"No one wanted to hurt your feelings," Randolph said. "Why are you making such a fuss? After my last visit here, I insisted Alice stop fueling that bit of gossip. Now you've managed to stir everything up again."

Ellen decided it was time to get to the gist of the matter and leave her part out of this. "Randolph, Cissy says Holton struck her. Are you aware of that?"

Randolph's cup hung in midair. "What? You can't be serious. No man of consideration hits his wife."

"Cissy's eye was still faintly bruised when she arrived," Ellen said.

"Is this true, Cissy?" Randolph demanded, his jaw jutting forward.

Cissy burst into tears.

"The truth, Cissy," Randolph insisted.

It wasn't until Randolph addressed their sister so sternly that it occurred to Ellen that Cissy might be lying. She began to feel angry before her sister even answered.

"Oh, very well. Holton and I were arguing. I tried to push past him. He stopped me and I stumbled and bumped my head against the molding."

So Holton hadn't struck Cissy. It had been just an accident.

"Cissy, how could you—" Then she stopped before her anger got the better of her. "Why would you mislead me about something as serious as that?"

"Cissy, you *married* Holton," Randolph said. "He isn't perfect. No one is," Randolph admitted. "If Holton ever does intentionally harm you, you are to come to me immediately and I will deal with him. But I fail to see why you've made a big fuss and started people talking again for nothing."

"It wasn't nice to find out from Alice that the gossip about Holton and Ellen was true," Cissy said resentfully.

"That's why you're acting this way?" Ellen asked.

"Alice told you that, did she?" Randolph looked displeased. "We'll deal with that when we return home."

Ellen gazed down at her child, wishing her siblings could return home immediately. Her life was here now, not with them. She wished them well but she did not care about gossip in Galena. She busied herself burping William.

At that moment, Randolph turned to Ellen. "As for you, Ellen, I think you're getting too thick with that Dutchman." Before Ellen could reply, he went on, "Cissy, I will accompany you home tomorrow. Another boat is expected to dock after breakfast. River traffic is humming before the Mississippi freezes. I will go to the General Store now. They offered to put me up again for the night." He kissed them both on the forehead. "I'll see you in town no later than eight o'clock in the morning." With that, he left.

Ellen went to the door and latched it firmly. She turned and faced her sister. "Celeste—I think it's time you started using your full given name—you are a married woman and yes, Holton squired me around town before you came home. But he chose you over me." Ellen was startled to realize that saying this aloud no longer held any pain for her. "Now you must be a wife to him, and not go around telling horrible lies about the way he treats you. After all, you chose him, as well."

And I choose Kurt.

The thought almost literally rocked Ellen back on her heels.

"Ellen, are you all right?" Cissy asked.

"I'm fine," Ellen said, sitting down slowly, suddenly imagining the family she and Kurt could make, with William, and Johann and Gunther. Her heart shivered with the thought.

I choose Kurt Lang. I'm in love with him, and I want to marry him.

Was there any chance he felt the same way?

Chapter Nineteen

Just after dawn, Kurt was in the barn milking the cows when he heard a man's voice call out, "Hello! Is this the Lang place?"

Kurt got up and looked out his partially open barn door. He was not surprised to see Ellen's brother in the clearing, looking around. After the disgruntled expression the man had turned on him yesterday, he figured this conversation was coming sooner or later.

He sighed and walked to the open door. "What can I do for you?"

The man marched over to him. "I'm Randolph Thurston, Miss Thurston's brother."

"*Ja*, I remember." The cow bellowed behind Kurt. "I am milking. You can come in." Kurt turned and went back to his stool, leaving the man no choice.

Randolph followed him inside. Kurt continued his work, not interested in making this conversation easy for Ellen's brother. "I have little time so I'll come right to the point."

"That will be best for both of us." The streams of milk hit the metal pail loudly, rhythmically.

"Every time I come to town, I find my sister Ellen in your company," Randolph said in a stiff, constricted tone.

"It is small town. People help each other when they can."

"The Ashfords say that you and she have people talking."

Kurt lost patience and rose. "What have you come to say?"

Ellen's brother glared but stood his ground. "Do I have to spell it out?"

Kurt leaned toward Randolph. "*Ja*, I'm just a stupid Dutchman. Spell it out."

"My sister's educated and has been raised to a higher standard—"

"Your sister is a fine woman—educated, kind and good. And I am not courting her." Kurt wanted to slam his fist into the man's face. He restrained himself. "That is your concern, yes?"

Randolph looked as if he were chewing cud like the cows.

"I am busy working. Do you need to say anything more?" Kurt asked.

"No. I just wanted to clear the air." Randolph turned and left with no further words.

Kurt clenched and unclenched his hands and then shook them out so he could continue his chore. He couldn't take his anger out on the cows.

He spent a moment gazing around the snug barn where his plow horse, two black-and-white Holstein cows and two brown goats would winter. When he'd come here, he'd lived in a tent. Now he had a good-size cabin, a barn, a full corn crib and root cellar. If Randolph Thurston had come to an empty piece of land this spring, would he have accomplished as much?

The cow lowed as if scolding him to get on with it. Kurt sat back down on the stool and began again, milking.

I am not courting Ellen. But I would like to.

There was no point in denying the truth. The memory of Ellen leaning against him last night rolled through him. *Ellen, dear Ellen.* But while the Ashfords had begun to view Gunther as acceptable, Randolph had made it clear that Kurt was not.

And although Kurt didn't care what Randolph Thurston thought one way or the other, he would never, ever want to make trouble for Ellen. That was exactly what he'd been trying to avoid since the very first moment he had found he liked her.

Sitting at the Ashford table after breakfast, Ellen let Amanda take William from her. An unusual lassitude gripped Ellen today. Breathing and speaking seemed to take great energy. In fact, it had since her revelation about Kurt Lang and her feelings for him.

"We'd best be getting ready for worship," Mrs. Ashford said.

Ellen nodded and leaned her head in her hand.

"You seem down, Ellen. Are you missing your sister and brother already?"

Ellen recalled the stiff farewells she'd exchanged with her siblings at the dock earlier, and shook her head.

"It's a shame they had to leave when Thanksgiving is just next week," Mrs. Ashford continued. "I'd invite you to eat with us but you'll probably be joining your cousin and her family, won't you?"

Ellen barely nodded.

"What *is* the matter?" The storekeeper's wife leaned across the table and touched Ellen's hand.

"I'm sorry," Ellen said, trying to come up with an explanation for her behavior that she could offer Mrs. Ashford. "I was actually trying to think of someone who could watch William during the schooldays. I need someone close, especially for the coming winter."

Mrs. Ashford looked thoughtful. "Maybe it's time Amanda quit school and started putting money away and filling her hope chest in earnest."

Dismay filled Ellen, galvanizing her. "Oh, no, she's the captain of one of the spelling teams. And she's doing so well. I'd hate for her to miss the spelling bee in the spring."

This halted Mrs. Ashford's counterargument. Evidently this woman wanted to see her daughter at the regional spelling bee—as did most parents. Spelling had become one of her students' favorite and most studied subjects.

"And you wouldn't want her to miss eighth-grade graduation," Ellen said, improvising. "I'm going to ask my uncle to come from Illinois to address our graduates."

"Your uncle who sits in the state legislature?" Mrs. Ashford asked with excitement in her voice.

Ellen nodded. "I plan on writing him soon."

"Oh, that would be wonderful!"

Ellen breathed a sigh of relief. It seemed

Amanda would be allowed to finish the eighth grade after all.

Suddenly Mrs. Ashford sat back as if startled. "Why don't I care for William during the day?"

"Oh, Mrs. Ashford, do you have the time?" This possibility hadn't occurred to Ellen.

"Why not? I've raised ten children. They've all married and scattered. Our son went all the way to California, so I am left with no grandchildren near. And your William is a good baby. He never fusses. Why, he'd be company for me during the long winter days."

Ellen gazed at the woman who had once called William disfigured. However, after watching Mrs. Ashford during the measles outbreak, Ellen had no hesitation. "I can't think of anyone who would take better care of him. I will pay you, just as I've paid you to take my dinners here." She let out a huge sigh. "Oh, thank you. That relieves me of such a worry."

As she discussed terms with Mrs. Ashford, Mr. Ashford came back from outside chores, rubbing his chilled hands together. "Time we were setting off to the school for worship. It's nearly ten o'clock."

The ladies quickly donned shawls and hats, and Ellen claimed William and they walked together through the barren trees to the schoolhouse. As they arrived, Old Saul was being helped down from his wagon. Smiling, he waved to her as he leaned on his son's arm. At his welcome, a feeling of gratitude suffused Ellen.

This had become her town. She was very aware that the school had become the center of the community, bringing people together, helping them help each other. She realized that she was important to this town, as the schoolmarm, the woman who would prepare the children for their future, for the town's future.

Since the measles outbreak, the town had been a bit divided and nervous, with some people even expressing concern again about Ellen raising William, a baby who seemed to appear out of thin air and could have come from anywhere. It was simply fear, that's all it was. Perhaps holiday cheer would bring the community back together again.

Then Ellen realized that, as the schoolteacher, she was in the perfect position to help the community reunite. And she had an idea.

She hurried through the gathering to Noah Whitmore and motioned to him that she wanted a private word. She murmured her idea to him and he instantly agreed. As she joined her family in their usual "pew," she glanced over her shoulder and noted Kurt, Gunther and Johann taking the bench in the rear that they seemed to favor. She waited to try to catch Kurt's attention, but he seemed very focused on the floor.

Ellen listened carefully to Noah's sermon on

loving one's neighbor as one's self, a theme that her idea dovetailed with quite nicely. At the end of the sermon, he paused before the final prayer. "Miss Thurston spoke to me before service today. She asked me to announce that this Wednesday, the day before Thanksgiving, the children will put on a brief program to commemorate the First Thanksgiving. Everyone is invited at two o'clock in the afternoon."

A buzz greeted this announcement—a happy buzz to Ellen's ear. She was already drawing up the program in her mind, which would emphasize gratitude to God and their common heritage as Americans.

And perhaps she'd remind people that pilgrims had been foreigners, too. She hoped she'd have a moment to talk to Kurt.

The hum of happy voices lifted Ellen's burden. A few mothers stopped her on their way out to tell her about the fun they were having learning the weekly spelling lists with their children. As she spoke with them, she could pick out Kurt's voice amid the many voices behind her. She soon realized she'd actually been seeking it.

"I did see him, yes," Kurt was saying to Martin.

"I tried to head him off," Martin said, sounding apologetic, "but he wouldn't take my word for it. He has this idea that you and his sister are . . ." Martin shrugged in an embarrassed way.

"Do not worry, Martin. He didn't say anything I

didn't know already." Kurt turned then and suddenly she and Kurt were facing each other. A new awareness of him shimmered over her.

The ladies bid her good-day and she stepped toward him, but he turned and headed for the door.

What had Martin been talking about with Kurt? A sense of urgency pushed her to follow him outside. "Kurt," she said, "Wait."

He didn't pause.

Then she did something she had never done— she pursued a man. She hurried after him into the nearly empty clearing. Very few people had come outside, as most wanted to finish their social time in the warm schoolroom.

Kurt finally halted by his wagon.

"Why didn't you stop?" she asked, holding her shawl tightly around her.

Kurt looked irritated. "You will catch cold—"

"Randolph visited you this morning and was rude to you, wasn't he?"

Kurt looked her in the eye. "It doesn't matter, Miss Thurston."

She could tell that whatever her brother had said had hurt Kurt, and she fumed. "I wish my family would learn to mind its own business."

Kurt said nothing, but Ellen could see the pain on his face and it nearly broke her heart.

"If you saw whom my brother married, you would see how silly it is for him to object to . . ." Suddenly she realized where her tongue was taking her, and she halted, swallowing words that should not now or perhaps ever be spoken aloud.

"Miss Thurston," Johann said, appearing at her elbow, "what kind of program will we be having? And what is Thanksgiving about?"

She drew her gaze from Kurt to the child. "I will tell you all about it in the morning."

"Let us go, Johann," Kurt said abruptly. "Say farewell to Miss Thurston. You will see her tomorrow."

Ellen watched as Kurt led his nephew away. It was not lost on her that he had not said farewell to her himself, nor was it lost on her that she had almost said, *If you saw whom my brother married, you would see how silly it is for him to object to my wanting to marry you.*

Shock tingled through all her nerves. She had almost told Kurt Lang that she wanted to marry him! But based on the interaction they'd just had, she got the impression that her brother had upset what had been growing between her and Kurt. She didn't know whether to do or say something. What could she say?

On Wednesday afternoon, Ellen stood at the front of the packed schoolroom, hopeful that this program would bring back the community's spirit of unity. The women and smaller children filled the benches while the men lined the walls. The standing-room-only attendance pleased her.

Nonetheless, she glanced again at the door, wanting to see one particular face.

Mrs. Ashford sat in the front row, holding William and doting on him. Every parent and most everyone else in town had come to see the program. Except for Kurt. Why hadn't he come to see Johann recite his piece?

From what she'd overheard between Martin and Kurt on Sunday, her brother must have asked Kurt to keep his distance from her. Would Kurt have agreed to such a request, such interference? Yet as a man of honor, he would never do anything that he thought might harm her reputation and Randolph might well have suggested this. The very thought of Randolph's interfering in her life made her want to growl. He had no room to be giving her advice.

Rising above her irritation, she forced herself to focus on the task at hand, and at her signal, Noah Whitmore stood at the front. "We will open with prayer."

Ellen listened to Noah's calm voice, his words setting the tone with a message of love and community. The tightness around her lungs loosened a notch. But she couldn't ignore her disappointment at Kurt's absence.

Then Noah was sitting down and she walked to center stage. "Welcome to the First Annual Thanksgiving Program at Pepin Community School."

Polite applause and some whistling followed her greeting.

"The students have worked very hard and I am proud of their efforts," Ellen said.

The back door opened and Ellen saw Kurt and Gunther slip inside and edge in beside the men who were leaning against the back wall. Joy surged through her, followed by trepidation. She cleared her throat. "We will begin by singing, 'We Gather Together.' "

The children filed out from her quarters and formed ranks, the oldest in the rear and the youngest in front. A few of the children forgot themselves and waved to their families.

Lavina came forward and led the hymn. Soon the schoolroom was filled with the heartfelt song, full of thanks for the bounty of the harvest, and praise for the Lord.

When the hymn ended, a pleasant sense of expectation expanded around Ellen.

The younger children sat down on the floor in a semicircle at the front, and Amanda stepped forward and began to read.

" 'One hundred and two pilgrims left Plymouth, England, in 1620 and sailed to the new world.' " As she read, three fourth graders donned paper hats in the style of the seventeenth century. " 'They settled near Cape Cod. There they met Squanto, an Indian of the Wampanoag or Massasoit tribe.' "

A fifth-grade boy with feathers in a band around his head walked over to the fourth graders and raised his hand in greeting. " 'Squanto had been kidnapped as a young boy by a sea captain and taken to Europe. He could speak English. He taught the pilgrims how to grow maize, beans and squash.' "

As the program continued, the door at the rear opened and a woman—a stranger—stepped in, scanning the room as if searching for someone. Ellen wondered who she was.

Amanda handed the book to another eighth grader who began reading, but the boy's voice trailed off as heads turned to watch the stranger. The woman was walking slowly up the center aisle, rudely studying the people in each row. People glared at her for disturbing the program. Ellen prompted the lad to start reading again.

"There he is!" the strange woman exclaimed and ran to Mrs. Ashford. The woman snatched William from Mrs. Ashford's arms, igniting an instant uproar. Ellen leaped forward and tried to wrest William from the woman's arms. "Take your hands off my son!"

With angry voices, people surged to their feet and converged on the woman and Ellen.

Kurt reached her first and wrenched William from the stranger. "What do you think you are doing?" he demanded. "This child belongs to Miss Thurston!"

The woman burst into loud tears. There was something false about her—Ellen did not think for a moment the weeping was real. "Who are you?" she demanded.

"I am the poor woman who was forced to leave my baby on your doorstep," the woman wailed.

Everyone quieted, watchful.

"Forced?" Noah pushed to the front. "Who forced you to abandon your child?"

The woman buried her face in a handkerchief and wept louder, as if she couldn't bear to tell her tale.

Ellen examined the woman from head to toe. She looked to be a few years older than Ellen, dressed in worn and not too clean clothing. A torn cuff caught Ellen's eye.

"Fate has been cruel to me," the woman said. "I'm a poor widow who lost her husband before my child was born. And then he was born disfigured so." She wept copiously.

Ellen gritted her teeth, holding back her words, letting the woman tell her story. She tried to remain calm, for nothing so far had registered in her mind to give any credence to the woman's claim.

"I found a man who would marry me, but I didn't think he'd want my baby, too, so I left him here."

More wailing and tears followed.

Ellen reached the end of her short rope.

Seething, she scanned the faces crowding around. Did they believe this woman?

Those who hadn't wanted this *disfigured* foundling in their town in the first place were nodding as if they did believe her. Ellen held her tongue, knowing anything she would say would be discounted.

But how could she put a stop to this?

"So," Noah Whitmore said, "you say that your husband died before your child was born, and since you wanted to find a new husband right away—before a proper year of mourning—you abandoned your child on Miss Thurston's doorstep?"

Ellen took heart. When the pastor put the situation in plain terms without all the weeping and histrionics, anybody could see that the story proved to be as thin as broth and did the woman no credit.

But the woman nodded, silently agreeing to these dreadful facts, her face still buried in her handkerchief.

"Do you have any proof?" Noah asked.

"Proof?" the woman replied with surprise, looking up. "What proof could I give?"

"*Ja*, a very good question," Kurt spoke at last.

"You don't sound like an American," the woman snapped. "What do you know about anything?"

Ellen swallowed a sharp retort, trusting Noah

to handle this. Kurt merely gazed at the woman, holding William securely in his arms.

"Before we could give you this child, we'd have to have something more to go on," Noah pronounced. "We know that Miss Thurston is giving the child good care, but we don't know you."

"Well!" the woman declared. "You can't prove that I'm not the baby's mother."

"Ma'am," Noah said, "the burden of proof lies with you. Bring someone or something to back you up and—"

The woman sent a scathing glance at Kurt and Ellen and then pushed through the crowd. When she reached the door, she turned dramatically and called, "I'll be back! You haven't heard the last of me. That's my child and I won't be denied!" With that, she swept out and slammed the door behind her.

"She didn't even say what her name was," Mrs. Ashford said in the quiet after the storm.

"Nor did she tell us where she's from, for instance, and how she got here to leave William in the first place . . . if she did," Noah added.

"The dustup about the foundling with a birthmark left on the Pepin schoolteacher's doorstep has become common knowledge up and down the river," Mrs. Ashford said. "People would come in and ask Ned and me whether it was true or not."

Old Saul cleared his throat. "Noah, I have

grave doubts about this woman's story—grave doubts. But time will tell. I will pray for clarity in this. I hope everyone will. Not every person is to be trusted."

Ellen heartily agreed with this but decided it best not to say anything. The truth will out, Shakespeare had said, and Ellen did not doubt him.

"Everyone," Ellen said finally in her best teacher voice, "the children haven't finished their program. Please be seated so all their hard work won't go for naught."

The crowd returned to their places, but the good feeling of the community coming together to give thanks had been spoiled, broken. At the end the children all bowed together and everyone applauded, but the zest had left the room.

Afterward, people milled around in groups, talking in low tones about the woman, not beaming and bragging over the children's program as Ellen had hoped. She roiled with frustration. Her plan to bring the community together again had been demolished by a woman she didn't believe for a moment.

The only bright spot came when she remembered that Kurt had wrested William from the woman and had defended her. But the way he would not look at her before he departed left her feeling even worse. Was this because of her brother's meddling?

Chapter Twenty

Wearing her best day dress of figured amber silk in honor of Thanksgiving at Martin and Ophelia's, Ellen wished she could get into the holiday spirit. She sat at the Steward's table watching Nathan and William, unable to tear her thoughts from yesterday's unexpected interruption at the school play.

The one person she wanted to talk to was Kurt. Also invited for the holiday, he and the boys were due to arrive at any moment. However, yesterday after the school program, he had made it clear that he did not want to speak to her. In some ways, she understood—it would have fueled the gossip about them even more.

Her only hope was that Kurt would drive her home from the Stewards'. Perhaps then, when they were alone, she'd have an opportunity to talk to him about William, and also find out what was bothering him.

Ophelia glanced at a list she had on the mantel and checked one more item off with her pencil. "Everything is done." She exhaled with satisfaction and untied her spattered apron.

Ellen smiled, but only with her lips; her heart remained weighed down. Would she be forced to take William away from here in order to keep him? Would she have to leave this place that had become home? Would she have to leave Kurt?

A knock sounded. Martin called out, "Come in!"

Kurt, Gunther and Johann entered, letting in the late November cold. The next few moments were taken up with exchanging greetings and hanging up coats and scarves. Ellen made a point to send Kurt a special smile. He merely nodded and then looked away.

Her spirits plummeted lower.

"It's getting cold. Maybe we get snow soon," red-cheeked Johann announced happily and then made a beeline to William, who was napping in his cradle.

Soon the seven of them sat around a table laden with bowls, one each of potatoes with a pool of melted butter, corn, dressing and a basket of yeast rolls. And a platter of wild turkey, Kurt's contribution to the feast.

Though the meal was wonderful, Ellen's appetite eluded her. She tried to keep all her anxiety inside. Tried but failed.

"Ellen, I know you're worried about William," Ophelia said finally.

Ellen felt ashamed for casting a shadow over the holiday meal Ophelia had worked so hard to prepare. "I'm so sorry."

"Nothing to be sorry about," Martin said. "If

that woman is William's mother, I'll eat my hat—and Kurt's, too."

"Why would she say he's her son if it isn't true?" Gunther asked, his face twisted with puzzlement.

Ellen had tried to come up with reasons but couldn't. She also tried to gauge Kurt's reaction but his expression had become shuttered as if he'd put up a wall between them. Why? And why did she feel empty, frail because of it?

"I don't know why that woman would claim William was hers," Martin said. "But it's just too fishy. Her husband dies and she immediately starts looking for another one? What kind of wife does that?"

"A wife who's left destitute," Ellen said. "Sometimes women don't have a choice."

They all looked to Ellen in surprise.

"But give up her own blood?" Gunther interposed. "That's not right."

Ellen listened to the arguments, all of which had already streamed through her mind over and over. Still, Kurt was silent.

"What will you do, Ellen?" Ophelia asked.

Ellen paused for a moment, and then said, "Maybe I should just go home to Galena. I have family and friends there who will support me," she said.

Kurt swallowed a sound of surprise.

At this, silence fell. Martin and Ophelia stepped

into the breach and began talking about their plans for a quick visit home before the Mississippi froze. "We haven't been home since we came north," Ophelia said. "Mother wants to see her first grandchild again."

"When do you leave?" Ellen asked.

"Tomorrow morning," Martin said.

This news surprised Ellen. "So soon? You didn't say anything."

"Mr. Ashford told us the river captains expect the icing over within the next month," Martin said. "It might come sooner, and we don't want to get stuck in Galena. A trip home by land in the cold isn't what I want for my wife and child."

Ellen got his point. Travel over land in the cold could endanger little Nathan. And with the threat of the imminent freezing of the Mississippi, the visit would be a short one, which they preferred.

"I will take care of your stock," Kurt offered.

"Thanks. I was hoping you would," Martin said, sounding distinctly relieved.

"Then we'll leave you the leftovers," Ophelia said. "I don't want the food to go to waste."

"I think I should come and stay here," Gunther suggested. "An empty cabin is not good."

"You're right," Martin said, giving Gunther a friendly slap on the shoulder. "We would be better off with someone staying here. Not just in case of a thief, but with all the hibernating animals foraging, a bear might break in easily and rip everything apart."

Kurt nodded, looking grateful. "You are thinking, Gunther."

Recognizing Kurt's pride in his brother, Ellen felt a pang. She missed talking to him about Gunther, about Johann. *I'll feel better after we talk on the way home.* Her ragged spirit yearned to be near him and she looked forward to sitting beside him on the journey home. She could bring up Randolph and somehow take the sting from his words. Or she could try.

But it did not turn out the way she'd hoped.

When the meal was finished and the dishes begun, the men went out to get wood. When they came back in, letting in a cold draft, Martin shed his coat and gloves but Kurt kept his on.

"Mrs. Steward, thank you for the wonderful meal. I must go home now. One of my cows is not well and I want to keep close watch on her."

His announcement hit Ellen right between her eyes.

Obviously startled, Gunther looked up from washing the large roasting pan.

"Yes, of course," Martin said, looking back and forth between Kurt and Ellen, and making it obvious that he, too, had expected Kurt to drive her home.

A few awkward moments passed. Ellen endured them, feeling discarded.

"I'll drive Miss Thurston home," Gunther offered, drying the last pan and setting it upside down on the table. "Johann can ride along with William in the rear. He'll enjoy it."

Kurt bid everyone goodbye without any special word or even a glance toward Ellen, and then shut the door hard behind him.

Soon, in the darkening afternoon, Ellen and William were bundled up for their chilly ride home. Johann carried the baby and Gunther got up on the cart bench first.

Martin and Ophelia walked Ellen outside. "You must have faith," Ophelia murmured close to Ellen's ear. "William will not be taken from you. That woman will have no proof. She didn't even give us her name. That's telling."

Ellen didn't say what she was thinking, which was that many in the community still would pressure her to give up William if it came down to it. But she found, as Martin helped her up onto the two-wheeled cart, that the sinking feeling dragging her down was not about the stranger who was lying about William.

Kurt, why have you turned away from me? This is more than Randolph's interference. It must be.

Then Martin leaned forward and said to Ellen, "I think you will be as happy as we are to have the river freeze."

Ophelia turned to her husband. "What do you mean, Martin?"

"Before he left, Randolph stopped by to have a few words with Kurt."

"You didn't tell me that," Ophelia protested. She looked to Ellen, and Ellen nodded, letting on that she'd guessed.

"Perhaps that has something to do with Kurt's demeanor today?" Ophelia asked.

Ellen found she couldn't even answer her cousin. Her brother's meddling could not be the cause of Kurt's distancing himself from her. She couldn't imagine him bowing to such pressure.

Martin put his arm around his wife, calling out a final farewell as Gunther turned the cart and headed away in the early autumn twilight. Ellen clung to the rocking bench, trying to understand what had gone so terribly wrong. On the way home, Ellen couldn't decide if she were colder inside from her distress or outside from the chill. Wind buffeted them and swayed the treetops. Dry oak leaves clung to the branches above and the sky stretched overhead, bleak gray.

"Miss Thurston," Gunther began, "I have finished reading the American history book you loaned me. Can we start our evening lessons again? I'll understand if you—"

Ellen was momentarily ashamed of herself for wallowing in her problems. "No. I want to help you keep up your studies. Do you want to come this weekend or wait till next week?"

"May I come Saturday afternoon?"

"Yes, we'll start learning more American geography. You can help me mount the new wall maps that just arrived."

"I'll be glad to help." The young man again fell silent.

Ellen tried to think of another topic of conversation, but all she could think was that Kurt had told Martin he'd expected Randolph's disapproval. Something else was at work here.

In the silence, Ellen remembered the many times Kurt had taken her home in this cart, and she'd rested against him. Had the sweet connection she'd felt with him ended? The bleak gray sky slipped inside her as angry words for her interfering brother flowed through her mind.

She had to find the courage to talk to Kurt . . . and let him know her heart.

Chapter Twenty-One

Saturday afternoon came, cold and clear, and Ellen welcomed Gunther and Johann. As she watched Kurt drive away in the cart without so much as a wave, loneliness welled up within.

Kurt's avoidance of her made her feel as cold as the December nights. He could easily have come in with Gunther today as he had in the weeks before Marta appeared and measles broke out. *If*

I don't know what's changed, what can I do to reach Kurt? When he came back to pick up the boys, she must find a way to speak with him privately.

After shedding coats and mittens by the door, Gunther and Johann went straight to the fireplace to warm their hands. "I wonder how much colder Wisconsin will be this winter," Gunther commented, shivering.

Ellen considered this. "I think the weather might be a bit colder here than my hometown. But it's nothing we can't handle." Memories of a few past blizzards came to mind and she added, "I should draw up guidelines for parents to follow when deciding whether to let their children walk to school or not. Frostbite and getting lost in a snowstorm are possible."

Even as she smiled to reassure the boys, her gaze shifted toward the door as if she expected Kurt to appear.

Johann hurried over to William, who lay on his back on a blanket in front of the fire, kicking his legs and trying to roll over. "Hey, William. I brought my horse and look, now I have a goat, too." The boy proudly displayed his carved toys above the baby's face.

Gunther suffered one more whole body shiver and then pulled a book from his pocket. "I read it, and learned so much. Is it true that Abraham Lincoln was born in a log cabin like we live in?"

Ellen smiled slightly. "Yes."

"Is that why the Ashfords have changed their opinion about me? Is it because they are giving me a chance to prove what I can do? That I could accomplish much, too?"

Ellen paused to consider her answer. "In a way. They are seeing what you do and how you behave."

"And that makes up for me being a foreigner?"

Ellen sighed. "Some people will always hold that against you, I'm afraid. But not all. When I first met you, you were very unhappy and it showed in your attitude and behavior. That has all changed now."

Gunther nodded seriously.

Ellen thought back to when Gunther had been so unhappy. Did it have anything to do with Kurt? She knew she shouldn't ask this of Gunther but she was tempted, especially since their conversation the other night, after the Thanksgiving meal.

Taking herself in hand, Ellen donned her shawl and led Gunther with his coat on into the chilly schoolroom. When school was not in session, she only heated her quarters. The next half hour went quickly as she and Gunther hung the maps of the United States and the world. On his pad of paper, Gunther sketched a crude map of the thirty-seven states and ten territories plus Oklahoma, Indian territory and the newly purchased Alaska. Then, the lesson finished and the two of them, very chilled by now, hurried back into her warm room.

"Look!" Johann exclaimed, pointing at William.

William grunted and rolled over, and crowed with his victory. Ellen clapped her hands and Johann sang an impromptu song, "William can roll oooooover! Oooover!"

She and Johann cooed over the baby, and Ellen was filled with joy at William's accomplishment. Then she looked at Gunther's face, which was dark with some murky emotion she could not identify.

Before she could say anything, he got up, buttoning up his coat. "I will bring in more wood." After snagging his hat, he was gone.

Ellen didn't hesitate. She tightened her shawl and pulled on wool mittens. "I'll be right back, Johann."

She found Gunther bent forward in front of the woodshed, pressing both hands flat against its door, his distress obvious. "Gunther?"

He swung around.

She saw tears in his eyes and took another step forward.

He held up a hand, fighting for control. She waited, shivering.

"Bad things," he began when he could command his voice, "happened to us in Germany."

Ice crackled around Ellen's heart. She tried to think of what to say, some comfort to offer. But she desperately wanted to know what kind of bad things he was talking about. Did these bad things have anything to do with how Kurt had pulled away from her?

Gunther wiped his face with the back of one hand and folded his arm, tucking his hands under. He leaned against the woodshed doors. "When we watched William roll over, I remembered when Johann's mother died. He had just learned to roll over." The young man's voice broke on the last word.

"My parents both died last year," Ellen said, trying to say: *I know how you feel.*

"Then last year my father died and that was the worst—"

"Gunther!"

At Kurt's shout, Ellen jumped and swung around.

Kurt leaped down from Martin's pony cart, his chest heaving as if he'd been running.

"We go home *now!*" Kurt barked. "Where is Johann?"

"He's inside with William," Ellen said as calmly as she could, hoping her tone would help soothe Kurt.

"I'm getting more wood for Miss Thurston," Gunther said combatively, opening the shed door.

Kurt walked past Ellen as if she weren't there and called out, "Johann! Time to go home! *Now!*"

Ellen didn't budge as Kurt disappeared into her quarters. Moments later, he returned with Johann behind him. "Hurry and put that wood inside," he

298

said to Gunther, who had come out of the shed with an armload of wood. "We go home now."

Gunther halted. "I'm not going home with you, remember? I'm staying at the Stewards' place. And before going there, I'm expected to help Mr. Ashford around the store this afternoon and take supper with them. Then I'll go back to the Stewards' and do the milking. I will ride to church with you tomorrow."

Gunther's polite but firm tone impressed Ellen. He no longer was the surly teenage boy she'd met only months ago. She turned her attention to Kurt, whose face registered a storm of anger. He turned and marched toward the cart.

"See you tomorrow, Miss Thurston! Goodbye, Gunther!" Johann called as he ran to catch up with his uncle.

Ellen held open the door for Gunther. She wanted to ask him to finish telling her what had happened in Germany, but neither of them spoke as he knelt and stacked the wood neatly by the door.

"Thank you, Gunther."

"You're welcome, miss." He looked at her. "My uncle is still sad."

Ellen nodded, unable to speak.

"I will see you later at supper with the Ashfords."

After Gunther left, she slowly unwrapped her shawl and hung everything neatly on the pegs by the door. Then she prepared a bottle for William and fed him. She looked down at the chubby, happy face, her heart aching for the man she loved. "Kurt is very sad," she told William. "What hurt him, little one? What awful thing happened in Germany to force him to run all the way here to Pepin to escape it?"

On Sunday morning, Kurt stood in the school-room, singing along with the hymn. But the peace he'd begun to feel in this room on previous Sundays had vanished without a trace.

"There is a balm in Gilead
To make the wounded whole . . ."

Gunther sat with him and Johann, but anyone could see his brother wanted to sit with the Ashfords. The boy thought himself in love.

In love. Bile rose in Kurt's throat.

Did love really exist in this dark, hurtful world? His traitorous eyes sought out Ellen, who stood alone toward the front of the room.

What had Gunther told Miss Thurston about what had befallen their family? The heat of shame rolled through him in waves.

He alone carried the full weight of the past. Johann and Gunther's youth protected them. *I'm so tired, Lord.*

"There is a balm in Gilead
To heal the sin-sick soul . . ."

Even as Kurt sang, he was sure there was no

balm in Gilead for him. He would carry this weight till he died. Only then could he lay it down.

His mind rebelled at this curse, remembering the joy of holding Ellen close, of breathing in her floral scent and cradling her softness within his arms. That had been a balm to his wounded heart. But that could never happen again. She didn't need a wounded soul like his.

Noah prayed, and the service ended.

"Come," Kurt told the boys. "We go."

People gathering to speak to the pastor on their way out blocked the doorway. Wanting to escape before Ellen came anywhere near him, Kurt chafed. But he waited till he and the lads could make their way into the aisle and then approached Noah. As usual, Kurt said, "Thank you for the good sermon."

Noah gripped Kurt's hand but didn't relinquish it. "We appreciate how Gunther has pitched in to keep things safe at the Steward's while they're gone."

"*Ja.*" Kurt nodded, extracting his hand from the pastor's grip.

"Do you need any help putting up enough wood for the winter? Gordy and I are going to clear another field before the first good snow and could use you and Gunther. You'd get a share of the wood." Noah searched his eyes as if reading his heart.

Kurt edged a step away, nodding. "Thank you."

"Come over later or tomorrow morning and we'll talk it over."

Kurt hurried his two boys through the door into the chill wind. And then he felt a hand claim his sleeve.

Ellen Thurston stood before him. "May I have a word with you?"

"It is cold and we must get home," he replied and turned away.

"It is cold indeed when a friend turns his back," she said.

He swung around, aware of people all around them, hurrying to their wagons or heading home on foot. "What do you need?"

"To talk to you."

"We have nothing to say to each other."

"I have much to say to you," she said plainly, her beautiful eyes beseeching him.

It hurt just to look at her. "I have no time for talk."

Kurt turned and climbed up onto his wagon bench. Johann looked shocked, his mouth hanging open. "Get into the back, Johann." Kurt untied the reins. "Come on, Gunther. It's cold."

Gunther sent Miss Thurston a sympathetic look and then glared at Kurt, but he climbed up on the bench.

Kurt slapped the reins and without a backward glance turned his wagon and started up the track.

Against his will his mind replayed the hymn. *There is a balm in Gilead to make the wounded whole . . .*

When they arrived at their cabin, both Johann and Gunther wordlessly got off the wagon. Kurt unhitched the team, rubbed them down and put them out to graze the dry grass. He looked at his barn and cabin, and thought that what he'd been told about America had proven true so far—there was free land, and a hardworking man could make a place for himself.

A few feet from the cabin door, Kurt halted. His unruly imagination drew up an image of Ellen in a crisp, white apron, standing in his doorway, telling him to hurry inside where warmth and a good meal awaited him. The imagined picture beckoned and then mocked him. Searing pain made him gasp and bend over, resting his hands on his knees. How could mere emotions hurt so much?

Finally, he straightened and went inside where he and Gunther ate lunch in an unfriendly silence. Johann looked worried but said nothing until he asked to be excused to go out and play. Kurt nodded.

The moment the door shut behind Johann, Kurt and Gunther faced each other.

"Why did you act like that today? Rushing us off?" Gunther asked.

Kurt ignored this. "What did you tell Miss Thurston about what happened in Germany?" Nausea rolled through Kurt.

"I only told her bad things happened there," Gunther said with a defiant edge to his voice. "You heard me, didn't you? And why shouldn't I tell her that?"

"Why?" Kurt thundered in German. "Why don't I want everyone here to know what happened at home? Are you crazy?"

Gunther stared at him. "Even if I told Miss Thurston, do you think she would repeat it to anybody else? Don't you know what kind of lady Miss Thurston is by now?" Gunther struck the table with his fist. "Are you the child here or am I?"

Kurt leaped to his feet, breathing fast and hard. "You will not talk to me like that."

Gunther rose and gazed at his brother with pity. "I am living in the here and now. I am Gunther Lang," he pronounced the words the American way. "I am learning to be an American. I will never return to Europe. Nothing we left behind would draw me back there. And nothing that happened *there* can touch me *here*."

Gunther's words ricocheted in Kurt's mind, and he could not reply.

"We watched little William roll over yesterday by Miss Thurston's fireplace and it reminded me of losing Maria." The lad stopped and obviously swallowed down his emotion. "Because Johann had just rolled over for the first time the day Maria died. She was too ill to see Johann that day. The fever had already taken her husband and she was leaving us, too." Gunther bent his head for a moment, struggling visibly for control. "I can never talk to you about what happened because you don't want to talk about it, won't talk about it. But it happened to me and Johann, too. It didn't just happen to you."

Kurt silently admitted the truth of that. His throat shut tight. Sweat dotted his forehead.

I can't bear to talk about it.

"I don't take pleasure in talking about it. But if I had told Miss Thurston all that happened to us —losing Maria and her husband, the way our father lived . . . and how he died—she would say nothing to anybody about it. She is not the kind of lady who gossips. I trust her. Why don't you?"

Kurt swallowed and tried to come up with words but couldn't. Stark, uncompromising shame and loss riddled him.

"I've made up my mind," Gunther said. "I am going to court Amanda for the next two years till I'm eighteen and can stake my own homestead. Then I will ask Amanda to marry me. *I* am not going to let the past ruin my future."

The two of them stared at each other for a moment. Then Gunther went to the pegs by the door, drew on his coat and left.

Kurt felt ill, exhausted. He slumped into his chair and buried his face into his hands. As he thought of Gunther's words, the scene with Miss Thurston outside the school played in his mind.

I am unworthy of her, and not just because of her money or her uncle who sits in the Illinois congress.

The way his father died had stained Kurt and nothing would ever wash him clean. With a sinking sensation, he recalled the look on Brigitte's face when he'd told her about his father's death. She had jilted him then, just one week after the public announcement of their betrothal.

Sometimes he thought his father had planned everything to hurt Kurt and Gunther in the worst possible way.

Sometimes he wished his father lived again so he could pummel him, hurl abuse at him for what he had done. Kurt shook with a sudden rage, shocking himself.

Why, Father, why did you do that to us—after everything else you'd done?

Sitting alone in her quarters, Ellen had barely moved in the hours following her public scene with Kurt. Most likely people were gossiping about her brazen behavior over cups of coffee, laughing about the schoolteacher throwing herself at the Dutchman. No doubt they thought her pathetic.

It's fitting—I feel a little pathetic.

Ellen had declined Sunday dinner with the Ashfords and spent the rest of the gray day alone, caring for William—holding him close and rocking him soothed her battered heart. She pondered her feelings for Kurt, acknowledging that what she felt for Kurt was nothing like what she'd felt for Holton. She hadn't fallen in love with Kurt because of his handsome face, though he certainly was handsome. She'd fallen in love with him because he was working hard to help his brother become a man and to raise a motherless nephew. And Kurt had come to her aid so many times—when the community had tried to force her to give up William, and when William had convulsed and she'd been afraid of losing the baby. Hardworking, unassuming, caring Kurt had stolen her heart. Would she ever get the chance to tell him?

Ellen rose and laid William in his cradle. The sun had sunk below the horizon—winter nights came early now. She struck a match and lit the oil lamp, setting the glass cover in place just as a knock came at the door.

Startled, Ellen swung around. She'd heard no wagon arrive. No one had called out to her. So who had come out in the cold night to knock on her door? She reached the door and twisted the knob.

Chapter Twenty-Two

Ellen opened the door, letting in a gust of cold wind. A woman cloaked within a black shawl huddled at her door.

"Hello?" Ellen said hesitantly. Could it be that strange woman who might come a second time to try to wrest William from her?

The woman, hiding most of her face, glanced around in a furtive manner. Then she stepped forward, gently forcing her way inside. "You don't want me to be seen standing here. Please."

Ellen didn't recognize the woman's voice but her words surprised Ellen and she gave way, allowing her inside. Then she shut the door to keep out the cold. "How may I help you?"

The woman walked to the fireplace and stood before it.

Then Ellen noticed that under the shawl the woman wore a shiny red dress with a scandalously short skirt and black silk stockings.

Ellen was speechless.

A woman of easy virtue had come from the saloon to her door. In all her life, she had barely glimpsed—and certainly never spoken—to a woman outside her chaste world. The line separating decent from indecent women was sharp and vast, unable to be breached. Ever.

"I know I don't belong here," the woman said as if reading Ellen's mind. "But when I heard, I had to come. I reckon you can guess I come from the saloon. They call me Lila."

Not 'My name is Lila.' 'They call me Lila.' "I'm Ellen Thurston."

"I know all about you. Men talk at the saloon, you know . . ."

The woman trailed off. Ellen didn't know she'd been the topic of discussion at the saloon. The thought boggled her mind.

Lila rushed to reassure her. "I don't want you to get the wrong idea. Everyone said that you are a fine lady, smart and real kind to the kids—I mean, schoolchildren."

Ellen nodded, trying to figure out what had brought Lila to her fire.

"Well, and that's why I—" Lila began.

At that moment, William rolled over on the blanket and gurgled happily. He made a few attempts at pushing up with his arms, then gave up and swam with his legs.

Lila fixed her gaze on William, unmoving.

Ellen suddenly couldn't breathe.

"He's grown so much in just a few months," Lila whispered.

Ellen gasped silently. This couldn't be happening.

Lila dropped to her knees and reached for William. Just as Ellen was about to panic, Lila pulled back and began to weep silently.

Ellen could not think what to do but she couldn't bear the woman's distress. "Please, please don't cry."

Lila sniffed back tears and rose. "I saw you in town once, and you had such a sweet face and such fine manners. I knew you'd make a good mother."

"William . . . he's your child?" Ellen asked.

Lila nodded, gazing downward.

"Why are you here?" Ellen felt the earth giving way beneath her. *Do you want him back?*

"I don't want him back," Lila blurted out, as if she'd heard Ellen's anguish. "I hear some woman came and wants to take him from you."

Ellen's mind had slowed so that it moved with the speed of cold honey dribbling down the side of a jar. She couldn't sort out everything that was happening.

"You can't let that lyin' woman take him." Lila's voice got stronger. "You can't let nobody take him. I gave my baby to you. I wanted *you* to have him, *you* to raise him, don't you see?"

The woman's fervent plea woke Ellen up, her tension easing. "I do see, Lila. And I promise I will never let anyone take William from me. I might have to leave and go to my hometown,

Galena, however. There I have family and backing. My uncle is a judge."

"Good. Good," Lila said. "You do what you have to for . . . for William, all right? And you can't let anybody know he was born upstairs at the saloon. No one must ever know." Lila raised both hands as if in supplication.

"But many have guessed he might—"

"Guessin' ain't the same as knowing," Lila insisted. "If people know, he'll never live it down. That's why I just up and left him on your door-step so no one would ever know where he come from." Lila stepped close to Ellen. "You got to promise me. No one must ever know he was born upstairs at a saloon or his life will be a misery." Lila leaned toward her.

Ellen got the impression that the woman would have taken her hand but feared to breach the division that separated them.

This woman entrusted me with her child. Gratitude carried Ellen forward.

She grasped both the woman's hands in hers. "No one will ever know from me, Lila. I promise. I am so grateful. I didn't think I would make a good mother . . ." Emotion clogged Ellen's throat.

"Oh, no, I saw right away that you would be a sweet mother. I knew you'd know just how to take care of my . . . him."

Then Lila tugged her hands free and rearranged her shawl to hide within it. "Peek out and see if there's anybody around. I don't want nobody to see me."

Ellen obeyed and as she expected no one had come to her clearing. She motioned for Lila to come to the door.

Lila slipped past Ellen. "Thank you."

"Thank *you*. You've given me the most wonderful gift . . ." Ellen couldn't find more words to say.

"You give me the best gift. You love my son and you'll give him a chance for a good life." Then Lila slipped away, disappearing into the dark among the trees.

Ellen closed the door and rested against it. The facts that had just been revealed poured through her like a waterfall. Now she knew who had given up William and chosen her to have him and why. But she would never let anyone use it against him.

She knew what she must do.

Even if it cost her Kurt.

Sunday afternoon brought the first real snowfall. Ellen left Amanda in charge of William in her quarters and prepared to attend the school board meeting. She'd made her decision and would carry it out today. The Mississippi was freezing and she must take action now.

While the school board members followed the agenda, Ellen sat very straight beside Mrs.

Ashford near the front of the crowded school-room.

The men who had worked on the woodshed and had cut wood for the school had been invited to attend to receive public recognition. Ellen was very aware that though Kurt was part of this group, he had not come. Over the past few days, he had continued avoiding her. This made what she had to do both easier and harder.

Just before the board began the brief ceremony to thank the men, the door opened behind her. She didn't have to look back. She heard a few quiet accented words and knew Gunther and Kurt had arrived. Her stomach quivered like jelly.

"Miss Thurston, you said you had something to address," Noah said from the front of the room, sitting beside Mr. Ashford.

Ellen rose on trembling legs. She had decided that she must protect William at all costs, even if it cost her the only man she'd ever loved. "I am afraid that I must tender my resignation—"

Suddenly Amanda's panicked voice came from the next room. "No! No! Help! Help!"

Kurt was on his feet immediately, dashing toward the connecting door, just a few steps behind Gunther. As he passed Ellen, he grabbed her hand, pulling her along with him. The other men leaped to their feet and raced forward, too.

They entered the teacher's quarters to find

Gunther standing with his back to Amanda, protecting her, his fists raised. Amanda held William close and tight.

Kurt turned to see who Gunther was confronting and thundered, "You again! What are you here for?"

The woman who'd come earlier to claim William as hers stood in Ellen's quarters with a man who looked to be related to her.

"I am not letting you take William," Ellen declared, stepping to Amanda's side and putting an arm around the girl.

"Well, I brought my brother," the woman said, her chin reared up toward Ellen. "He'll tell you the baby is mine."

Kurt knew they were lying. He didn't know how, he just knew.

"If the baby is yours, why were you sneaking in here then?" Amanda asked accusingly. "You didn't even knock, just you came at me and tried to take William out of my arms!"

"You're lying," the brother said.

"Amanda doesn't lie," Gunther barked. "If she says it, it's the truth." Gunther clenched his fists and kept them raised.

"That's right," Mr. Ashford agreed from just inside the connecting door. "My girl doesn't lie."

The woman buried her face in her shawl. "Oh, everyone is against a poor widow!" she shrilled.

Kurt knew in his gut the woman was lying. How

could he convince others of this? And what had Ellen said right before Amanda cried out? *I am afraid that I must tender my resignation* . . . She was going to leave Pepin. She had said before she might go home to Galena to enlist the support of her family to keep William. And now she was going to go through with it.

At this realization, Kurt's heart raced so fast, sweat beaded on his forehead. Then he looked at Ellen and it was as if his heart stopped. In her eyes, he saw the same anguish he'd seen only once before in his life—in his sister's eyes, at the moment she realized she was dying and would leave her tiny Johann an orphan. The memory twisted inside Kurt, nearly forcing out a groan.

In that instant, Kurt knew he couldn't let Ellen lose William; he couldn't allow her to be wounded so deeply that something in her might die. But what could he do?

God, help.

Noah shouldered forward. "Let us all go into the schoolroom and discuss this civilly."

Along with everyone else, the two strangers moved with reluctance into the schoolroom. Gunther stayed protectively at Amanda's side and Kurt joined him, hovering near Ellen. He racked his brain. How could he protect William from this deceiving woman?

People encircled the main participants, not

sitting. A sense of watchfulness, wariness hung over them all.

Suddenly, before he knew he landed on a plan, Kurt found the words to say. "If you are this child's mother, you must prove it."

Every face turned toward him, most looking shocked.

"That's true," Noah agreed, "but how?"

Kurt glanced at William, and more words came to him somehow. "Everyone can see one of the child's birthmarks, but his mother would know where his *other* birthmark is."

Every face swung to the woman, who appeared perplexed, chewing her lower lip and frowning. The silent tension in the room rose higher, tighter. The expressions around the woman hardened.

"Well?" Noah asked.

She blurted out, "On his back."

With Amanda still holding him, Ellen lifted William's baby dress, revealing his smooth, unmarked back.

A growling swept through the crowd. Kurt felt it within himself. He clenched his fists and stepped toward the man and woman.

"Why have you lied?" Noah demanded.

The woman began weeping, but others took up Noah's question, insisting on the truth.

Kurt waited, moving closer still to Ellen.

"I heard about the child left on the doorstep

here," the woman said tearfully. "I'm not able to bear children. I just wanted to give this child a good home."

Rank disbelief met this. Anger and outrage at being lied to was expressed by a spontaneous hissing from the crowd.

"My new husband is expected to return any day to take us to a homestead in Kansas," the woman continued, trying to justify herself. "We would make a home for the babe."

When this speech met with no sympathy, the woman's brother blurted out, "She's got to have this baby or he'll know she wasn't—"

She hushed him sharply, guiltily.

Noah stepped forward then and asked, "How can we believe anything you say? First you say you bore this child and left him on the doorstep to look for a new husband. Now you say your new husband expects to see you with a child. None of this holds together."

"I've heard of women," Mrs. Ashford announced, "who tell men about to leave for the West that they are pregnant. But it's just a ruse to induce the man into marriage before he leaves. And then when he returns, what happens if there's no baby?"

More hissing followed this suggestion. Kurt began to wonder if the crowd might attack these two, who edged toward the rear doorway.

Noah addressed the town. "Lying, and attempting to steal a child does not recommend you to our community. In any case, God chose Ellen Thurston to raise William."

The pastor's words swayed popular opinion. Every head was nodding, scowling at the woman and her brother.

"If you'd been honest, matters could have ended differently," one of Ellen's most vocal critics said, glaring, disgusted.

Amid the crowd, a path to the schoolroom doors opened as if directing the disgraced twosome to leave.

"This isn't right," the woman said, raising a fist. "This isn't the last you'll hear of me," she blustered as she and her brother left.

One of the men slammed the door closed after them. "Good riddance," he pronounced.

Noah held up both hands to quiet the room. "Would everyone be seated, please?" The crowd moved to sit. "I think that we must put to rest this idea that Miss Thurston cannot keep this child. Did you hear her say she was going to tender her resignation?" Noah scanned the faces before him. "If you can't accept this child as hers, you will lose Miss Thurston from our school, our community. Is that what you want?"

"No," Kurt said aloud, along with many others. Ellen gazed at him with such gratitude in her eyes that he had to look away.

"Miss Thurston," Noah said, "you were going to

go home to better defend your claim to William, weren't you?"

"Yes, Ophelia's father is a judge. He would have given me his support," Ellen said, rising.

"Old Saul said that God had given William into this lady's care," Noah said. "We must let this matter rest there."

A man stood. "I been against the teacher keepin' the foundling. But I see today that was wrong of me. Those two were as shifty a pair as I ever seen. Don't you worry any more, Miss Thurston. You'll keep that child or I'll know the reason why."

Many added their agreement to this. Finally, Kurt began to breathe easier.

Noah proceeded with the public thanks to those who helped build the woodshed and the meeting ended on a positive note.

During the social period after the meeting, many men who'd never spoken to Kurt came up to him, surprising him with their congratulations and thanks for exposing the lying woman. They even shook his hand. He knew he'd always be "the Dutchman" in their minds, but something had shifted for them—he could see it in their eyes. Perhaps something had shifted inside him, too.

Finally, only Kurt, Gunther, the Ashfords and Miss Thurston remained. Mrs. Ashford sent Kurt an appraising look and said, "I think Amanda and Gunther and William should come home with us now. It's time you two had a talk," she said sternly.

And with that, Ellen and Kurt were left alone.

Without a word, Ellen led Kurt into her quarters. In front of the fire, she turned to face him. Her gratitude to him for saving William was tempered by a need to know, to come to an understanding of what had broken them apart. "You were wonderful," she said simply.

The words released something in Kurt, and before he could stop himself he had taken her into his arms. He held her, whispering, *"Liebschen."*

Ellen leaned back and looked up at him. "Why have you been avoiding me, Kurt? Was it Randolph?"

"He told me to stay away from you. That you're too good for me." At the time, the words had been very painful to hear, but Kurt said them now as if they were nothing—and they were.

Ellen didn't know whether to be relieved or infuriated. "But that is not what has kept you away, is it?" she pressed him.

Kurt exhaled loudly. "It wasn't just your brother. I already knew he didn't think me good enough for you."

"Then what?" She rested a hand against the mantel.

The light from the fire cast her in a glow, highlighting the golden strands in her light brown hair. She was so lovely. He must speak now, tell her everything. It was time.

"Ellen, it was because I did not *feel* good

enough for you." The old sorrow hung around his neck, threatening to weigh him down. But he reeled himself in, and focused on her. "Bad things happened to us in Germany."

"That's what Gunther said. But can't you tell me what happened there? Don't you trust me?"

"With my life," he said, resting a palm against her soft cheek for just a moment. Then he leaned forward and braced his hands against the mantel, gazing down at the low fire. "After a wasted life, my father gambled away our farm and then hanged himself in the barn."

Ellen gasped and then wrapped her arms around Kurt's shoulders as best she could, resting her head against his as he continued to stare into the fire. "Oh, Kurt, how awful for you."

Her words, spoken with heartfelt sympathy, released the pain in him. Tears flowed and he couldn't stanch them. They washed down his face, cleansing him.

"I found him. I will never forget the sight. And after . . . no one would speak to us. Or even look at us. Because he was a suicide, we couldn't bury him in the churchyard. My fiancée ended our engagement with a note tacked on my door. Gunther and Johann and I were left with just enough to pay for our fares and some money to start over. We left the week after."

Kurt straightened without breaking their

connection. He held her close and breathed in her sweet scent. "Ellen, my sweet Ellen."

"Yes," she murmured, "I am your Ellen. And you are my Kurt. I love you and will not let you go, no matter what," she said with all the fierceness she felt. "No one here needs to know what happened over there, Kurt. It wasn't your fault. When my little brother died, for years I blamed myself deep within. But it was false guilt, as is yours. There is no way you could have stopped your father. A son can't control a father."

Kurt received her words as absolution—at last. "You're right."

"God must think we're slow. We've blamed ourselves for losses we had no hand in. That isn't what He wants for us."

Kurt nodded against her.

They held each other a long, silent time and Ellen reveled in his strength and the very handsomeness that had at first made him suspect. With a lighter heart, she tousled his golden curls. "Kurt, you're too handsome to marry the old maid schoolmarm."

"Foolishness. You are a beauty. But you must know that I will always be *that Dutchman*," he said.

"And I'll always love *that Dutchman*," she said, stroking his cheek with her soft palm.

He clasped her to him again, thanking God for this woman, this special gift. He lowered his mouth to hers and kissed her as he had wanted to for so long.

Ellen drew his breath in and reveled in his gentle yet demanding kiss. She had never been kissed like this and with such love in all her life.

"Will you be my wife, *Liebschen*?"

Words she had thought she never wanted to hear. How foolish. Of course, what really mattered was the man who said them. "Yes, Kurt, I will be your wife." Joy enveloped her. She wanted to stand on tiptoe and sing.

Kurt laughed aloud as if he also couldn't contain his joy at this special moment.

She now knew the difference between calf love and real love. Kurt was her real McCoy.

Snow fell thick and fast on Sunday morning. It was almost time for worship to begin. Ellen dressed with care, wanting to look her best on this very special day. She finished getting William ready and then carried him into the schoolroom.

Martin and Ophelia had returned from Galena. They sat in their usual place but this time Kurt, Gunther and Johann had joined them, no longer sitting in the back. Already, people stared at this new arrangement, whispering to each other. But they had smiles on their faces, as if they were anticipating something. Ellen, unable to keep from smiling herself, walked over to the Stewards and the Langs. Kurt rose and lifted William into his arms. Then she sat beside him, feeling all eyes on her back. For the first time since she'd come to Pepin, the feeling was not a bad one.

Noah cleared his throat and everyone sat down, looking expectantly toward him. "Before we begin today, I think that Martin Steward has an announcement to make."

Martin stood and turned to face the congregation. "It is my distinct pleasure to announce the engagement of Kurt Lang to our cousin Miss Ellen Thurston—"

Clapping and whistles drowned out Martin's last words. "When's the weddin'?" someone called out.

Kurt stood and beamed. "In May next year. Right after school ends."

"That means we have to find a new teacher for next year," Mr. Ashford said, sounding surprisingly pleased.

Mrs. Ashford was weeping into a lace handkerchief. "I'm so happy. So happy."

Old Saul tapped his son, who then rolled the wheelchair down the aisle to Kurt. "I told you the day I met you that God had a plan for your life, a good one."

Kurt shook the large but frail hand. "You were right."

" 'A man who finds a wife finds a good thing,' " Old Saul quoted with a twinkle in his eye. "And you found a very fine one. God bless you both."

Ellen took Old Saul's other hand and the three

of them formed a circle of unity as Noah asked everyone to bow for a prayer of thanksgiving. At the end of the prayer, Old Saul said, "May God richly bless you with a love that grows and a family to love."

And everyone called out, "Amen!"

Kurt pulled Ellen closer to him, too proud for words.

She smiled at him and whispered, "I love you."

He bent close to her ear. "I love you, *Liebschen*."

Epilogue

April 18, 1871

The crowd sat on benches and in wagons that parked around the schoolyard clearing, watching Martin intently as he prepared to read the next word at the long-anticipated Pepin spelling bee. An especially lovely spring day cheered everyone, blessing the exciting event. Three other schools had arrived in midmorning to compete and now, after over two hours of spelling, only three students still stood on the makeshift platform in the schoolyard.

"Dorcas, you have won the spelling bee in the primary grade class," Martin said. "Please be seated until we have a winner for the advanced class."

People applauded as Dorcas sat down.

Both dressed in their Sunday best, Amanda and a boy from the Bear Lake School, Samuel Tarkington, still remained standing nervously on the platform.

Ellen held hands with Kurt as they sat on the first row of benches. She wanted to get up and shout, "You can do it, Amanda!" But she worked hard to hold herself with dignity, as a lady should. Johann sat with his fellow first graders, watching closely. Ophelia sat on Ellen's other side, jiggling Nathan, who was squirming on her knee.

"The word is *dichotomy*," Martin read from the approved list.

"Dichotomy," Amanda repeated. "*D-i-c-h-o-t-o-m-y.* Dichotomy."

"Correct," Martin said.

A burst of applause.

Martin turned to the boy. "The word is *euphonious*."

Samuel looked very white. Tension filled the school clearing. His family leaned forward. "Euphonious. *E-u-p-h-o-n-i-o-u-s.* Euphonious."

"Correct!" Martin said.

Excited applause from Samuel's school broke out.

"Hauteur," Martin said to Amanda.

"Hauteur," Amanda repeated, visibly trembling. "*H-a-u-t-u-e-r.* Hauteur."

"I'm sorry, Amanda," Martin said, sounding sorry. "That is incorrect."

Λ gasp went through thc crowd. Ellen tightened her grip on Kurt's hand. Amanda stepped to the side of the stage, waiting to see if Samuel would miss the word. She looked shaken.

Gunther rose from the bench, catching her eye.

She smiled tremulously back at him.

"Samuel, spell *hauteur*," Martin said.

The boy cleared his voice. "Hauteur. *H-a-u-t-e-u-r.* Hauteur."

"That is correct," Martin announced with enthusiasm. "Samuel Tarkington, representing Bear Lake School, is the winner in the advanced category and the last speller standing in the First Annual Southwest Wisconsin Spelling Bee."

Everyone rose and applauded, no matter what school they'd come to support. The applause went on and on till Mr. Ashford and three other men mounted the platform. Mr. Ashford held up his hands and the crowd settled down to listen.

"We are so happy that three other schools joined us in this first annual spelling bee." He shook hands with the other men who represented the three other school boards. "We intend to do this again next year and hope even more schools will be able to attend."

Then Mr. Ashford invited Samuel, his parents and teacher to come up to receive the large winning plaque. "Each year this plaque will be awarded to the winning school, engraved with the name of the winning speller, their grade, and the year."

The crowd applauded as Samuel accepted the plaque with a big grin.

"The top three spellers will receive ribbons." Mr. Ashford waved up Amanda and Dorcas, and hung a blue ribbon around Samuel's neck, a red one around Amanda's and a yellow one around Dorcas's. "Let's applaud all the teachers, parents and students who worked so hard to make this spelling bee a rousing success!"

The crowd rose as one, applauding, whistling and stomping their feet.

Ellen felt nearly lifted into the air.

Mr. Ashford continued, nearly shouting over the crowd, "I want to also announce that our teacher, Miss Ellen Thurston, was the person who came up with the idea for this spelling bee. Next month, she is going to marry Kurt Lang, one of our prominent citizens."

Not expecting Mr. Ashford to announce this so publicly, Ellen blushed. But at Kurt's insistence, she waved and smiled at everyone. Then Noah closed with prayer and Mr. Ashford invited everyone to partake of the potluck refreshments on the school grounds.

Ellen and Kurt stood together, receiving best wishes and compliments on the spelling bee. Finally, they walked together toward the food tables. "Prominent citizen," she murmured to Kurt with a smile.

Kurt chuckled, and pointed at Amanda and Gunther already sitting at a nearby table with the Ashfords. "He thinks we will be related."

Ellen laughed. "I think he's right."

Noah and his wife, Sunny, came up behind them in line. "We're so glad for both of you," Sunny said, with a smile that radiated joy.

Noah agreed, adding, "We've just received good news. My cousin Rachel Woolsey is coming from Pennsylvania in June. It will be good to have family nearby. Rachel is a wonderful girl."

Mr. Ashford overheard what Noah was saying, and he came over and asked, "Do you think she'd be qualified to teach?"

Noah shook his head. "No, Rachel is a notable cook and baker. She intends to start her own bake shop here."

Mr. Ashford looked surprised and many around them put their heads together to discuss this startling announcement. Ellen already knew all too well the challenges this unconventional woman was going to face in Pepin, but if the community could rise to the occasion for her, they could do it again for Miss Woolsey.

She looked up into Kurt's blue eyes and her love for him nearly overwhelmed her as he drew her hand to his lips.

"*Liebschen.*"

Then they made their way through the line, chatting with neighbors and filling their plates, just as their lives—soon to be joined together—had been filled with love.

Dear Reader,

I loved writing Ellen and Kurt's story. It's hard for us to believe today, but German immigrants or any immigrants (including, oddly, the Irish) who came from countries that didn't speak English were looked down on as second class, and often subjected to racial slurs. The racial slur used against Germans was "Dutch," which was a mispronunciation of what Germans called them-selves, Deutsche (pronounced *Doit-cha*).

It is always so interesting to research the language of a time period. For example, I had wanted to use the phrase "the real thing," but after some research, I discovered that phrase came into use much later than when this story takes place. I don't like to use phrases that aren't historically grounded.

So I substituted "the real McCoy," and dis-covered that this phrase came to be because of Elijah McCoy, an African-American born in Ontario, Canada, in 1844, the son of runaway slaves. Educated in Scotland as a mechanical engineer, Elijah McCoy settled in Detroit. He invented a cup that would regulate the flow of oil onto moving parts of industrial machines.

The term "real McCoy" refers to Elijah's oiling device. It became so popular that people inspecting new equipment would ask if the device contained "the real McCoy."

How about that?

The next heroine in this series will be Noah Whitmore's cousin Rachel, who wants to establish her own business. Again, businesswomen aren't uncommon now, but in 1871 they were! And wait till you see the unlikely hero who will claim her heart!

Lyn Cote

Questions for Discussion

1. What's the difference between infatuation and love, in your opinion?

2. Why did Ellen leave her home in Galena?

3. What impressed the Pepin community about Ellen?

4. What sad event had taken place in the past year in Ellen's life? Do you think this caused some of her and her siblings' troubles?

5. Why do you think people looked down on foundlings or orphans in the nineteenth century?

6. Why did Ellen think she wouldn't make a good mother?

7. Have you ever met a woman like Mrs. Ashford? Who was she and what was she like?

8. Why did Mr. Brawley object to his wife taking the job of caring for William at first? What does this say about the difference between life in 1870 and life today?

9. Measles has nearly disappeared from most of the U.S. but still rages in other countries. What caused this to change?

10. How did Gunther change over the course of this story? What do you think changed him?

11. Kurt carried a lot of sad emotional baggage. What was the source of his shame, and why was it so hard for him to get over it?

12. Is there anything in your life that you've had to work your way through emotionally? How did you recover? What helped you?

About the Author

Lyn Cote and her husband, her real-life hero, acquired a new daughter recently when their son married his true love. Lyn already loves her daughter-in-law and enjoys this new adventure in family stretching. Lyn and her husband still live on the lake in the north woods, where they watch a bald eagle and its young soar and swoop overhead throughout the year. She wishes the best to all her readers. You may email Lyn at l.cote@juno.com or write her at P.O. Box 864, Woodruff, WI 54548. And drop by her blog, www.strongwomenbravestories.blogspot.com, to read stories of strong women in real life and in true-to-life fiction. "Every woman has a story. Share yours."

Center Point Large Print
600 Brooks Road / PO Box 1
Thorndike ME 04986-0001 USA

(207) 568-3717

US & Canada:
1 800 929-9108
www.centerpointlargeprint.com